Praise for De~~n~~

"The Bennett siblings stole my heart in t~~...~~ ~~...~~ ~~...~~ of ~~...~~ Inn series. *Autumn Skies* is the perfect roundup to this series. The tension and attraction between Grace and Wyatt is done so well, and the mystery kept me wondering what was going to happen next. In *Autumn Skies*, Denise Hunter delivers another must read. Prepare to be swept away to the beautiful Blue Ridge Mountains in a flurry of turning pages."

—Nancy Naigle, *USA TODAY* bestselling author of *Christmas Angels*

"*Carolina Breeze* is filled with surprises, enchantment, and a wonderful depth of romance. Denise Hunter gets better with every novel she writes, and that trend has hit a high point with this wonderful story."

—Hannah Alexander, author of *The Wedding Kiss* and the Healing Touch series

"A breeze of brilliance! Denise Hunter's *Carolina Breeze* will blow you away with a masterful merge of mystery, chemistry, and memories restored in this lakeside love story of faith, family, and fortune."

—Julie Lessman, award-winning author

"*Carolina Breeze* was a book I could not put down."

—Cara Putman, bestselling author of *Flight Risk*

"Denise Hunter writes with a deep understanding of complex family dynamics in *Summer by the Tides*. A perfect blend of romance and women's fiction."

—Sherryl Woods, #1 *New York Times* bestselling author

"Denise Hunter once again proves she's the queen of romantic drama. *Summer by the Tides* is both a perfect beach romance and a dramatic story of second chances. If you like Robyn Carr, you'll love Denise Hunter."

—Colleen Coble, *USA TODAY* bestselling author of *One Little Lie*

"I have never read a romance by Denise Hunter that didn't sweep me away into a happily ever after. Treat yourself!"

—Robin Lee Hatcher, bestselling author of *Cross My Heart* for *On Magnolia Lane*

"Swoony, fun, and meaningful, [*Honeysuckle Dreams*] should come with a 'grab your fan' warning! Hunter's skill at writing sizzling romance combines with two reader-favorite tropes to deliver a story that is both toe curling and heartwarming."

—*RT Book Reviews*, 4 stars

"Denise Hunter's newest novel, *Sweetbriar Cottage*, is a story to fall in love with. True-to-life characters, high stakes, and powerful chemistry blend to tell an emotional story of reconciliation."

—Brenda Novak, *New York Times* bestselling author

"*Sweetbriar Cottage* is a wonderful story, full of emotional tension and evocative prose. You'll feel involved in these characters' lives and carried along by their story as tension ratchets up to a climactic and satisfying conclusion. Terrific read. I thoroughly enjoyed it."

—Francine Rivers, *New York Times* bestselling author

"Hunter has a wonderful way of sweeping readers into a delightful romance without leaving behind the complications of true love and true life. *Sweetbriar Cottage* is Hunter at the top of her game—a rich, emotional romance that will leave readers yearning for more."

—Katherine Reay, award-winning author of *The Printed Letter Bookshop*

"With her usual deft touch, snappy dialogue, and knack for romantic tension, inspirational romance veteran Hunter will continue to delight romance fans with this first Summer Harbor release."

—*Publishers Weekly* for *Falling Like Snowflakes*

"Hunter is a master romance storyteller. *Falling Like Snowflakes* is charming and fun with a twist of mystery and intrigue. A story that's sure to endure as a classic reader favorite."

—Rachel Hauck, *New York Times* bestselling author of *The Fifth Avenue Story Society*

"*Barefoot Summer* is a satisfying tale of hope, healing, and a love that's meant to be. Sail away with Denise Hunter's well-drawn characters on a journey that is at once romantic and compelling."

—Lisa Wingate, national bestselling author of *Before We Were Yours*

Autumn Skies

Also by Denise Hunter

THE BLUEBELL INN NOVELS
Lake Season
Carolina Breeze
Autumn Skies

THE BLUE RIDGE NOVELS
Blue Ridge Sunrise
Honeysuckle Dreams
On Magnolia Lane

**THE SUMMER
HARBOR NOVELS**
Falling Like Snowflakes
The Goodbye Bride
Just a Kiss

**THE CHAPEL SPRINGS
ROMANCE SERIES**
Barefoot Summer
A December Bride (novella)
Dancing with Fireflies
The Wishing Season
Married 'til Monday

**THE BIG SKY
ROMANCE SERIES**
A Cowboy's Touch
The Accidental Bride
The Trouble with Cowboys

NANTUCKET LOVE STORIES
Surrender Bay
The Convenient Groom
Seaside Letters
Driftwood Lane

STAND-ALONE NOVELS
Summer by the Tides
Sweetbriar Cottage
Sweetwater Gap
Novellas included in
Smitten, Secretly Smitten,
and *Smitten Book Club*

Autumn Skies

DENISE HUNTER

THOMAS NELSON
Since 1798

Published in Nashville, Tennessee, by Thomas Nelson. Thomas Nelson is a registered trademark of HarperCollins Christian Publishing, Inc.

Thomas Nelson titles may be purchased in bulk for educational, business, fundraising, or sales promotional use. For information, please email SpecialMarkets@ThomasNelson.com.

Scripture quotations taken from The Holy Bible, New International Version®, NIV®. Copyright © 1973, 1978, 1984, 2011 by Biblica, Inc.® Used by permission of Zondervan. All rights reserved worldwide. www.Zondervan.com. The "NIV" and "New International Version" are trademarks registered in the United States Patent and Trademark Office by Biblica, Inc.®

Library of Congress Cataloging-in-Publication Data

Names: Hunter, Denise, 1968- author.
Title: Autumn skies / Denise Hunter.
Description: Nashville, Tennessee : Thomas Nelson, [2020] | Series: Bluebell Inn romance ; 3 |
Summary: "From the bestselling author of The Convenient Groom and A December Bride (now beloved Hallmark Original movies) comes the third and final novel in the Bluebell Inn series!"-- Provided by publisher.
Identifiers: LCCN 2020015578 (print) | LCCN 2020015579 (ebook) | ISBN 9780785222804 (paperback) | ISBN 9780785222811 (epub) | ISBN 9780785222828 (audio download)
Subjects: GSAFD: Christian fiction. | Love stories.
Classification: LCC PS3608.U5925 A95 2020 (print) | LCC PS3608.U5925 (ebook) | DDC 813/.6--dc23
LC record available at https://lccn.loc.gov/2020015578
LC ebook record available at https://lccn.loc.gov/2020015579

Printed in the United States of America

20 21 22 23 24 LSC 5 4 3 2 1

Chapter One

Secret Service Field Office
Charlotte, NC

*R*eading people was part of Wyatt Jennings's job, and judging by the look on his boss's face, the news wasn't good. Wyatt forced himself to sit still as the special agent in charge lowered his considerable weight into the chair behind his battle-scarred desk.

In his midforties the SAIC's bull-like build matched his no-nonsense demeanor. He intimidated the tar out of Wyatt. The fluorescent lights gleamed off his bald head and did nothing to soften his nearly black eyes. He shuffled some papers, his lips set in a firm line. Did a soft side exist beneath that stone-cold facade?

"What's going on with you, Jennings?" Burke's gruff voice boomed across the small space. He folded his beefy arms and propped them on the desk. "Talk to me."

What was going on? Plenty, if Wyatt was honest. But he thought he'd done a stellar job of hiding his issues from Burke's eagle eyes.

Wyatt cleared his throat. "Well, sir, I took a bullet in defense of Senator Edwards."

"Bull hockey. Don't pull that with me. You've worked under me four years with never a problem. First to step up, no matter the job.

Work tirelessly like some kind of robot, not a word of complaint. And now this."

"Now what, sir?" Wyatt eyed him despite the way his heart knocked against his ribs.

"I'm not blind, Jennings. You've been slipping the last few weeks. Ever since the incident. You're distracted, short-tempered with your coworkers, zoned out on the job." His boss pinned him with a look. "And I found you asleep at your desk yesterday."

Wyatt hid a wince. That wasn't the half of what was going on inside. He'd always been an expert at managing his emotions, but the disquiet roiling inside since the shooting had taken on a life of its own.

"I apologize, sir. It won't happen again."

"You're right, it won't. That last assignment messed you up a little. Seen it before."

"I got shot, sir." He didn't know what else to say. He'd do it again, throw himself in front of a bullet to save a protectee. It was his job. His calling. And he was good at it.

"Surface wound. It's not the physical damage I'm concerned with. You need to take some time, get yourself together. I'm talking about a leave of absence."

White speckles danced in Wyatt's vision, from lack of sleep and desperation. "All due respect, sir, I don't need a leave. I have an exemplary record with the Service."

"No question. Let's keep it that way."

"I'll be fine. I just need a decent night's sleep."

"No doubt. Question is, why aren't you getting that? I know you have higher aspirations, and I aim to see you reach them."

It was true he was gunning for Presidential Protective Detail. But a leave wouldn't get him closer to that goal. Wyatt opened his mouth, searching for some explanation for his recent behavior. Some excuse that would make Burke reverse his decision.

"I'll leave you with this, Jennings. After your performance on the Edwards assignment, the higher-ups have you in their sights." His gaze sharpened. "You'll be moving up soon."

Wyatt straightened in his chair. "To PPD, sir?"

Burke gave a sharp nod. "You don't want anything to mess that up."

"No, sir."

"Four weeks," his boss said firmly.

"Four weeks, sir!"

"For starters. Then we'll reassess. Do a psych eval." Burke gave him that hard-eyed stare that had earned him a nickname no one said to his face. "I suggest you use the time wisely. A little counseling wouldn't be out of order. We got people for that." He shuffled some papers and rolled back from his desk. "Effective immediately, Jennings."

There was so much Wyatt wanted to say. Was desperate to say. But the Academy had trained him better. Like it or not, he was on a four-week leave. And even then he wasn't guaranteed reentry. A psychiatric evaluation. The thought brought bile into his esophagus. But then he'd be called up. Wyatt would finally get what he'd been working so hard for.

In the meantime, where he'd go or what he'd do, Wyatt had no idea. He'd been training for the Service one way or another since he'd studied criminal justice at Northeastern. Before that even, in high school—Hargrave Military Academy.

He couldn't even remember who Wyatt Jennings was outside of the Service.

But he was about to find out.

"You're dismissed, Jennings." Burke frowned at him.

He'd zoned out again. Wyatt rose to his feet with reluctance and said the only thing he could. "Yes, sir."

The familiar road twisted and turned around the Blue Ridge Mountains, following the shoreline of Bluebell Lake. Sunlight flashed on the water's surface, making Wyatt squint behind his sunglasses.

It had only taken twenty-four hours to realize he'd better tackle this problem like a foreign threat to one of his protectees. The Secret Service was all he had, all he wanted, so he'd better get his act together and quick. A few nights' sleep would be helpful, but the nightmares had been relentless.

Since he wasn't one to spill his guts to a stranger, he'd packed a bag, hopped in his Audi, and pointed it toward the place where his problems had begun. Probably should've booked a hotel, if there was such a thing around here. But it was September, off-season, so he should be all right.

The road curved to the left, and he passed the sign for the state park. Back in the early nineties, his father had set aside this piece of land. Before this place had been spoiled for him, Wyatt had fond memories of hiking and camping in those woods, thick with evergreen trees and night sounds. Bluebell had always felt more like home than Raleigh had.

After a few more curves he emerged from the mountains and into the town proper. Bluebell hadn't changed much. Someone had turned the fire station into a coffeehouse, and a few stores had sprouted up. He had fond memories of walking these streets, making ice cream runs to the Dairy Bar, fishing off the pier in Pawley Park with his dad. He didn't remember the colorful canopies or the tidy row of trees lining the streets, but he'd only been twelve his last summer here.

His respiration grew quick and shallow at the thought of that summer, his mouth going dry. He wiped a palm down the leg of his jeans. Out of habit he pushed back the memory. But he would have to stop doing that. It wasn't working anymore, not since the shooting. It was as if everything he pushed down during the day bubbled to the surface as soon as sleep left him unguarded and vulnerable.

His phone buzzed with a call. Ethan. He took it on his Bluetooth. "Hey, what's up, man?"

"You left Charlotte? You're on leave? What happened?"

"Wasn't my choice, believe me. Burke called me into his office yesterday."

"And I have to hear about this from Drewsky?"

Ethan had been Wyatt's best friend since they'd gone through twenty-eight weeks of intense training. You didn't make it through that hellish experience without forming lifelong bonds.

"Sorry, should've called." Wyatt progressed through town. He almost mentioned the promotion, then held back for some reason. "How'd your last assignment go?" Ethan had a temporary assignment protecting the pope during his stateside visit.

"Uneventful. You doing all right? I hate to tell you, but word around the office is you're losing it."

"Just a little trouble sleeping is all. I think I need to take a break from my routines. Chill out. I'll get it settled and be back before you know it."

Ethan knew better than to suggest sleep aids. Men who were trained to be on constant alert weren't about to render themselves helpless. At least Wyatt wasn't.

"Where'd you go?"

"Not far. A little lake town called Bluebell, tucked away in the Blue Ridge Mountains."

"Sounds quaint."

"Used to spend summers here with the folks when I was a kid."

"Ah. Does the Gov still summer there?"

"Not anymore. He stays in Raleigh year-round." The trauma of that last summer had spoiled the place for both of them.

"Maybe this is just what you need. A little R & R. Come back refreshed. You've been hitting it pretty hard for a long time. And that shooting . . ."

"It's what we're trained for."

"Sure, but not many agents actually find themselves taking a bullet. You did good, Jennings."

"Thanks, man." He rolled his left shoulder, the pain more a nuisance than a worry.

He was almost to the end of town when his family's old summer home came into view. It was as big and white as he remembered with a wide, welcoming front porch and neat lawn.

Only one thing was different: a sign reading Bluebell Inn. His eyes lingered on the words for several seconds before he pulled into one of the diagonal slots in front of the building.

"Listen, Ethan, I gotta run. I'll call you in a few days."

He ended the call, unable to take his eyes off the familiar sight. It appeared he'd get to see the inside of his old summer home. But did he really want to face the memories it might dredge up?

Chapter Two

*W*ould this meeting ever end? Grace Bennett stifled a yawn as her brother, Levi, droned on about the inn's finances. Beside her, Molly's phone buzzed. Her sister tucked a strand of her long dark hair behind her ear and sneaked a peek. Probably her husband, Adam. The two had been married in June and moved into Adam's beautiful lake home and were pretty much joined at the hip.

The siblings gathered in the inn's library as they always did for Death by Numbers. These days money wasn't so much a worry, but spreadsheets still weren't Grace's sweet spot. So she humored Levi while he did his thing.

"And that about covers it." Levi's blue eyes narrowed on them. "Now if you could both just pull your heads out of the clouds for a minute, I think it's time we talk about the inn's future."

They'd gotten the place up and running after their parents had passed away unexpectedly four years ago. It had been their retirement dream to turn their historic home back into an inn, and the siblings came together to fulfill that dream. At the time Grace was heading into her junior year of high school, Molly was almost finished with her hospitality degree, and Levi was putting his degree to work in Denver with a commercial construction company. Their parents' death had changed everything.

"What do you mean?" Molly asked.

"I mean, it's time we put the inn on the market."

That had always been the plan. With the influx of money they'd had two years ago, running this place had gotten easier. The restaurant was now full menu, much to Molly's delight, and they'd employed a few part-time employees to help manage it.

Molly cleared her throat. "Do you think we've been profitable long enough to appeal to buyers?"

"I think so." Levi started talking numbers but stopped when he must've realized he was losing them again. "So now's as good a time as any. What do you think?"

Grace smirked. "Someone's missing his honey bunch."

Levi's fiancée was the popular actress Mia Emerson—Grace still wasn't sure how he'd managed that—and they'd been together two years now.

"I understand completely," Molly said. "And I think putting the inn on the market now makes sense."

"But what about my business?" Grace had started Blue Ridge Outfitters last year at age twenty, running it out of the inn and storing her equipment in the shed out back.

Levi hitched a shoulder. "You always knew you'd have to move it eventually."

"But I won't be able to afford rent yet. I'm still building." Plus whoever was running the front desk also handled the rentals. In a retail space she'd need to hire extra staff.

"By the time the inn sells, it'll probably be next spring or even summer. And we should all come away nicely from the sale."

"That's true."

Technically Grace's outfitter business was already turning a profit, but that was because her overhead was almost nil. She was using her profits to purchase equipment: kayaks, tents, climbing gear, paddleboards, bikes. They weren't cheap. But the influx from the inn's sale would be a nice cushion.

"If you're both on board," Levi said, "I'll have Pamela Bleeker come out and appraise it, then she can list it."

Molly frowned. "Why can't we sell it ourselves and save the Realtor fee?"

"It'll take a lot of time and effort since our market reach needs to be national or at least regional," Levi said.

"Well, Grace is good with online stuff, and I can handle the showings." Molly blinked dramatically. "Some say I have amazing social skills."

Levi rolled his eyes. "That's up to you two. My plate's full with wedding stuff."

With Levi's wedding here at the inn less than three weeks away and Mia filming in LA, he'd had no choice but to step up to the plate.

Molly looked at Grace. "We've got this covered, right, Sis?"

"Sure, I'm game."

The chime on the front door alerted them to an arrival.

"Meeting adjourned. You're on deck." Levi nodded to Grace as he stood and gathered his papers. "I have errands to run."

Molly rose, addressing Grace. "I'll be out back weeding if you need me. Try not to."

Her siblings slipped out the back door, and Grace made her way down the hall. They weren't exactly booming with business, it being a weekday and off-season. In fact, they had only three rooms full at the—

Her thoughts halted at the sight of the man in the lobby. Though her approach had been silent, he was already staring at her as she came into view.

It wasn't his good looks that arrested her attention—though he had those in abundance—but his air of intensity.

"Hi there. I'm Grace, one of the innkeepers." Her words wobbled.

She slipped behind the desk, glad for the buffer. "How can I help you?"

"Saw your sign as I was passing by. Looking for a place to stay." His voice was low and pleasantly rumbly.

He appeared to be in his thirties. She scanned his face and altered her opinion. Midtwenties with the confidence of someone older.

"I think we can help you out." Grace opened the appropriate window on the computer.

"It's probably too early to check in."

"The rooms have already been cleaned, so it's no problem. How long will you be staying?"

"Not sure. A few days, maybe a few weeks if possible."

She tried to act unaffected, but it was hard when he was sizing her up with emotionless eyes. She was suddenly conscious of her messy ponytail and freshly scrubbed face.

"We're all clear except the weekend of October third. We have a private wedding scheduled."

"If I'm here that long, I'll figure something out."

"Great." She quoted the weekday and weekend rates.

"That's fine."

Grace took his card and information. *Wyatt Jennings—nice name.* She tried to keep her eyes on the screen, tapping the keys with fingers that were oddly clumsy. Her heart, too, seemed to be doing some weird kind of flutter, and the discomfort left her hoping Wyatt Jennings might limit his stay to a few days.

He stood a few feet from the desk, hands at his sides, posture rigid, gray duffel bag at his feet. He was dressed casually, but his clothes were crisp and neat, not a wrinkle in sight. He wore that tucked-in black T-shirt like a second skin, the short sleeves hugging an impressive pair of biceps. A tattoo peeked out from beneath one of the sleeves.

Stop staring.

"What brings you to the area?" she asked, by way of making conversation.

He ran his fingers through his short, almost-black hair. "A little R & R."

She paused a moment, waiting for him to expound, but he didn't. If she were Molly she'd keep at it until she knew the man's city of origin, marital status, and social security number. But she wasn't Molly.

"Well, this is a great place to rest up, especially this time of year. The weather's still nice, but the trails and lake aren't swamped with tourists."

She clacked away, hitting wrong keys and backing up to delete her mistakes. She was vaguely aware that his gaze shifted around the lobby and the connected living room. She had a feeling if she asked him to close his eyes and recount the visual details of the rooms, he might score better than she did.

"All right, Mr. Jennings," she said when she finished. "We're all set."

"It's just Wyatt."

When his eyes returned to hers, the full impact of his attention made her lungs empty. His brown eyes were set deep beneath a pair of masculine brows. He was neither frowning nor smiling. She wondered briefly what that might look like. The smile, not the frown. She already knew she didn't want to see him unhappy.

She slid his key across the desk. "Wyatt, then. I'm Grace, one of the owners. Maybe I already said that." She paused, but when he simply slid the key into his back pocket, she went on. "Let me give you a little tour before I show you to your room. You can leave your bag behind the counter if you'd like."

He didn't really seem like the tour type—or the inn type for that matter—but he followed her down the hall anyway.

"The Bluebell Inn was built in 1905 and was the town's very first inn. It featured ten bedrooms. Early on it was a stagecoach stop, then for years it housed the post office, till it was sold in 1978 and turned into the governor's summer home." She nearly added that he shared a last name with the governor, but that seemed like the kind of trivial detail he wouldn't care about. "My parents purchased the home when my siblings and I were young, so we had the pleasure of growing up here."

Unlike Levi and Molly, she always skipped over the part about their parents' deaths and their desire to fulfill their parents' dream. She could do without the pity.

The hallway's walls closed in, the space almost buzzing with Wyatt's presence. She was grateful to enter the more open space of the library.

"My brother, sister, and I run the place now, and I also run an outfitters business in my spare time."

He gave her a long look, which she felt to the tips of her lime-green toenails. Her gaze fell to the duffel bag he'd carried with him.

"Um, this is our library, obviously, and you're welcome to use it and borrow books if you like. Let me show you the restaurant." She gave him a smile—unreturned—as she passed him on the way back out. A clean masculine scent wrapped around her and, unwittingly, she drew in a deep breath.

She gestured toward the back door. "The lake's out that way, of course. We have a small boat that's available on a sign-out basis and a pier with a bench, a favorite spot to watch the sunset." He did not seem like the sunset type.

"I'm not sure if you're familiar with the area's natural attractions, but pamphlets are in the lobby, and someone is almost always at the desk. We're happy to help with recommendations, directions, or anything else you need."

As they passed through the lobby she gestured toward the small glass dome on the desk. "Our cook, Miss Della, is famous for her sweets. Every afternoon you'll find complimentary cookies here." Remembering his stellar physique she added, "And also, fresh fruit."

They proceeded through the living room, and she stopped at the French doors leading to the restaurant.

He scanned the space, still saying nothing.

She headed back toward the lobby. "Breakfast is included in the cost of your room, and we also have a lunch and supper menu, which comes in handy. You'll find a lot of restaurants close during the week or on rainy days or, you know, when the owner has a hangnail."

Very professional, Grace. She winced.

"If you'll follow me upstairs, I'll show you to your room."

When she made the turn to the second floor, she paused, mostly to make sure he was still there. "Any questions so far?"

"Is there a workout room?"

"Um, no, but we have an arrangement with Jim's Gym. You can use it since you're staying here. Also the yoga studio in town."

His eyebrow arched, he gave her a long, steady look.

Okay, no on the yoga. "There's a pamphlet downstairs with details."

She continued up the stairs, then down the hall, and stopped at the first door on the left, room seven, tucked into a little alcove.

She gestured toward the door, giving her best professional smile. "And here we are."

He slid past, almost brushing her in the tight space.

Her smile wobbled as her breath caught. "Um, please let me know if I can be of any assistance."

He gave a nod.

Grace turned away, fighting the strange urge to scurry back down the hall.

Chapter Three

Grace had two tasks in mind as she hunched over the laptop's keyboard. Okay, three. One, she needed to find an affordable space for her business, preferably in downtown Bluebell. Two, she needed to know at which sites to list the inn. Three, she had to distract herself from the noises coming from Wyatt's room overhead. She'd already figured out from the repetitive noises he must be working out. She briefly considered bringing him that gym pamphlet, but there was a line between helpful and overbearing, and she liked to stay on the right side of it.

Why was he at the inn? He wasn't their usual customer. They catered mostly to couples from young to elderly, or sometimes families with small children. Maybe he was here to hike—there were certainly plenty of trails to keep him busy. Maybe he hadn't wanted to bother with an Airbnb. Maybe he liked starting his day with a full stomach.

And maybe it was time to get down to the real question at hand: Why was she so fascinated with him? It wasn't just his pretty face. She'd come across many of those. Perhaps it was the confidence he exuded. Or the way he seemed so at ease—not with his environment necessarily but with himself.

And how could she even know these things from their brief encounter?

Grace scowled at the screen. She was failing monumentally at number three.

She slipped off the stool and wandered into the dining room to see if Miss Della needed help in the kitchen. When the siblings decided to open the inn, Mom's best friend graciously offered her outstanding cooking skills—and, occasionally, some unsolicited advice. But that was mostly reserved for Grace, the baby of the family.

She found Miss Della rolling out a lump of pie dough, her dark hands working the roller with expert precision. Her short, wash-and-go hair called attention to her wide-set brown eyes and high cheekbones.

"Need help with lunch, Miss Della?"

"You're just in time, sugar. I need your steady hands. Wash up."

Grace did as asked and joined her at the floured-up counter where a flat circle of dough awaited.

"Grab the pastry cutter and make me some nice strips for the lattice top."

Grace took the fluted wheel by the handle and started slow, precise lines through the dough, listening to Miss Della talk about a new roast recipe she was trying out for supper tonight.

The wheel in Grace's hand swerved out of line, and she winced at the crooked path. She wanted to fix it, but reworking the dough would make the crust tougher. She'd do it anyway, except Miss Della would disapprove.

When Grace finished the job, she carefully wove the strips into latticework while Miss Della buzzed around the kitchen, stirring pots, whisking gravy, and checking the oven. Grace made sure the strips were evenly placed across the cherry pie filling. Four strips in, the dough ripped and Grace gritted her teeth as she gently pinched it back together. But there was no making it perfect again.

When she finished, she surveyed the uncooked pie with a scowl. "All finished."

"Thank you, honey, that looks splendid."

"It looks terrible."

Miss Della surveyed the pie from the stove where she was stirring the green beans. The imperfections were so obvious Grace didn't bother pointing them out.

"Honey, it's just the way I wanted it. If it was perfect it'd look like it came from a Sara Lee box."

"If you say so."

"I do." Miss Della scooped up the pie and placed it in the oven. "And now it'd be a big help if you could fold napkins for me. Jada got held up at her other job."

When Grace slipped into the dining room, Molly was already setting the tables.

She looked up as Grace began working alongside her. "Oh, good. I could use the help. Did you get a chance to look into listing the inn?"

"I found some promising sites. It'll probably take hours to do the listings. We should set up a few more professional shots too. We've made updates."

"Good point. I can write something up for the listing. It's hard to believe we've finally reached this point. In one way it seemed like forever, but in retrospect, it went quickly."

Their parents' deaths had forced them to make a decision: sell the house and move or finish the remodeling their parents had started and open the inn. It had been a monumental task, and they'd all sacrificed a lot to make it happen.

Grace folded a cloth napkin with military precision. "Now you can spread your wings and fly—all the way to Italy. Is Adam still on board with your plan?" Molly's dream of running a bed-and-breakfast in Tuscany went back a long way, but there were two of them now.

"He supports my dreams 100 percent. He can write from anywhere, and he can fly back for book tours."

Adam Bradford was a writer of love stories, perennial bestsellers, with one of his novels made into a movie so far. He was also one of the most down-to-earth people Grace knew. And he really brought out the best in Molly.

"It's been quiet around here this afternoon," Molly said. "Anyone check in?"

"Just the guest who arrived as our meeting was winding down."

"How long are they staying?"

"It's only one guest—and he wasn't sure how long. A few days or a few weeks. He's leaving it open-ended."

For the dozenth time in the last hour, an image of Wyatt Jennings flittered into her mind. Those dark eyes, so serious and observant. Did he make everyone feel like an ant under a microscope? She tried to tell herself it had been an unpleasant sensation, but that wasn't entirely true. Otherwise Grace wouldn't be anticipating their next meeting, now would she?

"That's interesting," Molly said. "What brought him to the area?"

"He didn't really say." But judging by his well-used duffel, the tennis shoes, and yes, the physique, she guessed his idea of R & R included a lot of exercise.

Molly was staring at her, head tilted in that knowing way.

"What?" Grace asked.

"How old is he? Is he married? Single?"

"I don't know. I didn't ask."

Molly gave a smug grin. "So, young and single."

Grace gave her a wry look.

"That blush told me everything I needed to know."

"I'm not blushing." Grace ignored the heat flaring in her cheeks as she grabbed another starched napkin and started folding. What had gotten into her? And who was this man who'd had such a ridiculous effect on her?

"A blush *and* a vehement denial." Molly was studying her face. "Very interesting. I gotta get a load of this guy. I've never seen you react like this to someone you've barely met."

"I've had boyfriends," Grace said a titch defensively. She was twenty-one after all.

"I'm not saying you haven't. I'm just saying no one's really swept you off your feet yet."

"My feet are firmly on the ground and will remain so. There's only room for one romantic in the family, and that spot's already taken. And now Levi has joined the ranks of the happily-ever-after crowd, and that's fine. But leave me alone. I'm happily single, and I want to focus on getting my business off the ground."

"So what's he look like?"

"Did you hear a word I just said?"

"What's his name? You have to know that at least."

"Wyatt Jennings."

"No wedding band? Or telltale white line around the ring finger?"

Grace spared her a glance.

"What? That's important information."

"I don't think so," Grace finally said. "Not that it matters."

"What's he like?"

"We exchanged all of fifty words, Molly." And about forty-nine of those had been hers.

"Well, your first impressions then. Come on, dish. We never get to talk boys." Molly's intense look told Grace she wasn't letting this go.

"Fine. I don't know. He was quiet."

"Ooh, the strong, silent type. Did he ask any questions about the area? That can tell you a lot about a person."

"He asked about using the gym."

Molly waggled her brows. "So he's fit then?"

The image of his muscular biceps leapt into Grace's mind, complete with the little bit of ink peeking from his sleeve. What was the tattoo?

"Eye color?"

"Brown." Grace let that slip before thinking twice.

Molly's eyes gleamed with glee. "You noticed."

"You can't help but notice." Grace turned her attention to the napkin. "You'll see."

The silver stopped clinking as Molly stilled. "Okay, you can't not explain that comment."

She was like a lion chewing on a bloody carcass. Grace expelled a breath, trying to formulate what it was about him. "I don't know, he's very . . . intense, I guess. He takes in everything."

"Including you?"

Grace ignored her.

"So he's an observer?"

"Yes, but not just that. It's like he's, I don't know, wired for 240 or something."

"What does that even mean? He's hyper?"

"No, the opposite. Wired on the inside, like super alert or something. He's actually kind of eerily still and quiet—and maybe a little guarded."

Molly arched a brow. "That's a lot of impression from fifty words."

Grace started to reply just as Molly's gaze darted past Grace to the doorway.

Just as a throat cleared. A very male throat.

Grace sucked in a breath. *Please, no.* Her eyes widened on Molly, hoping against hope it was their brother with a frog in his throat or something.

Molly's eyes, equally wide, swung back to Grace. Her expression told Grace everything she needed to know.

How long had he been standing there? How much had he heard? And why on earth hadn't they shut the door? Grace's face heated a degree or ten. It had to be a veritable beacon by now.

"Is the restaurant open for lunch?" he asked, in that low, yummy drawl.

Molly gave Grace an *Oh!* look before her eyes swung back to Wyatt, her lips curving into a professional smile. "Of course. Come on in and have a seat anywhere. I'll let Miss Della know you're here."

Grace gave her sister a pleading look, nuanced with desperation. *Don't you dare leave me!* But Molly raced for the kitchen as if a swarm of bees were on her heels.

Thanks a lot, Grace telegraphed to the back of Molly's head.

Grace resumed folding the napkin, her fingers now trembling. She messed up and started over. She kept her back to the doorway, giving the flame in her face time to extinguish. She heard a chair scrape the floor in the corner of the room. Heard it squeak as his weight settled into it.

She glanced toward the kitchen door, willing Molly to return quickly.

She didn't.

Long seconds ticked by. One napkin folded. Two. Finally, the last one. She placed it on the table and turned to leave, lifting her chin a notch and arranging her expression into a bland smile.

Wyatt was facing the entry, so she could hardly avoid eye contact without being rude.

"Have a nice lunch," she said as she scuttled from the room.

"Will do."

She could've sworn the corner of his lips twitched before the menu came up to block his face. When she'd dreamed of seeing his smile before, this wasn't at all what she'd had in mind.

Chapter Four

*W*yatt stared at the unfolded trail map from the comfort of his car. It was possible he'd underestimated the difficulty of his objective in Bluebell. He thought he'd find the place he was looking for in the court records or in the police station's records. But the former hadn't turned up the details he needed, and the latter had been destroyed in a flood.

The desk sergeant he'd spoken with was eager to help once Wyatt showed his badge, but there was nothing the man could do. The file was gone, and the officer on duty all those years ago had since passed away.

Wyatt surveyed the trail map. He'd forgotten the thousands of acres that surrounded the little town. Had forgotten how many miles of trails wound through those mountains. He'd only been twelve that summer and was following his mom, not paying attention to where they were going.

But he knew there'd been a waterfall nearby. And a rock formation he could still see in his mind's eye. That was how he'd found his way . . . afterward.

He looked up at the trailhead, at the sign that read Lone Creek Falls. Had to start somewhere.

He exited his car, shouldered the backpack, and checked the

position of his Glock. He didn't anticipate trouble, but he'd learned long ago that a weapon was excellent prevention.

He started up the trail, glad for the absence of tourists. His company this evening came in the form of nattering squirrels, tweeting birds, and scurrying chipmunks.

The sun was still burning hot, and the shade of the woods was a welcome reprieve, as was the breeze that rustled the treetops. The air was heavy with the scent of pine and the earthy smell of decaying leaves. Strangely, these were not the smells that triggered him. Instead, it was the scent of wood smoke on clothes, which thankfully wasn't present at the moment.

He turned his thoughts to the lake house—the Bluebell Inn now. Though the exterior looked largely the same, the interior had undergone radical changes, particularly the upstairs. Still, it had been easy enough remembering his mother trotting down the stairs or his dad lounging on the front porch with a book. They'd spent a lot of time outside during those summers, Wyatt swimming or fishing, his mom never far away. And of course, they'd also gone camping regularly.

He shoved the thought from his mind with the determination of a Navy SEAL. He'd have to let his mind go there eventually, but not until he found the spot. Then he would make the memory his playground. He was, after all, trained to do the very thing others ran from.

For now he could find better things to think about.

An image of the pretty innkeeper danced into his mind, loosening his muscles, turning up his mouth. He'd been intrigued from the moment he'd seen her striding down the hall. By way of keeping his mind occupied, he tallied up everything he knew about Grace Bennett so far.

She was young—twenty-one or twenty-two. She wore her heavy

mane of honey-blonde hair in a ponytail, a few wisps framing her perfect oval face. A thick fringe of lashes bordered her eyes, which at first glance appeared clear blue. But a closer inspection turned up flecks of silver and an interesting ring of amber around the pupil. One eyebrow arched slightly higher than the other, giving her a sardonic look. But he had yet to see if her personality bore that out.

Her nose was straight and unassuming. Her lips full and pouty. There was the tiniest scar on her chin, left of center.

When she was nervous she covered by standing tall and lifting her chin, but if that didn't give her away, she had another tell—she rubbed her lips together as if she'd just applied lip gloss.

She was a blusher. That had been a surprise. In the dining room she'd tried to hide her face, but the tips of her ears had given her away. She was probably as embarrassed at having been caught discussing a guest as she was about the content of her dialogue.

He'd heard some interesting things and admittedly took perverse pleasure in making eye contact with her as she tried to sneak away.

Wyatt's phone buzzed with a call as he headed up a steep incline. He was surprised he even had a signal. He dug the phone from his pocket and saw his dad's picture on the screen.

He paused only a second. "Hey, Dad. What's up?"

"Not much. I was getting ready to head into a meeting and thought I'd check in with you real quick. How's the shoulder doing?"

"Fine. Told you it was nothing."

"Well, the papers sure made it sound like something."

"Yeah, well, sensationalism sells."

"What are you doing? You sound a little winded."

"Working out." He hadn't told his dad about the leave, and he sure wasn't telling him where he was. Paul Jennings had finally moved on with his life, had even remarried a nice, if slightly vapid, woman named Valerie who supported his political career.

They caught up on the extended family, and Wyatt did his best to give an update on his own life without lying. They made tentative plans to meet for the holidays—probably at Valerie's request—which seemed like eons away.

When Wyatt got off the phone, he felt a prick of guilt for hiding his whereabouts. But he didn't want to worry his dad. As he did with everything else, Wyatt would handle his demons on his own.

ℓ

Grace headed out to the shed to get the tandem bike she'd just rented to a couple. The tandem had been a popular addition to her rental equipment, and tonight's weather was perfect for a romantic bike ride.

She said hello to Robin, the photographer who was already taking pictures of the lake view from the inn's backyard. Things were moving fast. And while the idea of having her own location was exciting, it was also a little scary . . . Molly and Adam moving to Italy, Levi heading to LA to be with Mia. Grace would be left behind in Bluebell all alone. Even her best friend, Sarah, was away at college, and Grace wasn't sure she'd come back here when she graduated.

She gave her head a hard shake. No reason to feel sorry for herself. She had far more than she deserved.

She unlocked the shed, pulled out the bike, and gave it a thorough cleaning. One nice thing about new digs would be having a decent place to store and display her rental equipment.

When she reached the sidewalk, the honeymooners were waiting for her there. "Did you decide where you're going?"

"I think we'll just play it by ear." The man straddled the front seat, holding the bike steady for his bride.

"We're working on our spontaneity," the pretty woman said.

"Yes, we're *planning* to be spontaneous."

"It's a thing." The woman shrugged, an adoring gaze focused on her husband.

"Have fun, you two. If you have any problem, my number's on the card." Grace watched them ride away, a little wobbly at first. The woman squealed, and the man teasingly chided her for not doing her part.

Grace couldn't help but smile at their backs. They didn't look much older than she was, and they'd already found their special someone. She was surrounded by happy couples.

But that was all right. Her brother and sister deserved to be happy. They'd given up a lot for Grace. They never once held it over her head, but she saw their sacrifices. Even now Levi was still here, taking care of things, when he should be in California.

It was a lot to live up to. What if her business failed? Levi had told her she should go to college, and she pushed back. But what if he was right? Fifty percent of businesses failed in their first five years—why should hers survive while others' flopped?

Enough with the negativity. She'd have a nice influx of capital once the inn sold. And hers was the only such business in the area. The off-season would be the challenge—as it had been for the inn. But if she gave it her all, surely that would be enough.

As she turned toward the shed, a whirl of red caught her eye. The approaching minivan—a '96 Chevy Lumina—anchored her feet to the ground. The model was unique. Even fourteen years ago you didn't see many of them around.

Grace's mouth dried. Her heart fought to explode from her chest.

It was coming from the direction of town, going slow. Too slow.

It couldn't be him. He was still in jail and would rot there. The sun, low in the sky, reflected off the windshield, obscuring the driver. Blinding her.

The adrenaline flooding her system screamed *fight or flight*, but she couldn't seem to do either. She could only watch in horror as the vehicle pulled to the curb directly in front of her.

Chapter Five

*L*one Creek Falls was a dead end. The pines weren't thick enough, the terrain was too hilly, and the falls were higher and broader than the one he remembered. Wyatt had reached the trail's end and turned right back around.

Once in his car he followed the curve of the shoreline, heading back toward town, back to the inn. The sun was low in the sky, and it was too late to set off on another trail. He'd study the maps of the area and do more research online. He'd narrow it down more. There were only two popular waterfalls, but he was starting to think the one he remembered probably wasn't one of them. Not big enough to be a tourist attraction.

Tomorrow he'd go to the library and see if he could find the old articles. See if they mentioned exactly where it had happened. He should've started there.

When he reached the inn he pulled into a slot out front. He grabbed his backpack and exited the vehicle. When he stepped onto the curb he caught sight of Grace to the right of the inn.

She was standing just off the sidewalk, staring straight ahead. All the color had fled her face, leaving her shockingly white. Her eyes were wide, her shoulders hunched as if her head was trying to disappear into them.

He moved to her side, recognizing the glimmer of fear in her eyes. "Grace?"

She didn't reply. Didn't even blink.

He followed her line of vision to a faded red minivan a dozen feet away. He stepped between her and the vehicle. Made himself big, his hand automatically on his Glock. His eyes locked on the driver's door.

It opened slowly, creaking with age. An orthopedic shoe appeared beneath the door. A moment later the slight frame of an elderly woman emerged from the van. She closed the door and slid open the door behind it. A little girl leapt out of the van. She took the woman's hand, and the two of them headed down the sidewalk, going toward town.

Letting his hand fall, he turned back to Grace.

She was still staring at the van, her breaths fast and shallow. Shock?

He set a hand on her shoulder, dipping down to make eye contact. "Grace?"

Her eyes darted to his, still wide.

"Sit down."

"I'm fine."

"Do as I say." He led her to the curb and she sank onto it.

He dropped down beside her, took her wrist, noting her cold hand, and found her pulse. He counted for ten seconds. Her other hand was pressed to her stomach. She was breathing through her mouth. Rapid pulse.

Her eyes locked on his, panic mounting there. "Don't feel so good."

"Purse your lips like this. Breathe slowly through your mouth."

She did as he said.

"In . . . two . . . three. Out . . . two . . . three. Just like that. Keep going. You're doing great." He breathed with her. When her eyes drifted away, he pulled her back to him.

Slowly the color returned to her face. The panic faded from her eyes.

"Better?" he asked a few minutes later.

She sat up straight, folded her arms over her stomach. "Yes. Thank you. I don't know what that was, but I'm glad it's over."

"You were hyperventilating. Happen before?"

"No." She rubbed her lips together.

He believed her, but something had likely brought this on. Some medical conditions caused hyperventilation, but this seemed situational, brought on by shock or panic.

"Did you know that woman?"

"What woman?"

"The one in the van. You were staring at her."

She looked away from him. "Never seen her before. I'm fine now. Are you a doctor or something?"

"EMT."

"That's handy. I, uh, I think I'm good now." She started to rise to her feet. "I should get back to—"

"Easy." He took her elbow when she wobbled, standing with her. She was through the crisis, embarrassed now and seeking escape.

She disengaged from him and lifted her chin, professional smile in place. "I'm fine now. Thank you again. I appreciate your help."

"No problem," he said, but she was already walking away.

Chapter Six

*W*yatt woke with a sudden jerk. His heartbeat thudded in his ears and the suffocating heat had him shoving the covers away. The gray veil of daylight filtered through the gap in the curtains. He'd almost made it through the night without a nightmare.

He ran a hand over his face, the dream lingering like a bad odor. As usual it had been all too realistic, but he was bound this time, hands and feet. If only he really had been. Maybe then he wouldn't feel so guilty.

He pushed out of bed. He had a lot to do today. In the shower he spent a few extra minutes appreciating the inn's excellent water pressure. He thought of Grace's episode last night. What had provoked it? He hoped she felt better today.

He dressed in hiking clothes, stocked his backpack with water, and headed downstairs. The steps creaked in a familiar way, and he ran his hand down the railing nostalgically. He used to be so happy to get here that he'd wake up early every morning for a week or two. Dash down the stairs to find his mom in the kitchen making pancakes or on the porch enjoying a cup of coffee with his dad.

But his family wasn't at the forefront of his mind today. How would Grace respond to him after yesterday? Would she be über-professional to compensate for her embarrassment, or would she avoid him altogether? Hard to manage when you worked the front desk.

Wyatt was headed to the town library first, but he'd purposely avoided looking up the address. As he took the last stair, however, he discovered the person behind the front desk was not Grace and deflated.

The twentysomething man looked up from a spreadsheet wearing a congenial expression. "Good morning."

"Morning."

He looked to be in his midtwenties and dressed professionally in a polo and khakis. He was tall and fit with dark hair and bright-blue eyes. Something about his smile reminded him of Grace's.

"I'm Levi, one of the innkeepers."

Ah, the brother. "Wyatt."

"Checking out? Or is there something else I can help you with?"

Sounds of movement thumped from above. Wyatt looked at the ceiling as if, by sheer force of will, he might make Grace appear.

He stepped up to the desk. "I was planning to hit the library today. Is it within walking distance?"

"Only about ten minutes." Levi pulled out a town map. "We're here. You follow Bayview into town, make a right at Church Street. It's two blocks down on your left. You can take this. GPS is spotty around here."

He took the map. "Thanks."

"Do you have time for breakfast?"

His stomach was already twisting at the savory aromas emanating from the kitchen. But before Wyatt could respond, footfalls sounded on the steps, more than one pair. Grace and another woman made the turn on the landing and continued down.

He didn't miss the way Grace's steps stuttered as their eyes connected.

She lifted her chin. "Hello."

"Morning."

"I'm Molly, Grace's sister." The brunette popped out from behind Grace. She bubbled from the inside out with energy and warmth.

"Wyatt. Nice to meet you."

"We didn't really get a chance to meet yesterday in the dining room."

Grace cleared her throat, giving her sister a warning look.

"I hope you enjoyed your meal," Molly said. "Nobody puts out a spread like Miss Della."

He opened his mouth to reply.

"You should definitely have breakfast this morning," Molly continued. "You don't want to miss the blueberry streusel muffins. Or the homemade granola. Well, about anything Miss Della makes is wonderful and—"

"Heading out on another hike?" Grace's professional demeanor was in place with a little color in her cheeks.

He much preferred the high color to the ashen look of last night. "Eventually. I'm heading downtown to the library first."

"Grace can show you the way." The words erupted from Molly's mouth like a geyser. "She was on her way to check out a rental space for her business, in town. It's right on the way, isn't it, Grace?"

Grace nailed her sister with a look. "I wouldn't want him to miss out on Miss Della's breakfast."

"Actually, I'm not hungry just yet."

Grace blinked at him.

"Perfect!" Molly bounced on her toes. "There you go then."

A beat of uncomfortable silence passed.

Grace mushed her lips.

The brother glanced between Wyatt and Grace.

"Great," Grace said finally. "It's not far. Are you ready then?"

Wyatt hitched his bag higher on his shoulder. "Whenever you are."

e

Grace headed down the porch, Wyatt on her heels. At least she thought he was. The man was as stealthy as a mountain lion. She'd planned to slip out of the house unnoticed, and she certainly hadn't planned on escorting Wyatt into town.

He made her nervous. All she'd done so far was embarrass herself in front of him. He probably thought she was a loon. Maybe she was. Who had a panic attack at the sight of a feeble old lady?

But it hadn't been the old lady. It had been the van. The one that had riddled her childhood with nightmares. The one that had caused her to miss so many days of second grade that she'd been held back.

Even after all these years some things still triggered her: the sound of tires squealing, the first scent of summer in the air, the crunch of gravel under her feet. And now the van.

She shook away the memory. She'd been through counseling as a child. Her doting parents and concerned siblings were almost smothering. After months and months of remembering, she just wanted to forget. She finally told her family to stop. If she wanted to talk about it, she'd bring it up. They finally acquiesced. It had been years since there'd been a single reference to that early summer day.

But Grace had not forgotten.

Heaven knew she'd turned those memories over and over in her mind last night. But she wasn't letting them intrude on her daytime too.

The morning was pleasant, at least: sunny, midseventies, slight breeze.

She hit the sidewalk and turned toward town. Wyatt came beside her, street side, and matched his pace to hers. Her heart gave a heavy thump at his sudden nearness.

"So, tell me about your outfitters business."

Grace was relieved at the neutral topic. "I started it last year, running it out of the inn, basically. I have a decent web presence and have managed to accumulate some quality equipment. We'll be selling the inn shortly, though, so I need to find a retail space for it."

"Why are you selling the inn?"

"That was always the plan—get it established as a business, then sell it. My brother will be moving to California—his fiancée lives there—and Molly wants to move to Tuscany and eventually open an inn."

"You're the only one staying here then?"

She'd expected him to react to the Italy thing. Most people did. Grace shrugged. "It's home."

"Your parents live here?"

"They passed a while back."

She felt his gaze on her for a long moment. "Sorry to hear that."

"So, yes, it'll be just me." Even she heard the forlorn note in her voice. What would Bluebell be without her family? She guessed she'd soon find out.

"You'll miss them, your siblings."

"Of course. But I have friends, and this is a close-knit community. Sometimes too much so, if you know what I mean. What do you think of the area so far?"

He nodded as they crossed the street. "Nice. Scenic. Plenty to do."

"Where'd you say you were from?" she asked even though he'd never actually said.

"Charlotte."

"Born and bred?"

"Originally from Raleigh. Were you born here?"

"A Bluebell girl through and through."

"You like to travel?"

"Sure, I've been here and there. But mostly I like it here." She flashed a saucy smile at him.

"Fair enough."

"What about you . . . world traveler?"

He slid her a sideways look, the corner of his lips tipping up. "Here and there."

"Are you trying to be an enigma, or does it just come naturally?"

"Comes pretty natural."

She laughed.

"You seem awfully young to own a business—two businesses."

Grace cocked a look at him. "Is that your way of asking my age?"

"I'm usually more subtle."

"I have no doubt." Grace took a step up the curb and turned right, leading them down Church Street. They had to walk fairly close to fit on the sidewalk, and she caught the scent of his woodsy cologne.

"You're not going to tell me?" he said finally.

"You haven't asked."

"How old are you, Grace?"

"I'm twenty-one, Wyatt. How old are you?"

"Ancient."

"You're aging well. Not a gray hair in sight. Come on, now, I told you."

"Twenty-six."

Grace widened her eyes dramatically. "You're right. Positively ancient."

He skirted a root that had grown through the sidewalk. "What made you want to open an outfitters business?"

She hitched her shoulder. "I've always been active and outdoorsy, and I saw a need in town for such a place."

"Sounds like a big challenge."

"I like a challenge." She gave him a look from the corner of her eye. Had that come off flirty? She hadn't meant it to. She didn't think. "But to be honest, I mostly do the fun stuff, and my brother handles the financial side. He's teaching me, but I'm not a natural with numbers and spreadsheets. How about you? How'd you become an EMT?"

He paused long enough she wondered if he was going to answer at all.

"I'm actually in security. The EMT training was part of that."

Security? She had about a dozen questions. For starters, what kind of security? Did he work in a prison? At a bank? Was he a policeman? A sheriff? But she wasn't Molly. She wouldn't push for answers. He obviously liked his privacy, and she could respect that.

"What's your next hike?" she asked instead. "You should definitely head up to Stone Gap Bridge before you leave. It's a swinging bridge stretched across a deep canyon, a popular tourist destination."

"Sounds treacherous."

"You strike me as the type of guy who might like an adrenaline rush."

His lips twitched. "Just might."

They crossed another street and passed the coffee shop. She waved at a couple of women drinking on the patio. "Church friends."

"Where do you attend?"

Gracie pointed up the street at the white structure with the traditional steeple. "Right there. First Community Church."

"Ah. The famous church of Church Street."

"The very one. Do you attend anywhere?"

"Not for a while." His tone said *subject closed*.

She sensed his silence held a story, and she'd love to know it. But he was a stranger, only passing through, and she was just the innkeeper.

The library was just ahead, and Grace found herself reluctant to part ways.

"You'll have to stop in at the coffee shop sometime. It's really good. Their frappés are amazing. I know, I hate to be a cliché—that's such a basic girl drink. But my opinion stands."

"You're not a basic anything, Grace."

Oh really? She arched a brow his direction.

His lips curled in an almost smile, and she wondered what he looked like when he really went all out and showed his teeth and everything. She hoped to put a real smile on his face before he left town. She had a feeling he could use a little levity in his life.

Her footsteps slowed as they reached the Bluebell Public Library.

He glanced up at the old brick building, at the American flag fluttering in the breeze.

"Well, here we are. Thanks for the escort. And good luck on the retail space."

"Thanks."

He treated her to one of those intense looks before he headed up the sidewalk with that purposeful stride that was already becoming familiar.

l

Wyatt settled at the microfilm machine, armed with the appropriate slides. The librarian had helped him find what he was searching for and instructed him on the machine. He found himself reluctant to dive into the old newspaper articles.

He'd rather think about Grace. He'd enjoyed talking with her; the walk went too quickly. She'd been open enough, a little feisty even, but she didn't push him when they'd touched on topics he preferred to avoid. He didn't expect good intuition and restraint in a woman so young, so innocent. A small-town girl.

Twenty-one. He shook his head. He'd been a numbskull at

twenty-one and wasn't sure he'd advanced much beyond that. But twenty-one seemed like a long time ago. He felt older than his age—always had—and given his job, he'd lived a comparatively worldly life. He'd parted with his innocence a long time ago.

Someone across the room sneezed, drawing his attention back to the machine. Enough stalling. He needed direction, or he'd spend the next few weeks trudging aimlessly around the mountains. He wasn't sure why he needed to go there for closure. Instinct just told him he did, and he'd learned long ago to trust that inner voice.

He placed the slide, adjusted the view, and scanned the local newspaper. It didn't take long to find the right issue—it was the day after it had happened.

The headline read "Governor's Wife Murdered on Camping Trip."

Wyatt swallowed hard and forced himself to review the article as if he were a subjective reader. He scanned the bits he knew all too well, searching for the exact location of the crime. But the journalist only named the Blue Ridge Mountains as the police hadn't released many details at that point. He moved on to the article in the next day's paper.

A fist tightened around his chest at the sight of his mother's beautiful picture.

It was a full five seconds before he could tear his gaze away long enough to read the article. It contained a few more details. The suspect was still at large. More background about his mother. Wyatt was also mentioned, but not by name, as he'd been a minor at the time.

Finally, in an edition a couple weeks out from the crime, an article declared that the culprit had been apprehended in Florida. A regurgitation of the crime turned up a few new details, but nothing regarding its location.

He kept going, searching for other articles, but the subsequent ones focused on the trial and prosecution of Gordon Kimball.

Wyatt turned off the machine. He'd learned nothing helpful, and the search had come at a cost. Sweat beaded his forehead, and his palms were cold and clammy. But the worst of it was the memories that had been stirred up. A necessary evil, he knew. He would have to dig it all up—feel it all—if he wanted to reach the other side of this and finally reclaim his life.

Chapter Seven

Molly smiled as she pulled the door shut, feeling rather smug about the way she'd set up her sister on a walk to town with the hunky guest. She stowed the dirty towels in the cart, pushed it into the laundry room, then started a load of sheets and towels. That done, she grabbed the bag of garbage and hauled it downstairs.

At the front desk Levi looked up from the computer. "Hey, you got a minute?"

"Sure, what's up?"

"Robin sent the pictures this morning. Did you see them?"

"Yeah, they turned out great."

"Did you get the listing written up yet?"

"It's only been a day, Levi."

"I know, but the sooner we get it online, the sooner we'll have a buyer."

"Somebody's eager to get out to LA."

"I have a prospective job—a commercial construction company. They want to interview me about a position that'll be opening up soon."

"Hey, that's great." The thought of Levi leaving for good weighted her chest. This was happening so fast. But it was the plan. She was leaving too. They'd all be going their separate ways. "I'll get the listing written up today."

"Thanks."

Molly picked up the bag of trash and headed toward the back door.

"Hey, one more thing," Levi said. "What's up with that Wyatt guy?"

"What do you mean?"

"It seemed like there was something strange going on between him and Grace earlier."

Molly lifted a brow. "That was just tension, Levi. Good ol' sexual tension."

He flinched, the thought of his baby sister experiencing attraction no doubt making his stomach heave.

"I was glad to see it going both directions," she said. "I haven't seen anyone turn her head like that before. That's some stare he has, huh?"

"What stare?"

"Never mind. You wouldn't understand. I'm taking this out, then heading home." She started down the hall.

"Wait. What do we know about him?"

Molly paused again. "We know he's a guest. And his name is Wyatt."

"That's it? And you just sent Grace out the door with him?"

"In Bluebell? In broad daylight? She'll be fine, Levi. She's not a child anymore."

"How long's he staying?"

She shrugged. "It's open-ended—and you're overreacting again. You said we should let you know when you're doing it, and I'm letting you know—you're doing it."

Levi shifted. "He seemed kind of secretive, that's all."

"During your extensive onetime conversation? People usually don't spill their life story upon first sight."

He pinned her with a look.

Well, fine. "*Most* people don't. I'm leaving now. Can you throw the load in the dryer in twenty minutes?"

"Sure." She could tell he wanted to say more, but he wisely held back. "See you tomorrow."

Two hours later, Molly sat at her kitchen table, frowning at the document on her laptop. She glanced out on the deck where her husband's fingers were practically dancing across his keyboard, feeling a moment's jealousy.

Sure, sure, he wrangled words for a living, but this was her beloved childhood home. She knew everything there was to know about it. Loved everything about it. Why couldn't she find the words to make others see how special it was?

She stared at the cursor blinking where she'd left off. She placed her fingers on the keyboard and wrote out the spiel they gave every new guest upon arrival. A nice long paragraph.

She reread it, finding it didn't feel right in print, not for a listing.

She placed her finger on the delete key and watched all the words disappear. Outside, the sunny deck and cushy lawn chairs beckoned. But Adam was working, very productively apparently, and she wasn't about to interrupt his flow.

Her gaze drifted around their lake house. He'd bought it when he moved here from New York. She'd thought he'd choose something new and modern like he'd had in the city, but this home was fifty years old and loaded with charm. They'd done some updating, but the two-story home retained its lovely character.

Settling in here after the wedding had been easy. She felt at home on the lake where she'd grown up. At home with Adam. She hated the weeks when he went on tour, but that was only when a new book released. The rest of the time was easy breezy. They'd settled into a nice routine. Most nights she cooked or he grilled out, and once a week they ate with Levi and Grace. Molly did the grocery shopping, and Adam took care of the lawn. They had a couple favorite shows they watched together.

All that would change when they moved to Tuscany. They'd have to find a new routine. But she was so grateful Adam was willing to move. She'd already started tackling the red tape necessary to own and operate a business in Italy. It was complicated, and she'd likely have to hire an Italian lawyer to help her muddle through it.

In the meantime she scoped out potential inns and homes online, but she didn't want to get her heart set on anything. It would probably take a while to sell their inn, maybe over a year.

The glass door slid open, and Adam slipped through, looking handsome as ever. His brown hair was windblown, and he had a few days' stubble on his jaw. He'd gotten new glasses a few weeks ago, and she was crazy about the way he looked in them.

"Ready for lunch?" she asked, eager for a distraction.

"Not just yet. I had a late breakfast. What are you working on in here?"

She heaved a sigh. "The inn's listing."

"It's not going well? What have you written so far?"

Molly peered down at the document. "Historic inn, nestled in the Blue Ridge Mountains, for sale." She gave him an exaggerated pouty look.

"All right . . . That's a nice start. *Nestled* is a great verb." He came behind her and rubbed her shoulders.

She moaned as his fingers dug into her tight muscles. She hadn't realized how tense she was. "How do you do it? How do you turn your thoughts and feelings into just the right words on paper? Everything I write . . . just doesn't do the inn justice."

"You're pretty close to the subject matter. Sometimes that makes it more difficult. Want a little help?"

"*Yes.*"

"Want me to just do it for you?"

She peeked up at him. "Would you?"

He laughed as he leaned down, pressed a kiss to her temple, and whispered in her ear, "There is nothing I wouldn't do for you, Mrs. Bradford."

Chapter Eight

*L*ater that night Grace took the bike and helmet back from the middle-aged woman. After a bit of small talk she said good-bye, then her eyes caught on the curb where the Lumina had pulled up the night before.

She stared at the empty parking space, a shiver of apprehension skittering down her spine at the memory. She wiped her sweaty palms down her shorts.

Ridiculous. The vehicle was nowhere to be seen at the moment, and she hadn't seen it since. Besides, it belonged to a harmless elderly woman. A sweet old grandma.

What was wrong with her? Sure, there'd been times when that childhood memory returned. Even freaked her out a little. But yesterday she'd had some kind of panic attack, and she could still feel the panic simmering beneath the surface.

And just below that was the other feeling she'd come to accept as her status quo. That she didn't quite deserve the good things in her life. That she maybe hadn't even deserved to live.

She knew she was dealing with survivor's guilt. But knowing it and making it go away didn't equate. She may have gotten away with her life that day, but she sure hadn't gotten off scot-free.

She put the bike away, locked up the equipment shed, and went inside the inn, the depressing thoughts on her heels like a murky shadow.

When she reached the lobby she spotted Levi at the front desk, clacking away on the keyboard.

He looked up at her arrival. "Hey. How was the retail space you looked at earlier?"

She shrugged on her way to the stairs, not in the mood for conversation. "It was fine, I guess."

"Is it a possibility? Think you could make it work?"

"I don't know, Levi. It needs a lot of help."

"Wait. What's wrong?"

"Nothing. I'm just tired. I'm turning in early."

"At nine o'clock? What kind of work does it need? We aren't exactly rookies when it comes to renovation."

"It's more the money than the work."

"You'll be getting a nice check when we sell the inn."

"Which I'll use to expand my business. I don't have an extra fifty thousand to throw into a building."

"What about a grant? I was reading a while back about state grants for new business starts. You should apply."

"I don't know. I'll check it out." She headed for the stairs.

"Sure you're okay? You seem down or something." He started to say something else, then closed his mouth.

"I'm fine. Just tired, like I said. Good night."

"Good night."

She was grateful that for once he hadn't pried. Molly was the nosy one, but Levi had his own special way of interfering. When their parents died he'd appointed himself guardian and lord over his sisters. He'd gotten better the past couple of years—after a sisterly intervention—but there was still room for improvement.

Once in her bedroom Grace showered and got into her pajama

bottoms and a top that read *Due to unfortunate circumstances I am awake*. She had the room all to herself now that Molly was married. She wouldn't admit it aloud, but sometimes she missed her sister's idle rambling and the bookwormy way she stayed up late reading whatever novel she couldn't put down. She didn't miss the messiness or the lamp shining late into the night, however.

If Grace were lonely for noise, her wish was soon granted. The family staying in the room next to hers returned, and their toddler began crying—screeching really.

Grace grabbed her laptop and started some tunes flowing through her earbuds. Now was as good a time as any to figure out how to fix her problem.

She began researching survivor's guilt. She got caught up in story after story of people who were living with the same problem she was experiencing. Trauma brought on by war events, mass shootings. Stories much worse than hers, which somehow only added to her guilt. At least she wasn't having nightmares, mood swings, and depression.

She turned her search toward overcoming the problem. What did she have to do? She immediately discounted counseling. Been there, done that. Most of the advice was about changing the way you think. Okay, she could work on that. But it seemed so passive. She wanted to *do* something. She wanted these feelings gone, and she sure didn't want another panic attack in front of a handsome guest.

Finally, she stumbled upon an extensive article from a psychology site that recommended turning guilt into helping others. Guilt made a person feel helpless—this she knew—while action, specifically helping others, made a person feel useful and purposeful.

Okay. Here was a plan she could get behind. Maybe it was self-serving, helping others to help herself, but hey, two birds, one stone. She would try to be more outwardly focused, on the lookout for how she could help others. That was really just the Christian way of life anyway, wasn't it? Love God, love others, and all that.

Having a plan made her feel better. She set her laptop aside, suddenly weary, and turned off her lamp.

Her thoughts immediately turned toward the conversation she'd had with Wyatt as they walked into town this morning. She enjoyed talking to him, bantering with him. Grace had never been talkative like Molly, but she'd always been quick on her feet with conversation. With Wyatt she'd met her match. He didn't say much, but what he said counted. He'd kind of flirted with her. And maybe she flirted back a little.

She hoped to see him the next day. And a few minutes later she drifted off with a smile.

Chapter Nine

*G*race heard footsteps on the stairs, and from her position behind the front desk, she tensed in anticipation. But a moment later the small family who'd been staying in the room next to hers appeared.

"Good morning. Checking out?"

"Yes, ma'am," the father said.

Grace made small talk as she completed the checkout process then handed them the receipt.

"Do you need directions, or are you all set?" she asked the father since their toddler was busy spilling juice on his mother's shirt and wiggling to get down.

"I think we're good to go."

Remembering her pledge to be more helpful, she asked, "Can I get you some muffins or coffee to go? They're orange spice today, and it'll just take a minute."

"No thanks. We're running a little late as it is."

"Well, let me get the door for you." She scurried from behind the counter. "Have a safe flight. We hope to see you again soon."

Once the family was out the door, Grace went back to the computer. She'd already bookmarked the top five commercial property sites at which to list the inn. She felt good about their chances of selling the inn on their own. She just needed that listing from her sister.

She texted Molly, who was due at the inn soon to clean rooms. *Do you have the listing written yet? I'd like to get it uploaded today.*

A moment later Molly texted back. *It's finished. But I already left the house. I'm at the coffee shop. I'll have Adam email it to you. Want a frappé?*

I'll wait to hear from him then. And no thanks.

She hoped managing the listing wasn't too time-consuming. Potential buyers would have questions before they'd travel here to tour the inn. But presumably a lot of them would be financial questions she could turn over to Levi. Not that he didn't have enough on his plate at the moment too.

With most of the guests checked out, she turned her attention to her own business. Several spaces were available downtown—that would be the ideal location. But all of them had been empty a long time, and there were good reasons for that. Renovations would be expensive.

There were also small homes on the outskirts of town that could work. But, again, converting them into retail space would be costly.

Levi had mentioned business grants. She did a little research to see what was available and found he was right. There were even grants specifically for the rehabilitation of old buildings. But upon reading further, she saw that many steps would have to be taken to have a chance at one of those grants. She read until she was completely overwhelmed and was glad for the distraction when Molly breezed in a while later, latte in hand.

"Good morning!"

"Morning. Adam hasn't sent me that listing yet."

"Oh! I forgot to ask." She pulled out her phone, her face sinking. "It's dead. I forgot to charge it last night."

"You can use my charger upstairs. I'll text him."

"I need to call him anyway. I forgot to defrost the chicken—he's grilling tonight. Are all the guests out for the moment?"

"All except Wyatt."

"Ooh, it's just 'Wyatt' now, huh? And is he the reason you're wearing makeup today?" Molly's gaze sharpened on Grace. "Is that a trio palette you're wearing?"

Grace rolled her eyes, making herself busy with the realty website. It was just a little neutral eye shadow and mascara. And okay, a little eyeliner. Also lip gloss.

"By the way, Levi was getting all up in your business last night, but I called him off. You're welcome."

Grace's lips slid into a rueful smile. "One hot guest and brother dear gets all bent out of shape."

A throat cleared.

Grace looked up, her smile falling flat.

Wyatt stood at the bottom of the steps. Of course he did.

Her face went nuclear. Darn the man. How did he get down those stairs without a single creak? It hadn't been done since 1920.

"Good morning," Molly said to Wyatt gleefully.

"Morning," he said, but he was staring straight at Grace, that enigmatic expression present and accounted for.

"I think I'll just . . ." Molly slipped past Wyatt and went upstairs.

Grace lifted her chin. "Do they teach that in security school?"

"Teach what?"

"How to enter a room without making any noise whatsoever."

"It's an important skill to master."

No doubt he'd already learned all kinds of things about Grace and her opinions. She'd really thought she was better at that whole aloof thing.

He came closer, shrinking the space, making Grace glad for the desk between them. Whenever he was near the air seemed to crackle between them. She'd never experienced that with a man before. Most of her dates—and her boyfriends—had been a little lackluster. Had made her wonder what all the fuss was about.

She wiped her palms down her khakis, glad she'd taken a little extra time to get ready this morning. And yes, she could admit, if only to herself, that Wyatt was the reason behind the sudden concern with her appearance.

Since he was studying the map on a nearby wall, she took a moment to study him. He was dressed to hike in boots and sturdy jeans, a backpack slung over his shoulder.

Remembering she was the innkeeper, she wandered over. "Is there anything I can do for you this morning? Besides embarrass myself, I mean."

His lips twitched just a little. "You seem to be making a habit of that."

"Not my usual MO, I assure you."

He turned to her. "What is your usual MO?"

"Oh, I don't know. Hang around in the background, all low-key, feet on the ground instead of in my mouth."

His gaze fell to her feet, and she was suddenly very glad Molly had talked her into a pedicure last week.

His eyes tracked back up to hers—those brown eyes. "Pretty feet, though."

She realized they were standing close, that countertop nowhere near. "You are flirting with me."

"If you couldn't tell I must be losing my touch."

She locked her gaze on the map, her heart having forgotten its usual rhythm. She'd always been direct. She just wasn't used to getting as good as she gave.

"Do you, um, need help finding someplace? I know the area pretty well. Even the far-lying regions. Though the best hikes aren't far at all. I guess that's what makes Bluebell so popular. And like I said, you really don't want to miss Stone Gap Bridge." One handsome guest, and she'd turned into Molly. She closed her eyes in a long blink.

"Maybe we can go there together."

Grace blinked. "Um, I do guided tours." It was true she hadn't done one yet. In fact, she'd planned to hire someone for that.

The corner of his mouth curled up as he looked back to the map. "That's not really what I had in mind. But for now, I'm trying to find a place I've been to before."

"You've been here before then?"

"Long time ago. Camping, east of Bluebell, I think. I remember a creek nearby and a waterfall, small one. There was a rock formation that was about thirty feet high. Lots of pine trees in the area. Any of that ring a bell?"

She wondered what he was looking for. "Well . . . we have three creeks running east. Lone Creek, Pine Creek, and Lost Creek." She pointed them out on the map. They all ran into the lake. "How big was the waterfall?"

"Just a few feet high, maybe ten feet wide. It was a long time ago."

"I can't think of anything like that nearby. That's pretty small. It might even be dried up this time of year."

"I hadn't thought of that."

"How far of a hike was it from town, do you know?"

"I think it was about a half day's walk—maybe a full day. Honestly, it could've been even farther."

"Okay . . . well, I'd recommend following each of the creeks from the lake. Some trails take you partway, but once you get past the touristy stuff, you might be on deer trails or even hacking your way through the forest. Also, Lost Creek is pretty wide. You get far enough away and tributaries flow into it." She pointed them out on the map. "The maps won't be very helpful after a certain point. If it's that far away, you should probably look at camping along the way. All the trekking in and out of the mountains will cost a lot of time."

His breath leaked out slowly. "This is going to be harder than I thought. I'm kind of on a schedule."

A frown crouched between his brows. It wasn't much, but for a guy with his poker face, it said a lot. She didn't know why he wanted to find this spot so badly, but it was obviously important to him.

She knew the area like the back of her hand. The mountains had been her escape whenever life got stressful or chaotic. Molly was scheduled at the front desk at ten, and tomorrow was Grace's day off. She wouldn't even charge him, because she sensed this was a great opportunity for her too.

Ordinarily she wouldn't even consider it. Hiking alone in the woods with a strange man? No thanks. But her intuition told her she was completely safe with Wyatt.

"I can do it," Grace said finally. "I can help you find what you're looking for."

Chapter Ten

*W*yatt hadn't really wanted an audience as he faced his biggest fear, but he could always send Grace back home once he found the spot.

Despite her uncertain proposition, he didn't doubt her knowledge of the area. He also knew he might not have time to find the spot without her assistance. And he didn't have the equipment to go whacking his way through the forest or even for camping.

Did Grace often go traipsing through the mountains with strange men? He hoped not. "How much would you charge for something like that?"

She rubbed her lips together. "Um, I was going to do it on the house this time."

"And why would you do that?"

"Well, honestly, it would be my first guided tour. It'll be good experience for me."

"I still want to pay you something."

She waved him off. "I insist. I'd like to do this. And I have good camping equipment too."

"I don't doubt any of that, and I could sure use your help." But there was something more in her expression, something he couldn't quite gauge.

"But?"

He sensed her attraction, but he didn't think that was her motivation. If he did, he'd turn down her offer to be his guide. A little harmless flirting was one thing, but let's face it. She was too young for him—in years and in life experience.

That offer he'd extended before had been impulsive—an aberration. But she had those sweet blue eyes and that proud little chin, and he couldn't help but wish she were just a few years older, a few relationships wiser.

Maybe she really was seeking to build her résumé, so to speak. Maybe she was desperate to get away for some reason. Maybe some idiot boy was hounding her.

Maybe her reasons didn't even matter. "No buts. If you're game, so am I. And I appreciate your help." The smile that broke out on her face made his heart buck.

"That's great. Oh, I didn't mention I'm on duty for a couple more hours. Is that all right? I have tomorrow off though, so we'll have the better part of two days. With any luck that'll be enough."

"With any luck." He glanced at his watch. "I can wait awhile."

Grace glanced up the stairs. "I might be able to leave a little early. I'll need to get our gear together too."

"I can grab breakfast in the meantime."

"Perfect."

He gave her a nod and made his way through the living room and to the dining room. His day had just taken a big turn—for the better or worse remained to be seen.

ℓ

As soon as Wyatt disappeared through the French doors, Grace bounded up the stairs. She found Molly in Wyatt's room, making up the bed. Grace slipped inside and closed the door.

Molly gave her a curious look. "What's up?"

"Are you almost finished cleaning?" Grace worked the sheets across the bed from her sister.

"I just got started."

"Right. Well, you think you can keep an ear out for the phone?" There wouldn't likely be anyone coming in until later in the day since check-in wasn't till three.

"Why?"

"I have a guided tour, with Wyatt." No need to mention it was unpaid.

Brows raised, Molly looked at her. "I thought you weren't doing the guided tours?"

"I'm making an exception. And we'll be camping tonight, so we won't be back until late tomorrow. I didn't want anyone to worry."

Molly paused, the coverlet still in her hands. "Overnight? With someone you don't know? Are you sure that's a good idea?"

"Well, he needs a tour guide, and I haven't hired anyone yet. Besides, I thought you liked him."

"I do like what I know of him—which isn't very much. Grace, what do you know about him? Walking across town with him is one thing, but being in the mountains all alone with him is quite another. You'll have very little cell phone access."

Grace stiffened. "I can handle myself, Molly. Jeez. I never expected you to go all Levi on me."

"There's Levi and then there's common sense."

"I have plenty of common sense. And my bear spray. I may not know him well, but I trust him. He's a security officer, by the way. I'm sure those people go through rigorous background checks. Plus he's an EMT. I couldn't be safer."

Molly still seemed uncertain as she continued to adjust the covers. "That makes me feel a little better, I guess."

"You have all his personal information in the computer. Really, I wish you'd just trust me a little. I have good instincts about people, and I'm telling you, he's one of the good ones. Now, can you watch the desk for me or what? I'd like to have our equipment together before he finishes breakfast."

"Fine." Molly fluffed the pillows. "You're going to leave me to tell Levi about this aren't you?"

"Would you?"

"He's already suspicious of the guy."

Grace rolled her eyes. "Levi was suspicious of Adam."

"Good point." Molly set the pillows at the head of the bed, giving Grace a put-upon look. "Go on. Get out of here."

"Thank you."

She was already halfway out the door when Molly called, "But you better text me when you have a signal!"

Chapter Eleven

$\mathcal{G}$race was nervous about spending the better part of two days with Wyatt—but not for the reasons Molly had stated.

Having him behind her as they hiked was unsettling. She kept wondering how she looked in her jeans and if her hair was coming loose from her ponytail. Since when had she cared about such things? She'd never been like other girls. Hadn't fussed over who she was going to prom with or what she was wearing to this party or that event. She didn't even bother with makeup most of the time.

What was it about this man that made her care? That made her want to keep those chocolate-brown eyes fixed on her? She hated herself a little right now for that. And for single-handedly getting herself into this overnight camping trip. Her conflicting feelings made her dizzy.

It would be fine. He was obviously set on finding this particular spot, and the least she could do was help him do that.

She led the way on the marked trail following the rippling water of Lone Creek. The path was wide, paved, and ascended slowly into the hills. Towering deciduous trees rose above them, and a thick undergrowth sheltered the small critters scurrying about the forest floor. She breathed in the earthy smells of leaves, pine trees, and moss and caught a whiff of Wyatt's clean scent in the mix.

She stepped over a fallen tree, taking the time to hitch her backpack higher on her shoulder. Wyatt had taken the bigger of the two and managed the move like his pack weighed no more than a feather.

"Enjoy the paved path." She started off again. "It goes on for about four miles, then becomes a footpath."

"And after that?"

"A deer path, more or less. It's been a while since I've been out that far, though, so it might be overgrown. How long ago was it you were here before?"

"I was just a kid. But I have a good visual memory of the area. I'll know it when I see it."

They continued in silence, her footfalls and the chattering squirrels filling the quiet. She wondered again what drove Wyatt to find this area. But that was his business.

There was a lot she wanted to ask him. About his job, his life—and yes, his love life. But her job was to be his guide, not to pry into his personal life. If he wanted to talk, he'd talk, and she'd be happy to accommodate. If not, it was going to be a long, quiet two days.

"What was it like growing up here?" he asked as if privy to her thoughts.

Grace's first thought was of that terrible afternoon when the minivan had followed her down the deserted country road they lived on at the time.

"Pretty great really. I had loving parents, and we didn't want for anything. A nice, comfortable small town where everybody knows everybody, a lake to swim and fish in, and mountain trails to hike. Couldn't ask for much more."

"Some people think small towns are boring. Especially teenagers."

"It would be if you didn't like the outdoors."

"I guess you found the right business to launch. Did you like the space you looked at in town yesterday?"

"Loved it. Unfortunately, the building's as old as Methuselah, and it's been vacant awhile. It needs a lot of TLC. Did you find what you were looking for at the library?"

He paused a beat. "Mmm. Not really."

"Right genre, wrong author?"

"Something like that."

"I'm not much of a reader myself. I think Molly got all of the literary genes, though Levi likes to read a little too. Molly's husband is an author—writes under the pen name of Nathaniel Quinn."

"Sounds familiar."

"He lives in Bluebell now. Nice guy. They met when he came to stay at the inn."

"And your brother's engaged?"

She glanced over her shoulder. "How'd you know that?"

"He was on the phone discussing wedding plans when I passed him yesterday."

"Yeah, their wedding's coming up in just over two weeks. His fiancée lives in LA, and the wedding will take place here, so the planning's been a little tricky." She left out the part about his fiancée being a celebrity. They were trying to keep the wedding quiet to keep reporters away.

There was a nice lookout just up the hill with a grassy bank that overlooked the rippling water. "I'm about ready for a water break. How about you?"

"Sounds good."

At the designated spot she shrugged off her backpack, but it connected with Wyatt's shoulder.

He flinched at the impact, his lips going tight. He pressed his hand to the spot.

"I'm sorry," she said, even though she hadn't hit him hard enough to inflict pain. "Did I hurt you?"

"No, I'm fine." His hand fell away. "It's nothing."

Maybe he had a bad shoulder or something. In that case he probably shouldn't be carrying that heavy backpack. But he dropped the pack and rooted through it. He seemed fine. Maybe she'd jabbed him with something.

She mentally shrugged and went in pursuit of her own water bottle.

ℓ

By the end of the day Wyatt's shoulder was throbbing. Two days of backpacking had set him back. He'd also neglected the physical therapy regimen he'd been religious about before this trip. He needed to get back to it but suspected the injury was aggravated enough for now.

"I'll gather some firewood," he told Grace, scanning the small, primitive campground they just reached. "It'll get chilly tonight."

"I'll get out our supper."

"Sounds good." He grabbed his pack and headed up a path through the woods. They'd made decent progress today until they came to the deer path. It had been slow going, cutting through the underbrush.

He'd started to doubt his sanity. What if this was all a big waste of time? They wouldn't be able to go much farther tomorrow before they had to head back. What if he never found the spot? Or what if he did and it didn't bring the healing he sought? What if he was just as broken when his leave was finished? He couldn't entertain that thought. Not when he was about to be promoted to PPD.

Wyatt didn't bother looking for firewood as he walked. He was headed first to the creek. He had a day's worth of sweat, dirt, and cobwebs coating him, and he couldn't wait to shed it. He was pretty sure Grace had already bathed when she disappeared for a bit after they'd set up the tents.

She was in good shape, he'd give her that. They'd hiked, mostly uphill, for hours and not a word of complaint. She was a good traveling companion—chatty when he was, quiet when he wasn't. It went back to that good intuition he'd noticed before. She hadn't even pried him for information about this place he was searching for.

Did she even know about the murder that had happened somewhere in these mountains fourteen years ago? Probably not. She'd only been a child at the time, not likely to be scanning newspaper headlines or watching the eleven o'clock news.

When he reached the creek, he ditched his pack and took a few minutes to stretch out his shoulder. The creek was deep enough here for a swim. And no one was around, even at the campground, so he stripped off his clothes and went in.

ℓ

Grace set out some of the food Miss Della had packed for them—peanut butter sandwiches, chips, granola bars, and bananas. The old campground had grills, but Grace hadn't been sure of that, so she played it safe. There were napkins, paper plates, even instant coffee and coffee cups. God bless Miss Della.

The sound of a thumping bass hit her ears just before the rumbling of an engine. A pickup truck approached from the dirt road, turning into the campground. Looked like they had company. There was still plenty of light, but the shade of the trees made it seem later. She couldn't make out who was inside the extended cab.

The truck slowly wound around the dirt lane, then stopped and parked two sites away from theirs. There were at least a dozen spots, all of them open, so the proximity seemed overclose. But maybe they fancied the idea of company.

When the doors opened, three guys spilled out, wearing jeans and T-shirts, mid- to late twenties, she guessed. They greeted her with waves and smiles before they got down to the business of unloading things.

She couldn't make out their quiet chatter, but judging by a glance or two, and some guffawing, she got the feeling they were talking about her. A prickle of unease squirmed down her spine. Maybe this would be a good time to check in with Molly. She pulled out her phone, but of course, there was no service.

Might be time to go after some firewood herself, and if she stumbled upon Wyatt, all the better. She slipped away, glancing back to make sure no one was following. Adrenaline had shot into her bloodstream, making her heart beat obnoxiously fast. Her breaths quick and shallow, she heard every snap of the twigs beneath her feet, every rustle of underbrush.

She was being ridiculous. But she was glad Wyatt was here. She was strong, but that wouldn't amount to much against three grown men. And she'd left her bear spray at the campsite.

She picked up sticks as she walked, scanning the woods for Wyatt. But she didn't glimpse his white T-shirt anywhere. She heard the rippling of the creek and went toward the sound. She'd washed up earlier, best she could. Maybe Wyatt had decided to do the same.

She came through the clearing and found him right there on the bank, facing the creek, wearing only jeans. His short hair was damp against his neck, and droplets of water peppered his skin.

The rushing water had covered the sound of her approach, so she took the opportunity to appreciate the broad slope of his shoulders, the artful curve of his muscular back. She could see part of the tattoo on his bicep now, some kind of symbol she didn't recognize. Her eyes homed in on his shoulder where a circular scab was surrounded by pink, puckered flesh.

She must've made a sound because he whipped around.

A matching wound appeared on the reverse side of the same shoulder. She blinked at the wound. "Is that a . . . ?"

He grabbed his shirt off a rock, and her eyes caught on the possessions remaining there. Boots, socks, and a black pistol.

She stepped back, her eyes darting to his.

He was watching her, expressionless. Calm as you please, he shrugged into the shirt, then grabbed the gun and slipped it into a holster inside the waistband of his jeans. He sat on the rock and proceeded to put on his socks.

She tightened her arms around her small bundle of kindling. She'd been with him all day and had no idea he carried a gun. Why would he have a gun? Sure, he was in "security," but there was nothing to protect himself from out here. Wildlife, mainly bears, could be defended against with the bear spray she carried—she'd mentioned that before they left the house.

And then there was that bullet wound on his shoulder—what else could it be? Of course, he could've been shot in the line of duty. It was time for a few questions, even though she was half afraid to hear the answers.

"You carry a gun."

"I have a concealed-carry permit."

"Okay, but why are you carrying out here? And who shot you?"

He gave her a long, searching look before he proceeded to tug on his boots. "Look, I can see you're a little shaken up. There's no need to be. I was shot on the job. The guy who did it is in jail."

"Is it loaded?"

"Yes."

She stared at him, wishing he'd look at her so she could read his eyes or something—not that they ever gave much away. But he was looking down, tying his laces.

He might very well be telling the truth. Then again, he might just be a good liar. How did she know if he was really in security? And what did that mean, anyway—security? She'd told Molly he was a security officer, but she supposed the mafia might consider themselves in security too, or a hit man or a random thug for that matter.

Wyatt gave his laces a final tug and looked up at her. His gaze roved over her face, and she had a feeling he saw a lot with that one sweep.

"I carry because I never want to be caught off guard. I don't want to be vulnerable in the case of a threat, and I don't want innocent civilians to suffer because I couldn't protect them."

She took in his unwavering expression and his unthreatening posture. She hoped he was telling the truth. For better or worse she had bet her life on it when she'd set off on this adventure. And now she had nothing to protect her but three burly guys who seemed like more of a threat than Wyatt did.

He held her eyes captive with that invisible magnetism he seemed to possess in spades. "I would never hurt you, Grace."

The sticks in her arms began snapping. She loosened her grip. "Right. Okay. Well . . . supper's ready. We'd best get back."

Chapter Twelve

*B*ack at camp Grace and Wyatt settled at a picnic table and ate,
mostly in silence. From the other site the delicious aroma of
grilled burgers carried to her nostrils, teasing her senses. It was getting darker, the shadows pressing in on the campground.

One of their neighbors let out a guffaw, drawing Wyatt's attention. "You didn't tell me we had neighbors."

"We have neighbors."

His eyes slid briefly to hers, then back to the men.

So she was feeling a little bristly. She didn't much like feeling
vulnerable, and now she was out in the middle of nowhere with three
strange men and a mystery guest who carried a loaded gun. And she
had no one to blame but herself.

"Doesn't look like they're staying the night. No tents."

Grace glanced over, making out a cooler and snacks. Wyatt was
right. They could have tents in the truck bed, but they would've set
those up before they lost daylight. They'd already laid a fire with wood
they'd brought along. It was burning bright, sizzling and snapping
in the relative quiet.

A tall, dark-haired guy manned the grill while the other two sat
on the tabletop, swigging beer and chatting. One of them, the more
attractive one, wore a baseball cap and had a sturdy build. The other

sported longish blond hair and a beard and looked like he might've already eaten too many burgers.

They seemed harmless enough, just a few friends enjoying the great outdoors. The tension seeped from her muscles.

"Long way to come to grill out." Wyatt was still staring at their neighbors.

"Depends where they're coming from."

"Did they have to set up so close?"

"Maybe they like to socialize."

Just then the guy with the cap looked at them—at her. His gaze swung to Wyatt next.

"No doubt." Unsmiling, Wyatt held the man's gaze for a long moment.

"Lighten up," Grace whispered. No need to make enemies of them after all.

The guy finally gave Wyatt a nod, then turned a smile on Grace. "Want to join us? We have a couple extra burgers, some hot dogs. Luke made brownies—they might be edible." He got an elbow from the other guy on the table.

"No thanks," Wyatt said before Grace could answer.

"We brought plenty of food," Grace added.

"Suit yourself." The guy turned back around.

Grace gave Wyatt a look. "You got something against burgers? You could be a little friendlier."

"I said 'thanks.'"

"They have brownies. And he's kind of cute." Why did she say that?

His face unreadable, Wyatt looked back over at the table. A moment later he began cleaning up his trash. "I'll start the fire."

Grace finished her meal in peace. When she was done she bagged her trash and pushed it underneath the log teepee Wyatt had made along with the dried bark he'd collected.

"Somebody was an Eagle Scout."

He took out a lighter, thumbed it, and the tip lit with a *snick*. The kindling caught fire quickly and slowly spread to the smaller logs.

Grace took a seat on a nearby log, shucked her boots. *Ah, much better.* She had blisters forming on her heels. It had been a while since she'd worn the boots.

She crossed her arms against the breeze. It would get down to the low sixties tonight, and a fire would go a long way toward chasing off the chill. What were they going to do until bedtime? Wyatt wasn't exactly talkative, and though she had a lot more questions about who he was and what he did, he'd probably answered them as thoroughly as he planned to.

She was still a little miffed about that. Seeing that gun had unsettled her, and she didn't like being unsettled. It made her question things. Like what was so significant about this place he was searching for? Was something buried there? Treasure? Stolen money? A body?

A country song kicked up at the nearby campsite, something by Keith Urban. The guys were now settled at the table, wolfing down their burgers in the waning light, their chatter and laughter carrying over.

Wyatt sat across the fire from her, carving something from a small block of wood he'd pulled from his pack. She couldn't deny he looked handsome in the firelight. Handsome and slightly dangerous. But maybe that was the flickering shadows—or the knowledge that he was packing.

She remembered his promise that he'd never hurt her. The fervent look in his eyes. If he was a liar he was a darned good one.

The campfire's sparks shot into the sky, then sputtered out. The smell of smoke was a pleasant reminder of many childhood bonfires and campfires. She'd camped at least once every summer with her dad and Levi. She missed her dad so much. Missed both her parents. Sometimes it was still hard to believe they were gone.

She glanced at Wyatt, wondering about his parents, his childhood. He was aloof and hard to read. She could practically feel the silence getting heavier. "What are you making over there?"

"A cross."

"What for?"

"Something to do." The quiet scraping of the knife filled the silence.

Okay then. She checked her watch in the firelight. It was only nine thirty. She'd never wanted to knit, but she was starting to wish she'd learned how.

"How do you feel about the area we're in?" she asked. "Is it feeling familiar at all?"

"It's too hilly. I think the area I'm looking for is higher up in the mountains."

"Maybe tomorrow then."

"We won't have a lot of time; need to leave time for our return."

"There's a road that loops up into the mountains about a half mile from the creek. We can take that back—it'll be a lot faster."

"That'll help." He kept whittling. Didn't seem to have anything else to say.

Grace pulled out her phone and opened a game. She probably shouldn't waste the battery, but she had to occupy herself somehow.

She was fifteen minutes into *Angry Birds* when she heard Wyatt shift. His attention had zeroed in on something behind her.

Grace turned as the guy in the ball cap appeared in their circle of firelight. He offered her a smile and a small paper plate. "I know you brought your own food, but I thought you might enjoy a couple brownies."

She took the offering. "Thank you."

"I'm Evan by the way."

71

"Grace. And this is Wyatt."

Evan gave Wyatt a nod.

The two guys remaining at the campsite were sniggering, making Grace feel like she was in the middle of a sixth-grade camp dare.

"Luke actually makes a pretty good brownie. I was just giving him a hard time earlier."

Grace took a bite of the brownie. "It is good. Tell him thank you."

She offered the other to Wyatt, but he shook his head and went back to whittling.

"Where you from?" Evan asked.

The laughter down the way was louder. The beer had been flowing awhile.

"Bluebell. How 'bout you?"

"Me and my buddies are from Tennessee, but we're staying with a friend in Hollis for a while."

"If you're hoping to make it back tonight, you've got a bit of a drive." Grace hoped Evan was the designated driver because it sounded like the other two were already hammered.

"Yeah, we do. I'll let you get back to your . . ." He glanced at Wyatt. "Evening."

"Thanks again for the brownies."

Evan's friends got louder as he returned to the site, some of their conversation carrying over. Enough to know they were talking about her. One of them made a vulgar reference to what he'd like to do to Grace.

Her face heated.

Wyatt's hands froze as he stared at the guys, a muscle flinching in his jaw.

Maybe they noticed because Evan shushed them and their chatter grew quieter.

"You shouldn't eat food from people you don't know," Wyatt said.

"Yeah? You ate my food."

"That's different."

She picked up the second brownie and took a big bite, enjoying the rich chocolaty flavor as much as she enjoyed the way Wyatt scowled at her.

"Have you always been defiant?"

She smiled around the brownie. "Little bit."

"Well, better hope they're not 'special brownies.'"

"Special . . ." Midchew, she looked down at the remaining piece, her appetite suddenly gone. She assessed her mental faculties. Was she feeling a little funny? She didn't think so, but maybe it was too soon to feel the effects. She forced herself to swallow the bite.

Wyatt's low chuckle carried across the site. His smile—the first she'd seen from him—was a little crooked, and surprisingly, a dimple flashed on the left side. If she'd thought him attractive before . . .

"It's not funny," she said, even though the throaty sound of his laughter sent tingles down her spine.

"It's a little funny." He chuckled again and went back to whittling. "The look on your face."

It took everything in her to keep from smiling in return. He looked so different when he laughed. He should do it more often. Then again, maybe it was better if he didn't. She didn't need to be attracted to some out-of-towner who carried a gun, sported a gunshot wound, and had a mysterious job in "security."

She glanced at the time and checked her phone again for a signal. No bars, even when she got up and held the phone in the air.

"There's a signal up by the creek," Wyatt said. "Not much of one, but something."

"I should try to call Molly." Wouldn't hurt for him to know someone knew and cared where she was. She fished a flashlight from her bag to save the phone battery. "Be back in a minute."

He jerked his chin in a nod.

She slipped past him and headed down the trail. She hoped she could reach her sister. If Molly knew exactly where Grace was, it would ease both their minds. It took a little longer to reach the creek in the dark. She checked her phone and found only one bar. Maybe enough.

She placed the call, the sound of the rippling creek mingling with other night sounds—the high-pitched chirp of crickets, the intermittent call of katydids, and the lonely hoot of an owl somewhere in the distance.

"It's about time," Molly said by way of greeting. "I was just telling Adam I hadn't heard from you all day. I was getting worried."

"You know how reception is out here."

"Is everything all right? Is Wyatt behaving himself?"

"Of course. Everything's fine. We set up camp before dark—we're staying at that old campground by Lone Creek."

"Okay . . . Is anyone else there?"

"A few guys, hanging out."

"Somehow that doesn't make me feel any better."

"I'm fine. Wyatt's in security, remember? And he also carries, so we're well protected." She wasn't sure why she added that. Maybe she wanted someone to know just in case.

"What? He has a gun? Grace, I don't like this at all. You don't know the man. Is he there now listening to our conversation? I'm coming to get you right now."

"Jeez, chill out, Molly. Everything's fine. He's sitting by the fire whittling something. We're going to head farther up into the mountains tomorrow, then we'll return by way of the road. We need to make the most of our time so don't look for me to come home until dark."

"No, I don't like this. Let me come get you. I can be there in less than thirty minutes."

"And then what? I desert our guest after I agreed to accompany him? And let him think we believe he's some kind of psycho? This is my job, Molly. Just let me do it."

"I'm telling Levi."

"Seriously? I'm not a child anymore. I told you I'm fine, and you'll just have to trust me."

Adam murmured something to Molly in the background, probably trying to talk sense into her in his unique Adam-like way. A long silence followed, the night sounds pressing in.

"I still don't like it," Molly said finally.

"I know you don't, but I can take care of myself. It's going to be fine. You'll see."

"I'd better see. And you'd better be here before dark, and I want you to check in when you can."

"Yes, Mommy."

"It's not funny. I'll be too worried to sleep tonight."

Grace rolled her eyes. A twig snapped somewhere nearby, making her head spin. "I have to go," she said more quietly. "I'll check in tomorrow when I can."

"You'd better."

Grace disconnected, her eyes still glued to the spot up the trail where she'd heard the noise. Another twig snapped and footfalls sounded. She reached for the flashlight, her heart thumping out a tattoo. It wouldn't turn on. She reached for her phone instead.

"Wyatt?" she called even though he'd probably never walked that noisily in his life.

A moment later a dark shadow emerged from the woods. Her breath stuttered.

"Guess again." It was the tall, dark-haired guy, the one who'd been grilling.

"What do you want?"

He laughed. "So demanding."

"Stop right there."

"Relax, darlin'," he slurred. "Just came out to keep you company."

"I'm fine. You can go back to camp now." She'd already taken one step back, and she added another as he neared. But with the creek at her back she couldn't go far. Would Wyatt even hear her if she screamed? The night sounds were loud. And a cry for help would also bring this guy's pals, who'd no doubt defend their friend.

"My boyfriend'll be here any minute," she said with confidence. "You don't want to mess with him."

He guffawed. "That ain't your boyfriend. How stupid you think I am?"

An honest answer wouldn't help her cause. He was blocking the trail, but if she played it cool maybe she could get past him.

She lengthened her spine and lifted her chin. "I'd better get back. He'll be waiting for me." She stepped boldly around him, her heart pounding in her ears, drowning out the warbling of the insects, the rippling of the creek.

She thought she might make it past until a viselike grip clamped around her arm.

Chapter Thirteen

*O*ne of the goons was missing. The tall one with the mean eyes and dirty mouth. Maybe he'd only gone off to take a whiz, but something in Wyatt's gut rejected the thought.

He'd only stepped inside his tent for a moment. Wyatt cursed himself for letting his guard slip and rushed down the trail. He hoped the guy's buddies wouldn't notice his departure and follow. The portly left-handed one was probably too drunk to care, but Evan was sober. Wyatt could easily take both of them even without his Glock, but Grace's presence could complicate matters.

He didn't use his flashlight. The moonlight was adequate, and he wanted the element of surprise. He made quick, quiet work of the path, his ears tuned for human sounds.

A few moments later he heard a voice above the rushing of the creek. Grace. "Stop it. Let go of me!"

Wyatt quickened his steps. Nearing the creek, his eyes homed in on the shadowy forms. The idiot had Grace in his grasp, a hand over her mouth. She strained against his hold.

Wyatt rushed forward, his unexpected appearance distracting the guy.

Grace wriggled free. Wyatt took advantage of the sudden clearance to deliver a cross punch.

The man's head flew back. He rebounded quickly and attempted a jab.

Wyatt blocked it with one arm, grabbed the guy's jaw with the other, and twisted his head, leading him to the ground. Wyatt dropped his knee onto the guy's throat. He checked on Grace, a still shadow. "You all—?"

"Look out!"

The tackle came from out of the blue. A fist slammed into Wyatt's gut. He hit the ground.

Wyatt pushed the considerable weight off and sprang to his feet. He waited for the drinking buddy to get up, then faced off against him. He could bring the guy to his knees without so much as a bruise, but where was the fun in that?

"Shouldn't have done that," Wyatt said.

"Oh yeah?" Idiot Number Two wore a smug grin. "Let's see whatcha got."

Number One was coming around, but Wyatt had a minute or two. He threw a cross punch, pivoting at the waist. The guy tried to block it, but he was too slow. The strike landed with a satisfying *thwack*. His head jerked back and to the side.

Wyatt pulled back his fists, waiting in a defensive position. "Still want to defend a man who was assaulting a woman?"

Instead of answering, Number Two surged forward with a growl, going for a tackle. Wyatt easily dodged him, and the man flew past, barely keeping his footing. He cursed a blue streak. And fool that he was, he barreled forward again, head aimed for Wyatt's gut this time.

Wyatt braced his feet in a fighting stance and, on impact, pivoted and shoved the man's shoulder, adding to his momentum. He hit the ground hard and didn't get back up.

Wyatt shook his head. If the man had a lick of sense he'd stay down.

But Number One was back on his feet, eager for more trouble. Mean eyes glinted in the darkness. He was taller than Wyatt and probably figured that to be an advantage.

"You need to mind your own business," Number One said with a grunt.

"You need to learn some manners."

The man jerked his head toward Grace. "This your sister? We're gonna have some fun with her once I take care of you."

A surge of disgust coursed through Wyatt, but he kept his expression blank. "Give it your best shot, buddy."

The guy sprang forward, going for Wyatt's legs.

Wyatt hooked his arm, elbow bent, around the man's head, cupping his jaw, and twisted his body, bringing Number One to the ground easily. He lowered his knee to the man's neck and looked up just in time to see Grace knocking Number Two on the head with something as he was getting to his feet. The man slumped back to the ground.

Grace dropped the object and skittered away, flapping her hands.

Wyatt gave her a nod. "Not bad, Bennett."

"All right, I give." Number One tried to squeeze out from under him. "Let me up."

Another shadow burst out from the woods, and their brownie buddy came to an abrupt halt, surveying the scene in silence.

"Want to join the fun?" Wyatt kept his knee on Number One's throat in case he had new ideas.

"I'll take a hard pass," Evan said.

"Good to see someone has a functioning brain cell. You'd best round up your friends and head out of here. They've worn out their welcome. This one manhandled the lady." Wyatt jerked his head toward Number Two. "And that one came to his defense."

Evan swore, his eyes sliding to Grace. "Real sorry 'bout that, ma'am. And here I came along to keep them out of trouble."

"You might think about finding some new friends." Wyatt cautiously eased his knee away from the guy, who grabbed his own throat and started hacking.

"Come on," Wyatt said to Evan. "I'll help you take them to the truck."

Chapter Fourteen

Grace slumped onto the log as Wyatt shut the truck's passenger door. She was shivering, but not so much from the chill in the air. She'd never witnessed a real fight, much less been a participant. Her heart was still knocking around her chest like a pinball.

She pressed her palm to it. She could still feel the place on her arm where that guy had clamped it. When he'd put his meaty hand over her mouth, she'd thought she was done for.

The panic evaporated the second she saw Wyatt coming to her rescue like an avenging angel. She nearly sagged to the ground in relief. He handled the man—both of them—as if, well, he really was in the security business. His swift, compact movements left little doubt that he could've put an end to it even quicker. As if he was merely toying with them.

She'd never doubt him again.

The two men hadn't put up a fight as Wyatt and Evan helped them back to the campsite. Grace was just glad to see them leaving.

The truck started with a roar and began rolling away. There was a flash of movement from the driver's side as Evan waved. She waved back. He'd obviously felt terrible about what his friends had done.

Grace's eyes slid to Wyatt as he returned to their site, no more than a stealth shadow moving in the night.

"Are you all right?" She thought he'd only taken the one sucker punch to the gut. But it had been dark, and everything had happened so fast.

"That's my line. Did he hurt you?"

"No." Grace absently rubbed her arm. "You showed up just in time."

Wyatt sank onto the log beside her. "Sorry I let him slip past me. That was sloppy."

Grace blinked at him. He acted as if her safety was his job. And from where she was sitting it looked like he'd handled the situation like a pro.

"Are you kidding me? You saved my life back there. Or at least my virtue." She shuddered at the thought.

"You managed pretty well yourself."

"He was really strong." She'd felt so trapped against his chest. But then she remembered her contribution at the end and breathed a laugh. "I'm just glad I didn't kill the other guy. That was a heavy rock."

"We made a good team."

He obviously could've handled things fine without her, but it was nice of him to give her credit.

"We'll need to report this when we get back to town."

She didn't want those guys victimizing another woman. "Yeah, let's do that."

Silence settled around them for a long moment.

Then she voiced the question that had been rolling around her head since the second guy showed up. "Why didn't you draw your gun back there?"

"They weren't carrying, and I knew I could handle them."

"*All* of them?"

He hitched a shoulder. "If necessary. Come on, two of them were drunk."

"How'd you know they weren't carrying?"

"There are tells."

"Such as?"

"Bulges under the clothing. Security checks—little touches or adjustments to the gun when they move around. A sagging pocket. Lots of things."

Grace shook her head, staring long and hard at him. "Who are you, Wyatt Jennings?"

l

Wyatt put her question on hold long enough to pull his jacket from his backpack and settle it over Grace's shoulders. She'd been shaking since back at the creek. Probably from shock, but there was also a nip in the air.

He grabbed a few logs and laid them carefully on the fire, then sat back down, still considering her question. For the first time ever he found himself wanting to open up to someone. Wanting to spill all his secrets. Tell her he was damaged and troubled and that his job, while extremely rewarding, had lately stressed him to the breaking point.

He wanted to tell her that while he liked being alone, he was lonely. Hungry for the kind of intimacy he'd never shared with another. That he'd been most loved by his mother, but she was gone and he hadn't felt quite the same since.

But Grace was young and innocent, and their relationship—strictly business—was only temporary.

"You don't have to tell me anything," she said when the silence stretched out too long. "I can tell you like your privacy."

The fire snapped and popped, the new wood catching the flames. The smell of wood smoke scented the air.

Grace snuggled into the jacket. "And I take back all the bad things I said about you."

He arched a brow. "What bad things?"

"Okay, maybe they were just thoughts."

"You going to enlighten me?"

She deliberated for a moment, rubbing her lips together, a frown popping out on her forehead. "No. Definitely not."

"I save your life and virtue and don't get to know a thought or two?"

"Some things are best left unsaid. Besides," she said saucily, "if you get your privacy, I get mine too."

He considered that. "Disappointing, but fair."

"Unless . . ."

The fire bathed her in a soft golden light. Man, she was a pretty woman. He wished, just for a moment, that he lived in Bluebell. That he wasn't so far past her in age and experience. That he was toting a little less baggage.

"Unless," she continued, "we could take turns. You share something, I share something, and so on and so forth."

He was more tempted than could be considered smart. He didn't need to develop any kind of intimacy here. Although he surely wouldn't be around long enough for that to happen. Besides, after all the excitement, he was keyed up. Neither of them would be able to sleep for a while. "Three things."

She tilted her head thoughtfully. "Okay, three things. You go first."

He gave her a mock scowl even as he considered what to say. There were many things he could tell her. Inconsequential tidbits about his life, experiences, and various foibles. His coffee addiction. His boundless curiosity. His weird habit of ironing every stitch of clothing.

"My mom passed away."

Grace's face fell.

He instantly regretted dumping something serious onto the moment.

She settled a hand on his forearm. "I'm so sorry. How long ago?"

"Long time. I was just a kid. I'm way past the grief stage."

"Still, it's hard. My mom died too. Four years ago, in a car accident. My dad died at the same time."

His heart squeezed tight. "That's really tough, Grace. You were seventeen?"

"Eighteen. Starting my junior year. My brother came home from Denver, and my sister dropped out of college to come home and open the inn. That's the only reason I was able to stay and finish high school."

Now that he'd gone and dropped something so private, he was more than happy to shift the focus to her. "You grow up fast when a parent dies."

Her eyes sharpened on his. "*Yes.* You experienced that too? Even though you still had your dad?"

"He worked a lot, but he did his best. It must've helped you, having siblings. You must be close, the three of you."

"Sure." She smirked. "They're great . . . when they're not in my business or bossing me around."

"Sounds like a pretty typical sibling relationship."

She seemed to realize she was still touching him and pulled away. He missed the slight weight of her hand on his arm.

"Do you have brothers or sisters? Oops. I guess it's my turn now. I feel like I need to come up with something really profound."

He slid his gaze sideways and got stuck in her eyes. They looked dark blue right now, and he could see the flicker of flames in their depths. A tight cord of tension drew between them. The pull was strong and carried the promise of something better.

Wyatt broke eye contact and grabbed a stick that lay at his feet. He poked at the fire. "You just told me about your folks. So that probably means it's my turn again." What was he doing?

"Fine by me. Go ahead then."

He gave the fire another poke, watched sparks shoot up into the sky and fade away into the heavens. He stared at the moon as a cloud moved in, shrouding it. "Sometimes I wonder where God is."

The moment of silence betrayed her surprise. "Wow. You're really good at this game. But I think that's normal, isn't it? I mean, sometimes I wonder too. I think everyone does when something's gone wrong, and He doesn't fix it right away, or at all. Like when my parents died, I definitely felt that way. I guess that's where faith comes into play."

He studied her for a long moment. "Smart girl."

She looked away. Rubbed her lips together. They looked especially full in the firelight, and he wondered what they tasted like.

Forbidden fruit, that's what. "Your turn."

"Okay, let's see. All right. I've never told anyone this, but . . . I'm a little jealous of my sister. I mean, I love her to pieces, but that's just it. *Everyone* loves Molly. She's so good with people, and she's positive no matter what happens. Sometimes it's annoying, but really, I wish I could be more like her. If you tell her I said that, I'll deny it until my last breath."

How could someone so amazing want to be like someone else? Grace was ambitious enough to start her own business. Generous enough to help him, a virtual stranger. She was gutsy enough to hit a full-grown man over the head with a rock. And she wasn't full of baloney like a lot of people, spouting frivolous words just to flatter or pacify. She was straightforward, and in a world full of people who played head games, that was a quality he appreciated.

"I don't know you all that well," he said, "but so far I think you're pretty perfect just the way you are."

The words seemed to suck the oxygen from the campsite. Maybe he shouldn't have said that. It gave away too much. But he couldn't regret letting Grace know she was special.

"Thanks," she said softly, gazing into his eyes with a look of surprise. "That's kind of you to say."

He pulled away from her sweet gaze. He'd known all along what his last secret would be. "Guess it's my turn. I told you I'm in security, but that's not the whole truth. I'm a Secret Service agent."

Grace laughed in disbelief.

He turned slowly and just stared at her, watching silently as realization registered. As the humor fell from her face.

Finally her eyes widened and her mouth slackened. "You're serious. Well, no wonder you can fight like that. That is so cool. So do you protect the president or whatever?"

"Agents do a lot more than just that. Some handle federal investigations like fraud or computer hacking. Currently I protect visiting heads of state and other high-profile officials. I'm working my way up to presidential detail."

"That's amazing. The competition for that must be insane, not to mention the training."

"It's fairly rigorous."

"Why do I have the feeling you're understating it?"

She wasn't wrong. The year he'd applied there'd been sixteen thousand recruits and two hundred had made the final cut.

"It's all making sense now. How serious you are. How you're always calculating and measuring until it makes you want to squirm—and all the while you're wearing the straightest poker face ever."

He hiked a brow. "I think some of those bad thoughts are starting to come out."

"That was the good stuff."

He laughed. She was always surprising him in the best of ways. "Yikes."

Maybe the firelight was deceiving, but he could swear she was blushing a little.

"What a job—you risk your life every day. The bullet wound," she said suddenly. "You did get that in the line of duty."

"Like I said."

"It looked fairly recent, so you must be off work while you're recovering." She jerked toward him. "You're the one who took a bullet for Senator Edwards."

She was a sharp one. "Bingo."

"I can't believe you're here in Bluebell. At our inn. It was in all the papers. You're practically famous."

"I prefer to remain in the background."

"Of course, your job. I completely get that. You must've hated being all over the news."

"It's settled down now, thankfully."

"What does your tattoo mean? The one on your bicep."

"It's a Celtic symbol for 'guardian.'" He gave her a wry look. "And now I think I'm all out of revelations. It's your turn."

"If there's a winner in this game, it's definitely not me. I feel downright boring now."

"Don't knock boring." Besides, she seemed pretty adventurous to him.

There was a long pause while she gave the last revelation some thought. He understood. Each piece of information was like giving someone a glimpse into the window of your life. What piece of yourself was safe to give away? That depended on how much you trusted the other person.

"I, um . . . I have a lot of guilt," Grace said finally.

She was staring at the fire now, fiddling with the zipper of his jacket. He waited her out.

"Something happened when I was little. Something I never really talk about. Someone died and I didn't, and deep down I feel like it should've been me. Sometimes I feel guilty for just . . . being alive."

"Survivor's guilt," he said softly.

She looked at him. *"Yes."*

"Big load to carry."

"It weighs a million pounds."

He knew. After all, wasn't he carrying the same weight? The guilt from doing nothing while some monster took his mom's life. He deserved to feel guilty. But Grace didn't. He was certain her circumstances didn't warrant the punishment she'd imposed upon herself.

He was equally sure nothing he could say would make her feel better. It was something she needed to process on her own.

"That's hard. I'm really sorry you're dealing with that."

She gave him a befuddled look. "That's not the response I expected—kind of dreaded, actually."

"What'd you expect?"

"That you'd try to fix it."

"I would if I could. Sometimes it's best to work things out on your own."

Her eyes searched his. "I completely agree."

He wondered what she hoped to find. What she was thinking. Feeling. The attraction went both ways, that much was obvious. He knew, for instance, that if he leaned toward her and placed a kiss on those sweet lips, she'd respond in kind. But he shouldn't lead her on.

He turned away, gave the fire one last stir. Then he rose to his feet. "I'm going to turn in. We need to get an early start tomorrow."

"Yeah, I think I will too." Grace stood, removed the jacket, and handed it back to him. "Good night."

"Night, Grace."

As Wyatt zipped his tent closed and settled in his sleeping bag, his heart was still beating out a wild rhythm.

Chapter Fifteen

*G*race snapped awake at the sound of thunder. It was pitch black, and rain pattered the roof of her tent. She'd paid a mint for these waterproof tents, and it looked like they were going to be tested tonight.

She used her phone's flashlight to check the seams. So far so good. There was no dampness on the floor either. She turned off the light and lay back in her bag.

She'd checked the weather before they left. The storm on the radar had been a substantial one, but it was supposed to have passed north of here. Obviously it hadn't, and if the weather had otherwise stayed the same, they were in for a lot of rain tonight and tomorrow.

But if Wyatt decided to continue up into the mountains, they both had waterproof gear. It would be uncomfortable but doable.

Now that she was wide awake, her thoughts turned to earlier, by the campfire. To Wyatt's revelations. She'd thought he might tell her what he was searching for out here in the mountains. But he had other interesting disclosures. She hardly knew which one to focus on first. They'd all surprised her. As had his responses to her own confessions.

Wyatt was an interesting man, and the more she learned about him, the more intriguing he became. Just remembering the way he'd looked at her made her heart rate speed and her palms go sweaty—like she was a heroine from one of Molly's romance novels or something. Honestly, Grace had always dismissed the writings as fantasy. She'd dated plenty of boys, kissed a handful of them, and she never felt like that.

Like this.

The way Wyatt had stared at her in the firelight made her think he felt the same way. At one point she thought he might even kiss her. But he only turned away and poked at the fire. The letdown had been visceral. He probably thought she was too young for him. Or maybe he had a girlfriend back home. She felt a pinch in her chest at the thought.

She rolled over in her bag. If she wanted to have the energy to get through tomorrow, she needed some shut-eye.

Thunder sounded and lightning flashed, momentarily brightening her tent, and the rain picked up. Now if the tents could just make it through the night . . .

When Grace ducked outside the next day, Wyatt was already sitting by the fire, sipping a cup of coffee. It was just drizzling now, the leafy shelter overhead catching most of it.

"Good morning," she said, her throat rusty.

"Morning."

She cleared her throat. "Did your tent hold out?"

"Dry as a desert inside. Nice job picking the equipment. I woke up at one thirty to a downpour and never dreamed I'd make it to morning dry."

"I wasn't sure. They're supposed to be waterproof, but they've never been put to the test."

She felt a little self-conscious in broad daylight. Both from the revelations of the night before and from the state of her hair and face. She probably looked about fifteen.

She pulled up the hood of her jacket and took a seat across the fire. Wyatt brought her a mug of coffee, which, even though it was instant, smelled like liquid heaven.

"Thank you." She took a sip.

Wyatt looked up at the gray abyss. "In light of the inclement weather, I guess we should head back."

"Not necessarily. We have the proper gear. Our legs will get wet, but it's just water. I'm game if you are."

He studied her for a long moment. "You're not like any woman I've met before."

It was the first time he'd called her a "woman" and not a "girl." "Sounds like you've been hanging around the wrong women."

He cocked a brow. "I'm not touching that one with a ten-foot pole."

It rained all day, a slow, steady drizzle that seeped into Grace's jeans and dripped down her face. They had to cut their way through some of the trail, making for slow going. They stopped only for lunch and bathroom breaks.

As they climbed higher and walked farther, Wyatt's face took on a disheartened look. She'd so hoped he'd find what he was searching for—whatever it was—and as the day wore on, she started to realize that they might very well end the trek unsuccessfully.

Conversation had gotten sparse as the day wore on. Grace intuited his disappointment and didn't force it. She checked cell coverage periodically but struck out. Molly knew it was spotty out here. There was nothing Grace could do, though she did regret worrying her sister with the mention of Wyatt's gun.

By 4:30 Grace realized they needed to call it a day. It would take an hour to work their way over to the road through the thick woods, and even with the downhill shortcut, it would take at least two hours to walk home. The sun would set around 7:40, nightfall at 8:15, so that only left about forty-five minutes of cushion.

Wyatt stopped and took a swig from his water bottle. His hood covered his face to his dark brows, and his jaw sported a five o'clock shadow. Even sweaty and half drowned he was a sight.

"We should probably call it quits," he said.

Grace capped her water bottle. "I'm sorry. I know you're disappointed, but there's still Pine Creek and Lost Creek. And some high flat areas along both creeks that seem like what you're looking for."

"I'll find it eventually, one way or another."

"That's the spirit." She was out of days off this week, but he could use her equipment and move forward by himself. That thought left her a little sullen. She'd wanted to be the one to help him find what he was looking for. It was that nagging desire to be helpful. To prove—to herself, if nobody else—that she was here for a reason.

They began the cut over to the road. The going was rougher than she realized, the deer path overgrown with thorny brush and tree saplings.

She was relieved when they finally reached the road and no longer sure whether it was sweat or water running down her temples.

"It should be easy going from here." She led the way, walking along the side of the road to benefit from the shelter of trees. "If we keep a quick pace we'll make it in about two hours."

"That's about all the daylight we have left."

Realizing he was right, Grace stepped up the pace. It was tempting to walk on the road. Even though the asphalt was cracked and neglected, it was a better surface than the uneven ground with overgrown weeds. But the rain was coming down hard. They'd make it before dark. Just barely, maybe, but they'd make it.

New muscles made themselves known as Grace descended the steep, twisty road. Not surprisingly, there was no traffic. The road only led into the mountains, and no one wanted to be up here in the middle of a rainstorm.

They rounded another bend that offered a breathtaking view of the lake, even with the low-hanging clouds. The road dipped as it turned, then began leveling out before dipping again for a one-lane bridge.

At the sight of the bridge, Grace halted so abruptly Wyatt plowed into her back, bumping her a step.

He quickly steadied her. "Sorry, I didn't—"

Grace couldn't take her eyes off the bridge. The road going across was submerged under the rushing creek.

Wyatt's hands fell from her waist. "You have a plan B?"

She thought through the surrounding landscape, searching for any areas nearby where a crossing would be possible. But there was nothing.

"The creek's too swollen to cross anywhere. If we backtrack there's a road that cuts into this one. But it's an indirect route back to town. It would probably take a whole day to walk back that way—and that's if the bridge spanning the creek hasn't also flooded."

She pulled out her phone, hoping for a signal. The screen was black. Her stomach bottomed out. "Mine's dead."

Wyatt checked his. "I have a little power left, but there's no signal."

Grace glanced around them as if a phone booth or helicopter might materialize. But no matter how long she searched and deliberated, they really had only one option.

"Looks like we're spending another night out here."

Chapter Sixteen

Sunset had become a daily tradition for Molly and Adam when they were both home for the event. They loved sharing the wildly beautiful swashes of pinks and purples, and the quiet moment when the sun dropped behind the hills.

When she'd come home from the inn tonight, Adam had already put the chicken in the oven and set the table. So she started some rice and went to join him on the deck.

It was raining, so Adam had put out the retractable awning. Even though gray clouds shrouded the sun, the lightning put on a show of its own in the distance.

She settled into the seat for two and snuggled in beneath her husband's arm. She drew in the familiar spicy scent of his cologne, letting it comfort her.

"Long day?" he asked when she released a long sigh.

"It did seem long." Mainly because of Grace. Molly checked her watch for the umpteenth time. When she left the inn she'd made Levi promise to call her when Grace returned, so there was nothing else she could do. "How'd the writing go today?"

"It was a bit of a struggle, actually. My protagonist just will not do as she's told."

Molly smiled as he expounded on the problem. Adam liked to run through plot problems with her. She loved being involved with his writing, but he usually ended up working things out himself as he verbalized the dilemma. This time, the direction he'd planned to take the novel was not the direction he was headed.

He would eventually decide that the protagonist was right and he should just stop fighting it. So yes, she was paying attention—more or less.

Molly couldn't seem to get her mind off her sister. Grace hadn't reached out to her once today. Yes, yes, she knew the signal was almost nonexistent up in the mountains.

When she'd awakened to rain this morning, Molly had thought they would make their way back to town. Then when lunchtime had come and gone, she realized they must've gone ahead with the hike.

But now the sun was setting and Grace wasn't home. Should Molly have been more proactive about her fears? They'd already lost their parents. The thought of losing Grace was more than she could bear.

They didn't know anything about this Wyatt guy—and he was toting a gun.

The thought made her shiver.

"Are you cold?" Adam had already started to get up—to retrieve a throw probably.

She tugged him back as thunder sounded in the distance. "I'm fine. Just hold me."

He curled his arm around her, drawing her close, trailing his fingers down her arm. His touch still made her heart quicken. "What's wrong?"

"Grace hasn't come home yet, and she was supposed to be back by dark."

"Have you tried to reach her?"

"About a hundred times. Levi's supposed to call me when she gets home." She'd told Adam her concerns the night before after she'd talked to Grace on the phone. He did what he always did—talked her off the ledge.

But as she peered up at him in the waning light, she could see the concern in the way his forehead creased above his glasses. She had a tendency to overreact, but she could trust Adam for a levelheaded response.

"I'm sure she's fine. But let's pray for her."

Molly loved this about her man. While her first thought was worry, his was prayer. He offered a quiet, fervent prayer that hit all the points she was fretting over.

When he was done she squeezed his hand. "Thanks."

"She's probably just running a little late, with the rain and everything."

"I'm sure you're right." Her tone was heavy with reservations. "I didn't tell Levi about the gun. I didn't want to worry him needlessly, but now I wonder if I should've said something. If we should be doing something. I feel so helpless."

"Why don't we give it another hour? She said she'd be pushing it time wise, right? If it gets dark and she hasn't shown up, let's talk it over with Levi and decide what to do."

"Okay, you're right. That sounds reasonable." Adam was nothing if not reasonable. She'd never known such a trait could be so darned appealing. She looked at her husband. He hadn't shaved for a few days, and she liked the scruff on his jaw. She liked the shape of his lips too.

"What?" he asked when she continued to stare. His lips curled in a sexy half smile.

"I like you, Mr. Bradford."

"And I like you, Mrs. Bradford." He leaned forward and brushed his lips across hers.

As the sky darkened Molly and Adam moved inside. They had supper and cleaned up. Adam turned on the TV to a documentary, and Molly stayed in the kitchen, needing to burn off excess energy. She kept an eye on the time.

When it was good and dark outside and a full hour had passed, she set down the cleaning supplies and went into the living room. "It's been an hour. I'm calling Levi."

Adam muted the TV and watched as she pulled her phone from her pocket and made the call, putting it on speaker.

"Hey, Molly. I haven't heard from her yet."

"I'm getting worried. She said she'd be back by dark."

"I know, but they probably got held up from the rain or something. They're probably driving back right now."

She made eye contact with Adam, and he gave a little nod. "There's something I didn't tell you, Levi. I didn't want you to worry, but now I think you should know. Wyatt has a gun with him."

"What?" Levi snapped. "How'd you know that? Why didn't you tell me?"

"Grace told me on the phone yesterday. He told her he has a carry permit and he's said before he's in security. Grace didn't seem overly concerned about it, but I was. I offered to go pick her up last night, but she insisted everything was fine."

"And you waited until now to tell me? We need to call the police."

Molly's fingers tightened around the phone. "You're scaring me. I was telling myself I was overreacting—you're always saying I do that."

"We don't even know this guy, Molly. I'm calling Chief Dalton. I'll let you know what he says."

At the quiet *click* Molly disconnected the call and looked at Adam. He patted the seat beside him, and she went to him and sank onto it.

"I really thought I was making too much of it. But if Levi wants to call the police, I know I have good reason to worry."

"Or good reason to keep praying," Adam said.

She leaned into the warmth of his embrace and did just that.

Chapter Seventeen

*H*er sister was going to kill her when she got home.

Grace and Wyatt had backtracked to an overlook that had a small picnic shelter. The stone fireplace was useless to them without dry tinder, and they wouldn't be able to pitch their tents on the concrete floor, but the shelter would keep them out of the rain at least.

Grace ducked behind the privacy barrier she'd rigged with one of the tents and changed into dry clothing, still fretting about Molly. Not only had Grace been unable to reach her sister all day, but now she was staying out an extra night.

Molly had one of the biggest imaginations known to mankind. She probably had Grace dead and buried under a pile of decaying leaves by now.

At least Levi and Adam were sensible. They'd suspect a delay, maybe even get word of the flash flood and talk some sense into Molly. But Levi could be overprotective too, and he definitely had a tendency to overstep.

Grace hung her wet clothes over the barrier, then pulled out her damp ponytail and combed through her hair, leaving it loose to dry. Finally she slipped on her jacket, wishing for something heavier.

When she stepped around the barrier she found Wyatt already changed and nurturing a small fire in the fireplace.

"Feels good to be dry again," she said. "Where'd you get the kindling?"

He took her in, and she wondered if he was noticing her hair down around her shoulders. She'd always thought it was her best feature, as it was long and thick and naturally blonde. Somehow the way he was looking at her made heat rise to her cheeks.

He turned away and blew on the fledgling flame. "Dug for pine needles, cut off some dry bark, found a dead tree under some heavy coverage. Not enough to last the night, but a few hours anyway."

She'd be glad for the warmth, and the light would push back the shadows.

Wyatt nursed the flame while she set dinner on the lone picnic table. Within a few minutes the small branches had caught fire, brightening the space, and he joined her.

She'd set out two granola bars and the last bag of chips. "I figured we'd save the apples and peanuts for morning."

"Good thinking. I'm collecting rainwater." He nodded to just outside the shelter where a nylon tarp from the tent was tied up. He'd rigged it to a funnel made from a potato chip bag and into a water bottle.

"Clever."

"Creek water's pretty muddy."

"Definitely not ideal."

"When that bottle fills up we can switch it out."

"At this rate, it shouldn't take long." She looked at him across the table. "Wyatt, I'm really sorry about this."

"It's not your fault."

"I feel like I should've prepared better or something."

"No harm, no foul. We're dry and safe. What's one more night?"

"I guess." She surveyed their supper. "Well, bon appétit. I'm sad to report that we're out of coffee, and I'm going to go ahead and warn you about my morning disposition."

"I'll be right there with you."

"At least we don't have drunk, disorderly neighbors tonight."

"There's always that."

Grace started on the granola bar, her stomach rumbling gratefully. She chewed each bite carefully, hoping her hunger would be satisfied with the meager fare.

"Will your family be worried when you don't turn up?"

She wasn't about to admit that her sister would be frantic by now. Wyatt was only starting to view her as an adult. "They know I can take care of myself."

"I'm sorry I dragged you out here. You could be warm and cozy in your bed right now."

"I offered, and I guess neither of us can claim responsibility for the flooded bridge—act of nature. I'm going to consider this a learning opportunity for future treks."

He gave her a long, steady look, his eyes dark as coal in the meager firelight. "And what is it you're learning exactly?"

"Pack extra coffee." Though she was thinking, *No more trips with handsome single guys whose eyes say one thing and actions say another.*

"And more water," he added.

"Dry clothes."

"More food," they said at the same time, then shared a smile.

The fire crackled and snapped, burning brighter, casting shadows over his beautiful face, emphasizing his angular features and deep-set eyes. Really, did a man need eyelashes that long?

"At least we have plenty of bug repellent," he said.

"True." She'd applied some as soon as they reached the shelter. Not sexy but necessary.

They finished the food all too soon, stuffing the trash into the bag they'd brought along, then they dragged the table closer to the fireplace.

Grace sat down and propped her feet on the stone hearth. A breeze cut through the open space, and she zipped her jacket to preserve warmth. Wyatt added a few more branches, then settled a couple of feet down the bench.

Her thoughts turned back to Molly, and she sent her sister a silent apology. At least she didn't know about last night's debacle. Grace remembered the man's iron grip on her arm and the helplessness that had risen in her. Feelings that took her back to that long-ago day when her heart thumped so hard she thought it'd beat right out of her chest.

She shivered.

Wyatt leaned forward, elbows planted on his knees. "Want your sleeping bag?"

She held her hands out to the fire as though temperature had been the cause of the shudder. "No, it's not that cold. The fire feels good."

Silence settled around them, punctuated only by the crackling fire. It was way too early to turn in. Though her muscles were fatigued, she wasn't the least bit sleepy. And something about Wyatt's presence made energy hum through her veins. It screamed danger, but she knew now he wasn't a danger to her physical well-being. Her mental well-being was another story, however.

An alpha male, Molly had called him. Grace knew what that meant in a general sense. But the men she'd had in her life—her dad, her brother, Adam—weren't so assertive and confident. At least she didn't see them that way. Wyatt didn't seem to need anybody.

She glanced over her shoulder at the concrete floor where they would bed down tonight. They wouldn't even have the thin walls of the tents between them. Would she lie awake half the night in her sleeping bag, buzzing with this energy of awareness?

And what would they do until bedtime? She'd learned a lot about

Wyatt last night, but there were other key things he hadn't revealed. He wouldn't give them up easily though.

Grace gave him a sideways glance. "Are you up for another game, like last night?"

"We should've brought cards." He leaned back against the table-top, propping his elbows on it. His hand dangled mere inches from her arm. "I think I'm all out of profound revelations."

She lifted a shoulder. "We can change it up. How about direct questions this time? We can take turns."

He studied the fire, that enigmatic expression back in place. "I don't know about that."

"Come on. It's only eight thirty, and we have a long night ahead. What else are we going to do?"

The question was out before she'd thought it through. She was thinking it through now though. At least a dozen possibilities flashed in her brain, all of them sounding better than the game she'd suggested.

Her cheeks flared with heat.

He turned toward her just a bit, not enough to make eye contact but enough to signal he was having the same thoughts.

She barreled on. "They—they don't have to be anything personal. Just like, you know, things an aunt might ask you at a family reunion."

"You obviously don't know my aunts."

She gave a nervous laugh. "A distant aunt, then, with good manners and excellent social skills."

He continued to stare into the fire, obviously considering it. Was he weighing his desire to know more about her with his need for privacy? Maybe that was wishful thinking. Probably he was weighing boredom against the risk of sharing too much with this child he was stuck with another night.

"All right," he said finally. "Three questions. And I reserve the right to pass once."

"You and your ground rules." She rolled her eyes. "Fine, but I have a pass too. I'll even let you go first. Ask away, Aunt Wyatt."

She stared into the fire, a thrill of anticipation passing through her. The questions themselves could be as revealing as the answers.

"Tell me about your extracurricular activities in high school," he said.

Grace frowned. That really was something an aunt would ask. But it also wasn't a yes-or-no question. It was actually a request, not a question at all. Open-ended, like he was panning for as much gold as possible with each scoop. And she wasn't calling him on it since he'd just set precedence.

"High school seems like so long ago," she said, because it was true and also because she was eager to add another point to the "woman" column. "Well, let's see, I played several sports early on: volleyball, softball, and I ran track. But after my parents passed I had to devote time to the inn, so I focused on volleyball."

"Part of that growing-up-quickly thing we talked about."

"Exactly. Suddenly there were extra chores and no parents to report to. Though Levi inserted himself into that position."

"I guess somebody had to. So volleyball was your favorite?"

"Definitely. And probably the sport I was best at." She ached to tell him about her achievements, about how hard it was when her parents weren't there to celebrate them with her. But she didn't want him to think she was too big for her britches.

"Is that all?" His voice was a low hum in the night.

"I'm not really the show choir type."

"I think you left out a few things."

She looked at him, searching for his meaning. But as usual there was no way to read his expression.

"You had the highest RBI average on your softball team. You set your school's record for the four-hundred-meter dash. And you were all-state in volleyball your senior year."

She blinked at him. How . . . ? "Molly."

"She's very proud of you." He sounded amused.

"Good grief." Grace wanted to slink under the table. What else had her sister shared while trying to pique his interest in Grace? "She's very nosy, and she doesn't know when to keep her mouth shut."

"You should be proud of your accomplishments."

"No one cares what you did in high school. It's real life that matters."

"Your history shows perseverance and discipline—traits that'll serve you well in life also."

"My turn." She was ready to shine the spotlight on someone else. Only she hadn't really thought about what she'd ask first. She most wanted to know if Wyatt had a girlfriend, but she'd save that one. Too obvious. She decided to ask him something equally as dull as he'd asked her. "Tell me about your favorite hobby."

If he was disappointed in the question it didn't show. "All right. I play the guitar. Taught myself when I was a teenager. Good way to relax."

"You didn't bring a guitar with you."

"I didn't come here to relax—at least not entirely."

She wanted to ask exactly why he had come here but suspected the question would make him retreat. "What genre? Do you write your own songs?"

He looked away. "You had your question; my turn."

"You *do*." She grinned, suddenly knowing it was true, even though his expression gave nothing away. "You write songs."

"Your question has expired."

"Are they love songs?"

"It's my turn, Aunt Grace."

She wasn't letting him off that easily. "My request was to 'tell me about your favorite hobby,' so songwriting falls under that category."

He spared her a long look. "Fine. I may have written a song or two. They're not especially good, and no, I'm not singing them to you."

She'd bet her right arm they were better than he admitted and couldn't help but wonder what exactly had inspired those songs. Women? And did he have a good voice as well? She suddenly wished he had a sister who'd spill all the deets to her.

"Favorite genre?"

"Country and classic rock. I know a few hymns too. And now it's definitely my turn. Tell me about your boyfriend."

She blinked at the sudden shift of topic. Now it was getting good. "What makes you think I have a boyfriend?"

"Come on. Pretty girls usually do."

She liked the *pretty*, but there was that *girl* again. "Well, as it happens, I'm single at the moment. I'm focusing on my business right now."

"Your most recent boyfriend, then."

It was sort of another question, but she'd let it pass in the event it might work in her favor later. "That would be Nick. We didn't date long, just five or six months, and then we decided we'd be better as friends."

He hiked a brow. "You mean *you* decided that."

"How do you know?"

"Admit it, it was you. No guy wants to be friend-zoned by a woman like you."

Woman. "Fine, technically it was me, but the feeling was mutual."

Wyatt chuckled. "Sure it was."

She poked him in the side. "It was."

He didn't even flinch. Although, small wonder, since his obliques were a cement wall.

"If you say so. And you still haven't told me about him, for the record."

She was happy to accommodate since her turn was coming next, and she wanted a nice, detailed answer.

"He works at the marina." She left off that he managed the office, preferring that he seemed more . . . physical than he actually was. "We've known each other for years, but we hadn't really had a conversation until I was over there seeing if we could work together on boat rentals for my business. In the end we decided it wouldn't work, but he asked me out, and I said yes."

"Where'd you go on your first date?"

"I'd like it to go on record that I'm allowing some flexibility in this line of questioning."

"Duly noted, Judge Bennett. Please proceed."

She almost wished she'd denied his request because her answer seemed juvenile. "He took me putt-putting."

"Putt-putting?"

"Hey, I won."

"He took you putt-putting."

"It was fun. And he was a gracious loser. Why, where do you take your women on first dates—Paris?"

"We're still on my question. Is that all? Did he at least take you out to eat afterward?"

He hadn't. And he'd presented a putt-putt coupon to the cashier, but there was nothing wrong with being frugal. "We had a Coke and sat and talked afterward."

"Guess that's one way to keep expectations low."

She poked him again. Maybe just because she wanted to feel those iron abs again. "It was nice. He was very nice to talk to. He was a good listener and ended up being super dependable."

"I'm starting to see why he got friend-zoned."

She gave him a mock glare. "My turn. Your question, right back atcha."

"Should've known that was coming." He shifted, his hand coming within a hair's breadth of her arm. "Currently single. Not really looking. Same as you, focused on my career."

She waited, but he didn't continue. "Because . . ."

"I travel a lot. Women tend not to like that so much."

"You still haven't told me about your most recent girlfriend."

He glanced at her. "Lauren. Met her at a friend's birthday party. Dated for almost a year."

"And . . ."

"And . . . she got tired of me not being around. Missing special occasions. It's hard to communicate while I'm on assignment—plus it's shift work. She finally had enough, like others before her."

"What'd you like about her? What initially drew you to her?"

He stared into the fire for a long moment. "She was beautiful and sophisticated. Savvy in the way of life. A good match for me."

Grace felt a pinch in her chest. No one would ever use those words to describe her. She was, perhaps, the very opposite of all that, meaning Wyatt wouldn't see her as a good match. It was nothing she hadn't already deduced, but his words cut nonetheless.

Chapter Eighteen

Thunder rolled in the distance, filling the silence between Wyatt and Grace. He'd meant to make a subtle point with his description of Lauren, who was Grace's polar opposite, but when hurt shadowed Grace's eyes, he instantly regretted it. There was nothing wrong with Grace's innocence and youth, and he hated that he'd made her feel inferior to someone who, in fact, couldn't hold a candle to her.

All the things he'd said about Lauren were true, but there was more that he hadn't said. That Lauren knew she was beautiful. That she brought her doctorate degree into every conceivable conversation. And that she was masterful at subtle manipulation. In the end he realized he'd been bored with her for a long time. And being released from the weight of her expectations had been freeing.

He couldn't imagine ever feeling that way about Grace . . .

He watched her stare at the flickering fire. Grace was honest and forthright. There was no manipulative undercurrent to their conversations. No guessing about what she was really trying to say. She was witty and real and beautiful in a way that didn't require three styling tools and a dozen different beauty products.

She was deserving of someone a whole lot less complicated.

He looked away. Why did he have to keep reminding himself of these things? And did he have the willpower to keep doing it?

He was sorry he'd opened this line of questioning, but he'd been curious about Grace's love life. Curious if she currently had a man in her life. If she was as inexperienced as he thought. He hadn't expected the burn of jealousy when she'd come so readily to Nick's defense.

These quiet conversations on their adventure had done nothing to quell his interest. The more he knew about Grace, the more he wanted to know. He wasn't usually so reckless, but she made him forget reason.

"Wyatt? It's your turn."

He'd zoned out there for a minute. He could think of at least a dozen things he wanted to know about her. "What do you want out of life?"

She blinked at him. "That's a weighty question."

"Take your best shot."

"All right." She crossed one foot over the other. "I want to make a success of my company and establish myself as a businessperson in this community. I want to be taken seriously. Someday I'd like a man in the picture. Someone who loves this town as much as I do. Someone who shares my faith, who has his own goals, and we can support each other, cheer each other on. I want to live in a small house, preferably on the lake, and I'd like kids someday too, a boy and a girl." She ducked her head. "That sounds really corny."

"Not at all. Continue."

"All right. Let's see . . . I want to go camping as a family every summer and go for walks around the lake and have date nights with my husband on Saturday nights. Oh, and a dog. I definitely want a big dog that can jump in the water and fetch sticks."

He'd intended to direct the question away from himself. Make her think about her goals so she could see how irrelevant he was—make them both think about how poorly he'd fit into her future. Because, yes, he knew she was drawn to him. As drawn to him as he was to her, and he needed to discourage that.

But instead she'd painted a picture that stirred up something in him. Something that made him remember his early years in Bluebell with his parents. Something that made him long for that quiet, simple, peaceful life where faith and family were everything. Someplace he could find rest and not be on constant guard. Vigilance was such a part of him he hardly knew how to relax anymore.

Still he could all too easily see himself in that picture she was painting, packing the trunk for a camping trip, pitching a stick to their dog, holding her hand on that long evening walk.

He shook the thought away. It wasn't like him to indulge in fantasy.

But he was impressed with Grace. She knew exactly what she wanted out of life. She'd thought it through.

She shifted. "That probably sounds really stupid to you, world traveler that you are. But I guess I just want what my parents had. And I want to feel worthy of all that."

He tucked the worthy comment away for later. "You make it sound really nice."

"My turn."

"Last question. Make it good." She'd probably turn the same question back on him. He was already formulating his answer, and it sounded pretty lonely after hers.

"What are you doing here?" She waited a beat. Waited for him to look at her. When he did, she said, "Why is finding this spot so important to you?"

His gut clenched. The question definitely didn't pass the aunt test, and he could see she was uneasy about asking it. He had his pass left and thought about using it.

But he wanted her to know this little piece of him. Maybe not everything, but she'd brought him up here, was giving it her best shot. And despite all the difficulties they'd faced—the rain, the extra night, the lack of food—she hadn't complained even once.

He gazed back at the fire, not wanting to see the pity in her eyes when he told her. "I told you last night that my mom died . . ."

"Yeah . . ."

"Well, she died out here. In the mountains." For some reason he couldn't bring himself to say *murder.*

Her body stiffened subtly. He could feel her gaze burning into the side of his face. But still she said nothing.

"I guess I want a little closure."

"Were you camping with her when it happened?"

"Yes." She was fishing for more information, but he'd kept the details under lock and key so long, he wasn't eager to let them out just yet.

"I'll help you any way I can. There's plenty of ground we haven't covered—those other creeks. We'll find it."

He looked at her finally, relieved to find no pity in her eyes. Only concern and hope. He grabbed on to the hope like a lifeline. "I appreciate that. You've been a real trouper."

She shrugged away the compliment. "Hey, this is what I do."

"You're one of a kind, Grace. I hope you know that."

Her eyes lit, her lips lifting just a little, enough for him to know his words had pleased her. The responding heady rush of pleasure made him want to say or do something else to provoke a real smile. A laugh. A touch.

Somehow during the course of their conversation, they'd shifted closer together, and his hand was almost touching her shoulder. His finger itched to trace a path down her arm. How would she react?

His self-control held out as the silence lengthened between them.

Her gaze fell to his lips.

His heart rate increased, his breaths grew shallow. Temptation crowded out his better intentions. Just one kiss. One taste. He wouldn't take it any further.

But no. It would be a mistake. It would hurt her in the long run. He made himself tear his gaze away. Pulled his elbows from the table, feeling the painful stretch of his deltoid where the bullet had penetrated.

He absently rotated his shoulder. He hated that the silence had grown awkward but didn't know what to do about it.

Grace took care of it for him. "How—how's your injury holding up?"

He stretched it, hoping he hadn't set himself back the past few days. "It's fine. Just a little tight."

The rain pattered on the rooftop. The thunder and lightning seemed to have moved on for now. Their meager supply of firewood wouldn't last much longer.

"Maybe we should go ahead and turn in." He stood slowly. "Get started at first light."

"Sounds good." Grace stood too, surveying their sleeping quarters. "Why don't we turn the table on its side and use it to block the wind?"

"Good idea." They worked in tandem to clear out the spot in front of the hearth. The fire wouldn't last long, but the wall itself was a good buffer.

He laid her sleeping bag closest to the fire, a safe distance away, then he rolled his out beside hers—also a safe distance away. He added a few more sticks to the fire as she wriggled into her bag, pulling her backpack close to use as a pillow.

"What's the plan for tomorrow?" He lay atop his own sleeping bag, propping his head on his pack. "You think the creek will be down?"

"Not if this rain keeps up. We'll backtrack a little and take that road I told you about. It might take all day, but if we get an early start, we'll make it home by nightfall."

The night beyond the circle of the fire was dark and quiet except for the drumming of rain. Wyatt closed his eyes, but he was wired from their conversation. From the look of want on Grace's face. From the tempting way she'd licked her lips. If he had an ounce less self-discipline, he would've tasted that mouth.

She wanted to help him, and he was tempted to let her. Tempted to let her do far more than he should. But future trips with Grace weren't a good idea. Even he had his limits.

Even with his eyes closed he was sensitive to every sound she made. The quiet rustling of her sleeping bag when she shifted. Every little sigh. But as the minutes wore on those sounds slowed and then stopped altogether.

He checked on her and watched the slow rise and fall of her chest. The feathery shadow of her lashes against her cheeks. He felt gratified somehow that she was at rest.

She was having better luck than he was. It was hard to sleep when he knew bad things could happen, even out here. When he might be the only one able to offer her protection. He touched his Glock, making sure it was still in its holster.

A moment later he slipped quietly out of his bag and went to switch out the overflowing water bottle. Afterward he lay down again, the smell of wood smoke on his clothes taking him right back to that night. Now, alone in his thoughts, he allowed them to come. Some of them. Just the parts before Gordon Kimball showed up.

He thought of the way they'd toasted marshmallows using sticks and the way she'd laughed when he told her about his last day of school. He'd always looked forward to summer at the lake, but it was the camping he liked most. His mom could dress up and impress his dad's political peers, but she was most comfortable in jeans, planting flowers around their summer home, puttering around the grounds.

Even all these years later the ache in Wyatt's gut yawned wide. He still missed her. Trying to shake the hollow feeling, he got up again and added the last of the sticks to the fire. The second water bottle wasn't quite full, but he changed it out anyway.

Grace was still sleeping peacefully when he returned.

He lay back down, ears straining for extraneous sounds. That summer night so long ago weighed on him like a lead blanket, smothering him with heat, making his skin break out in a sweat.

He had to redirect his thoughts. If he was going to keep up with Grace tomorrow, he needed some sleep. He lay there a long time, the day's tension gradually seeping from his muscles, his breaths slowing.

She was something. He'd learned a lot about her on this trip, and the more he knew about her, the more he liked and respected her. It seemed inconceivable that he'd only met her three days ago. He let his thoughts wander to Grace's picture of her future in Bluebell. And it induced a feeling so peaceful it was almost intoxicating. The cozy cottage, a gravel driveway, kids playing on a backyard swing set, the dog loping across a green lawn.

He had no idea what time it was when finally he succumbed to the lulling patter of rain.

His mom cried out, snatching him from the oblivion of sleep. Wyatt opened his eyes, but it was dark. So dark. A shadow hovered inside their small tent. A shadow so big Wyatt scurried to the corner.

"Run, Wyatt!" his mother screamed.

But he couldn't move. The shadow was wrestling with her. Wyatt could hear their movements in the dark, hear his mom grunting with effort.

The man called his mom a foul name. "Stop it, or I'll shoot the boy. How'd you like that, huh?"

In the sudden silence he heard the cock of a gun's hammer.

"No, please! I'll—I'll do whatever you want, just leave him alone."

His heart was about to explode from his chest. Fear pasted his tongue to the roof of his mouth. He had to do something. But what? The man was so much bigger and he had a gun.

A scuffling ensued as the man dragged his mom through the tent opening. Mom! his heart screamed, but his tongue was frozen.

Wyatt heard their footsteps outside through the grass and decaying leaves. The low pleading sound of his mother's voice. All of it fading into the distance.

He couldn't breathe. He couldn't think. He couldn't move. Please, God. Please, God. Please, God.

Chapter Nineteen

Something tugged Grace from slumber. She turned onto her stomach but kept her eyes closed, reaching for sleep. The hard ground beneath her reminded her where she was. The quiet patter of rain continued but was lighter now. The chill in the air made her huddle deeper into her sleeping bag.

A sudden movement beside her pulled her eyes open. Wyatt. His restlessness was what had woken her.

The fire had died out, the ashes glowing orange now but putting off no apparent heat. She recalled her conversation earlier with Wyatt. To that moment when she'd thought he was going to kiss her. Her lips had tingled with wanting. She'd never been one to move quickly, and she'd only known Wyatt three days. Yet she never wanted a kiss so badly.

When he'd turned away, the disappointment had been deflating. Was she that inferior to the women he'd dated? To *Lauren*? Did he still see Grace as a child even after all their conversation, after this backwoods adventure? She thought she'd proven that she was independent and capable. A grown-up at the very least!

But when viewed through the scope of his difficult past, her little crush paled in comparison. He was still mourning his mother. How awful that she'd died in some kind of camping accident, and he was still trying to find closure all these years later.

Grace understood all too well. But she'd had some things working for her in that department. Continuing to live in her parents' house after their deaths helped. Having her siblings grieve alongside her was a comfort. Bringing their parents' dream of the inn alive had been healing too.

But Wyatt had had none of those things. It saddened her that he was still trying to cope with his mom's death. When he'd disclosed his loss, she'd wanted to comfort him somehow. To mother him a bit. And that was so unlike her. That was Molly's way, not hers.

And yet, there it was. He brought a part of her to life—a part she hadn't even known about.

He flinched suddenly beside her.

She peered at his shadowy form, still moving in the darkness. She waited for her eyes to adjust. He lay on top of his sleeping bag. The shape of his form indicated he was on his side, but she couldn't tell which direction he faced.

He groaned in his sleep.

Maybe his shoulder was hurting. He might be lying on his injury. That couldn't be good. "Wyatt," she whispered.

His shallow breaths were her only answer.

She pushed up on her elbows. "Wyatt. You okay?"

He let out another moan and jerked onto his back. His head thrashed side to side.

This was not an aching wound. This was a nightmare. Heaven knew she'd had plenty of those. They'd plagued her childhood.

He was moaning more frequently, interrupted only by stuttering breaths.

She couldn't stand to see him suffer even in his sleep.

"Wyatt." She squirmed from her bag, inching over. If she could just nudge him a little, maybe he'd wake up enough to shift position. To dispel the nightmare.

"Wyatt." She shook his arm. "I think you're having—"

He struck out.

She flew backward, pain exploding in her head. And then his weight pressed her to the cement floor.

l

The feminine cry startled him from sleep. The nightmare evaporated instantly. Grace appeared in his vision.

Beneath him. Eyes wide in the darkness.

He was squeezing her wrists over her head.

He let her go. Pushed off her. The last five seconds played back in his head. He'd attacked her. He'd *hit* her.

"*Grace.*"

She was palming her cheek, breaths ragged, the whites of her eyes prominent.

His brain scrambled for purchase. He clambered for his backpack, his hands shaking. He fumbled with the zipper. Found his first-aid kit. Grasped the cold pack. Twisted until it popped and shook it.

He eased closer to Grace, then gently pressed the cooling pack to her cheek. It was too dark to see if her cheek was swelling. The memory of his strike played on repeat, the terrible *thwack* sound.

Regret squeezed his heart like a vise. "I'm sorry. I'm so sorry. Are you okay?"

"I—I think so." But by the halting way she answered he could tell her head was still ringing.

He gently cupped the other side of her face with his other hand. "I'm sorry." He couldn't say it enough.

"It's—it's okay. You didn't mean to."

"It's not okay."

"You were dreaming."

"Does anything else hurt? The back of your head? I think you knocked it pretty good."

"No, I—I don't think so."

She was partially on her sleeping bag. That may have saved her from a knot on the back of her head, because he'd tackled her pretty hard. He may have even bruised her wrists.

He looked her in the eyes, wishing for some light. "Are you dizzy? Nauseous?"

"Just a little headache. Man, you're fast. I hardly blinked and I was flat on my back."

"Not helping." He pressed her hand to the cold pack. "Hold that."

He grabbed his flashlight, returned to her, and shone it in her eyes.

She winced and turned away at the brightness.

"Sorry. I need to check your pupils."

She accommodated him, blinking. Her pupils were equal and reactive. Thank God. While he had the light he checked the wound and winced at the swelling and redness. She'd have a heck of a bruise in the morning.

"I'll be fine." She pushed the flashlight away from her face. "That's some backhand you've got, Jennings."

His breath left his body, his head dropping between his shoulders.

She gave a weak laugh. "I'm kidding. Stop torturing yourself. It was an accident."

He pulled the first-aid kit close and grabbed the packet of ibuprofen. He handed them to her with a bottled water, and she sat up to take them.

"What time is it?" she asked once she'd downed the pills.

He checked his watch. "Almost three. Sorry I woke you. Sorry I—" *Slugged you in the face? Tackled you to the ground? Scared the ever-loving snot out of you?*

"I'm a tough cookie." She squeezed his hand and lay back against her pack. "Must've been some dream."

The nightmare traipsed through his mind before he could stop it. At least he'd awakened before the worst of it. Before his mom's voice had gone quiet. Before the hours he'd cowered in the corner of that tent, trembling, listening desperately for her voice. Waiting for her return. "Yeah."

"Not uncommon after what you went through."

How did she—? Oh, she was talking about the shooting.

"I should've known better than to wake you like that."

He didn't want to talk about it. "We should probably get a little more sleep. Try to keep that cold pack in place."

He helped her back into her sleeping bag, noting her wince as she settled, trapping the cold pack between her cheek and the backpack. Then he dragged his own bag a few extra feet away just in case.

Weariness weighted his shoulders, but he wouldn't sleep any more tonight. He'd lie awake and make sure he wasn't a danger to Grace.

Chapter Twenty

*G*race stirred and pain stilled her movement. Her head ached. So did her arms and back—her whole body really. The night came rushing back. The nightmare, the strike, the lightning-quick tackle.

She opened her eyes to the soft gray light of dawn. A small fire burned in the fireplace and the rain had finally stopped.

She felt the puffiness of her swollen cheek. She tested her limbs and found them stiff and achy. Nothing a little movement wouldn't improve.

She glanced toward Wyatt's pallet, but he was gone. The place where his sleeping bag had lain was barren. The sight brought her fully awake. She pushed up. "Wyatt?"

The picnic table blocked the area behind her, and the frayed edges of night still clung to the woods around the shelter. She listened for sounds of movement but heard only the quiet drips of water falling from treetops to the padded forest floor.

Her heartbeat thrummed in her aching head. "Wyatt?"

A scuttling sound came from behind her.

"You're awake." He appeared above the picnic table, looking like he'd been up for hours. Upon sight of her, he flinched.

She touched her cheek. "That bad?"

"Bad enough I wish I had more ibuprofen."

"I have a packet in my bag." She scrounged around for it, because, yes, her head was cranking. She found the pills and downed them, then glanced up at Wyatt. For a man with a poker face, he was wearing regret this morning like a neon suit.

"Don't you dare apologize again. It probably looks worse than it feels." She didn't have a mirror to confirm that, but she couldn't stand that he was beating himself up over this. She knew he'd never intentionally hurt her.

She stretched. "What time is it?"

"Almost seven. The sun'll be rising soon, but we can wait till the painkillers kick in."

She pushed out of the bag, feeling every muscle ache. "Not necessary. We may as well pack up and hit the road."

"We're already packed except your bag."

She was on her feet now and looking around. Sure enough, his sleeping bag was rolled and attached to his backpack. The clothes she had drying were folded and lying on the hearth. The water collection system he'd rigged was gone. His backpack bulged with at least seven full water bottles.

"How long have you been up?"

"Awhile." He turned the picnic table upright and set down two apples and a bag of peanuts. "Let's fuel up and head out then."

Chapter Twenty-One

*A*ahh!" Grace said as they came down the hill that turned onto Bayview Drive. "Civilization at last."

It was late in the day. The sun had already set behind the mountains. The last of the pain pills had worn off long ago, and her head throbbed with each step. Otherwise, the walk had been easy.

"Now we just have to get to the trailhead where we left your car."

"It's not far."

People were out and about. Boats on the lake. Joggers out for evening exercise. People driving to restaurants for supper. She considered borrowing a phone, but they were almost home, and she didn't want to hear Molly squawking in her ear yet.

When they reached the car, Grace gratefully let the backpack fall off her shoulders, and Wyatt stowed it in the trunk with the rest of their things.

"Want me to drive?"

"Sure." She tossed him the keys and slid into the passenger side. She didn't realize how weary she was until her weight sagged into the cushy seat. She plugged in her phone, which was so dead it didn't even come on, then laid her head against the headrest. Oh, her bed was going to feel good tonight.

Wyatt started up the car and pulled onto the street.

"That was some trek, huh?" she said.

"You can say that again."

"I meant what I said before. I'm happy to help you figure out where to search next or whatever. There's a really detailed map at the library that might help narrow it down. We probably should've started there."

His grip tightened on the steering wheel, the bones in the backs of his hands fanning out in stark relief. "Haven't scared you away yet?"

"Are you kidding? You're pretty great in an emergency, you know. I just have to remember to keep my distance when you're sleeping."

Predictably, he winced.

She chuckled. "Seriously, I'm going to keep making jokes until you can laugh about this."

He grunted.

She was tempted to pull down the visor and check out the damage, but she didn't want to make him feel even worse. "I can't wait to take a hot shower and wash my hair."

"Food's number one on my priority list."

"I wouldn't turn down a cup of coffee either."

"Amen."

They rounded the lake and entered town, getting stopped at the only two stoplights in town. Grace checked her phone. There was finally enough battery power to turn it on. But by the time the phone was powered up, they were pulling into a slot in front of the inn. Home. Grace could've broken out into the "Hallelujah" chorus.

"I'll get the gear." Wyatt slid from the car.

Grace opened her door, got out, and groaned. Her muscles seemed to have seized up during the short ride.

She hobbled toward the back of the car, her phone buzzing in her hand, all the downloads coming in at once. Multiple texts and voice mails. Molly. She should probably go straight inside and—

From the corner of her eye a flash of blue caught her attention. Levi, barreling toward Wyatt.

The trunk shut with a slam, revealing Wyatt loaded down with gear.

Grace opened her mouth, a scream caught in her throat.

Levi's fist flew.

Wyatt stumbled backward.

"Levi!" Grace jumped between them, strong-arming Levi.

Her brother pressed in hard, towering over her, glaring at Wyatt. "Get out of the way, Grace!"

"Stop it, Levi! What are you doing?"

Wyatt bristled behind her. The packs hit the ground with a *thump*. "Step aside," he told her in a low growl.

Levi's face was red, a scowl pulling his brows tight. "What did he do to you? Did he hit you?" His eyes burned into Wyatt.

"No! Stop this right now. Levi! The bridge was flooded. We had to go around. Now back off, dufus, before he lays you flat on your butt!"

"And that shiner you're sporting? How'd you get that, huh? You run into a tree?"

"It was an accident. Step back, Levi!" She gave him a hard shove, but he hardly budged.

"And the limp? Was that an accident too?"

Grace leveled a glare at him. "I've slept on the ground for two nights, genius. Step. Back."

Levi's shoulders gave two more heaves before he lowered his gaze to Grace. Maybe he finally realized he'd made her honking mad, because he took one slow step back.

She exhaled and turned to Wyatt. His jaw was already meaty red, and his face was like stone as he glowered at Levi. Two days' scruff had given him a dangerous look. But neither of those things worried her half as much as the feral gleam in his eyes. Or the way he was braced, one foot forward, as if poised to strike.

"You okay?" Grace put a hand on his chest. Touched his jaw. "Wyatt. Look at me."

Long seconds later he dropped his gaze to Grace.

"You all right? Nothing broken?"

Some of the fire left his eyes.

"What on earth?" Molly came running from the house, sizing up the situation. "What's going on? Are you all right, Grace?" Her eyes zeroed in on her sister's face as her feet slowed. "Oh my gosh, what happened?"

"Our brother punched Wyatt in the face, that's what happened." Grace whirled around to her brother. "See, Levi? That's what reasonable people do when confronted with a set of circumstances they don't understand. They stop and ask a few questions!"

"You were supposed to be home last night. And Dirty Harry here has a gun."

Grace's eyes snapped to Molly. "You just had to tell him."

Wyatt stepped away from her, and she felt a prick of guilt for exposing him.

"We were worried!" Molly said. "You go off with a stranger—no offense, Wyatt—then you call and tell me he's carrying, and you don't show up when you're supposed to. Not for a whole day! Not a text, nothing. Of course I told him. Of course we were worried. You're our baby sister."

Grace let out a low growl.

"And then you come home with a shiner," Levi added. "What were we supposed to think?"

"I told you, it was an accident. And there was no signal. We would've been on time but the bridge on Cut Away Road was flooded.

We had to go all the way around. What would you have me do? Send Indian signals?"

Some of the starch left Levi's shoulders. "Well, we didn't know all that."

"You could've asked like a reasonable person before you started throwing punches."

"Agreed. He shouldn't have done that, especially since the man carries." Molly nailed Levi with a look. "But in all fairness, we were so worried we called Chief Dalton last night. The police and game wardens were out searching for you, not to mention us."

Grace palmed her forehead. "You what?"

"Maybe I should just go," Wyatt said.

Grace grabbed his sleeve. "No. You didn't do anything wrong. And you're not finished here." She faced her siblings. "If you had any idea how this man's come through for me the last couple days, you'd be thanking him instead of making accusations and punching him in the face, *Levi.*"

Her brother cupped the back of his neck, his sheepish look bouncing off Wyatt. "Sorry 'bout that, man. Guess I jumped to the wrong conclusion."

"You think?" Anger churned in Grace's stomach.

"I'm sorry too," Molly muttered. "I promise we're not normally this crazy."

"Great." Grace propped her hands on her hips. "Now that that's settled, we're going inside to ice his jaw. And you're going to call Chief Dalton and clear this up." She marched Wyatt right past them and into the house.

Two hours later, Grace was fed, showered, in her pj's, and in a much better frame of mind. Her siblings had wisely kept their distance while Grace heated up some chili and cornbread. Wyatt's jaw didn't look too bad after being iced. Either her brother didn't pack much of a punch or Wyatt had jaws of steel.

He'd been tense and guarded with her in the kitchen. She couldn't blame him. Not only had Grace blabbed to Molly about his gun, but he'd been attacked by his host. He'd continued to make overtures about finding another place to stay, but Grace thought she convinced him to stick around, at least for now.

In her en suite bathroom Grace dragged a comb through her damp hair, wincing as she glanced at her bruised cheekbone. The discoloration and swelling carried to her outer eye, making it look like a shiner. Makeup would help. She hoped.

A knock sounded at the door. Grace straightened from the mirror and went to open it, hoping for Wyatt.

Instead she got Molly, who stepped across the threshold and wrapped her in a hug. "I'm so glad you're all right. I was so worried, and Levi was too. I know he acted like an idiot, but don't be too hard on him. Between the two of us, he was the levelheaded one. I was ready to call in the National Guard."

"Never expected him to go all Rambo on us." Grace gave in to the hug. Was Levi an alpha male after all and she just never realized it? "I'm sorry I worried you. I shouldn't have mentioned the gun."

Molly pulled back. "Why did you?"

Grace led her sister into her room and plopped onto the bed. "I admit I was a little concerned at first, and maybe I wanted someone to know, just in case. But Molly, remember those guys I mentioned, the campers? One of them got me alone and harassed me. Manhandled me, actually, and I thought I was toast. Then Wyatt showed up and . . . let's just say he took care of the guy—of all three guys. He protected me, and he was really something to see."

"Wow. That must've been scary. Are you all right?"

"Yeah, I'm fine."

"That guy—is that how you got this?" Molly touched her tender cheek.

"No, that was—Wyatt was having a nightmare, and I woke him up and startled him. It was an accident. He felt terrible."

Molly studied Grace. "You're very protective of him. You got right between him and Levi. You were defending him against our brother."

"Only because Levi was in the wrong. Trust me, if Wyatt had decided to retaliate, Levi would've needed defending. Our brother would be in the hospital right now. But that's not who Wyatt is." She nearly told Molly he was a Secret Service agent but didn't want to break his confidence. "He's a good guy. A really good guy."

Molly's face softened. "A lot must've happened out there. I've never seen you quite like this."

Grace dragged her fingers through her damp strands. She didn't know how to put into words how she felt about Wyatt. And had no desire to figure it out right now, with Molly watching every thought flitter across her face.

"Levi called Chief Dalton and explained what happened, so everything's cool now. Is Wyatt angry?"

"I don't think so. He's not exactly happy though—can you blame him? And I really don't want him to leave yet. He has business here he needs to finish first, and I aim to help him."

Molly gave her an inquisitive look and then, miracle of all miracles, didn't press her about it. Instead she eased up off the mattress. "All right then. I'll see what I can do to smooth your friend's feathers. And I'll make sure Levi plays nice too."

"I'm really sorry I worried you," Grace said, because it couldn't be said enough. Levi's impulsive behavior didn't erase their suffering.

"I'm just glad you're all right." Molly gave her a wink, then slipped out the door.

Chapter Twenty-Two

*W*yatt had a few critical things to take care of this morning. When he looked in the mirror, he was relieved to see his jaw was only slightly discolored. Though Grace's brother had surprised him, Wyatt's training paid off. He automatically spun away from the punch, letting the hook pass through. The damage had been effectively minimized, and he'd managed to restrain himself. Barely.

The public library was closed today, and he was taking a break from hiking. His shoulder needed a few days off from backpack hauling. He rolled it, testing. He needed to go to the gym later, lift a little, and get back to his regular physical therapy. It wasn't lost on him that he was broken both physically and psychologically. A case could also be made for spiritually—which was why he'd decided to head to church this morning. The service he'd looked up online started at nine.

But he had something else he needed to settle first. He slipped out of his room and made his way down the hall. All was quiet behind Grace's door. He took the stairs silently, and when he reached the bottom he found just the situation he'd hoped for. Levi alone, working the front desk.

The man did a double take as Wyatt rounded the corner. He straightened to his full height—a few inches taller than Wyatt.

As Levi's gaze sharpened on Wyatt's jaw, he shifted uncomfortably and cleared his throat. "Good morning."

"Morning."

"Ah, about yesterday . . ." Levi lifted his chin a notch, reminding Wyatt of Grace. "I wanted to apologize again for jumping to conclusions."

"Accepted. Do I need to find somewhere else to stay?"

Levi blinked but didn't give an inch. "That depends. What are your intentions toward my sister?"

"I have no intentions toward Grace—if that's any of your business." He didn't know why it annoyed him so much that her siblings treated her like a child when he'd initially put her squarely in the same category.

"Does she know that?"

"I don't know. Maybe you should ask her," he said, because he knew Levi wouldn't bother. Grace would just tell him to butt out.

"She's young. And more vulnerable than you might think."

"She's an adult, and she wouldn't appreciate your talking behind her back. She's also quite capable of taking care of herself."

Levi's jaw clenched and his eyes flashed. He obviously didn't like being told about his sister by someone who'd known her less than a week. But Wyatt was right.

"Good morning!" Molly waltzed into the room, energized by her morning coffee? Or maybe a little manic. "How'd you sleep, Wyatt? Can I get you a seat in the dining room? Miss Della baked up her blueberry streusel muffins this morning, and you don't want to miss those."

Her gaze toggled between the men. "Everything all right here? Yeah? Wyatt, I also recommend the meat lovers' omelet. It's a fluffy, cheesy wonder you'll be dreaming about for weeks to come."

Wyatt looked back at Levi. "I was actually thinking about checking out this morning."

"Now, why would you go and do that? Grace said you have business here, and we're happy to assist in any way we can." Molly nailed her brother with a look. "Aren't we, Levi?"

He offered a wan smile. "Of course."

"Well, there you go then." Molly hooked her arm around Wyatt's and headed toward the dining room. "There's a seat right by the front window, and I'll get your coffee right away. Would you like some cream with that?"

"Um, no. Thanks." His head was spinning a little by the time Molly left for his coffee. Whereas Grace was like a balmy summer evening, her sister was like a whirlwind. And her brother a sudden storm front.

Maybe Wyatt should leave, but he wasn't letting some over-protective brother scare him away. He had business to attend to, and he wasn't quite ready to say good-bye to Grace Bennett.

e

"Seriously?" Molly asked as soon as she closed the front door behind the guests Levi had just checked out.

"What?"

Molly hitched her hands on her hips. "I walked into some kind of standoff between you and Wyatt. I thought we agreed you'd be nice. I thought we agreed you'd back off."

"That doesn't mean I have to trust him."

"Well, do you have to wear your feelings on your sleeve? He's a guest, and you need to treat him like one."

"Fine. I will." Levi ran his hand through his hair. "Have you sent Grace the write-up for the inn?"

"Nice change of subject. When would I have done that? She's been gone since Thursday."

"Well, do it now. We need to get this place listed."

"All right, all right." Molly texted Adam, asking him to email the document to Grace. "Done. What's wrong? You seem super stressed."

"Oh, I don't know. A missing sister, this inn, a long-distance relationship, a wedding I'm supposed to be planning."

"When's Mia coming?"

"Friday. She finishes filming on Thursday. We'll do the cake tasting, have the fittings, and go over the menu with Miss Della. It'll be fine. I'm just on overload right now."

"I can help. I'm good with weddings."

"I'll do the wedding stuff. You get the inn sold."

"Fine." She'd rather do the wedding stuff, but it wasn't her wedding. "I'm going to go clean rooms. And ease up on Wyatt. Grace trusts him, and we should trust her enough to give him the benefit of the doubt."

"Aren't you at least a little concerned?"

"I don't mean to throw the past in your face, Levi, but your track record with our boyfriends isn't the greatest."

"He seems a lot older than her—and not just in years. Besides, he's secretive and he carries. In security—what does that even mean?"

Molly crossed her arms. "Remember how I was supposed to remind you when you're butting in?"

His lips tightened. "Fine. I'll keep my opinions to myself."

She gave him an innocent smile. "That's all I'm asking."

Chapter Twenty-Three

Grace spent all Monday morning getting the inn listed at the online sites she'd pegged. Adam had done a beautiful job with the
write-up, but jumping through each page's hoops and listing the inn's
features repeatedly was time-consuming.

She finished just in time for her Realtor appointment. A house on
the edge of town that might work for her business had recently listed.
She jumped into her car and drove the short distance.

A few minutes later she pulled up to the curb. The one-story cottage squatted on a small, sloped lawn. It was near enough to the town's
center and the lake to make it a feasible option. The price wasn't bad
either. She wouldn't be eligible for that kind of loan now—and a grant
would never come through in time—but once the inn sold she could
pay cash and still have a little left over for renovations.

The Realtor was already there, so she met the petite woman on
the front porch. Pamela Bleeker sported a perpetual tan and wore her
beach-blonde hair short and fluffy. She was still attractive in her for-
ties and was known about town as a real go-getter.

Grace ascended the porch steps. "Hi, Pamela."

"Well, hello there, darlin'. You're looking well."

"Thank you." The makeup had helped disguise Grace's bruise,
but it was still visible. Pamela was too tactful to mention it.

"Well, you picked a beautiful day, and I hope we can find a nice spot for your business. This town needs some new options, and this precious little house is located just right."

"I'll give you that."

Pamela slid the key from the lockbox and unlocked the door. "Like I said on the phone, it's zoned for commercial or residential use. This nice wide porch would be a great place to display some of your rental equipment or sale items."

Grace had been thinking the same thing.

Pamela ushered her inside the empty house. "The high ceilings offer a nice open feel, don't you think?"

"I do like that." The wood floor was serviceable, and the windows let in plenty of light. Aside from the living area, the rooms were small and boxy and painted a garish shade of green. "Some walls would definitely have to come down."

"Well, yes, but that's cheap demolition. And, of course, you and your siblings have experience with that."

Grace didn't want to give too much away, but she could already see this house working out. See the open space that would display her hiking and camping equipment. See racks of quality hiking apparel where the living room currently was. See the checkout counter to the left of the door, where a dining room chandelier now dangled from a link chain.

A large garage was located out back where she could store her kayaks, canoes, and bikes. Lake access was free just across the street. It was an ideal location, and the interior had been recently updated.

She strolled through the house, taking in everything from the wood floors to the wall construction to electrical outlets. A small back bedroom would serve nicely as an office. It was right off the tiny kitchen, which she might be tempted to keep.

At the back of the house she saw a narrow set of steps. "There's an upstairs?"

"Just a little walk-up attic. It's unfinished, but it has super potential. Watch your step."

Grace took the stairs, which stopped at a short wooden door. She opened it up, went through, and pulled the string attached to a bulb. The space lit up. It was small and unfinished just as Pamela had said. But Grace could see the walls and sloped ceiling covered with drywall and sporting a fresh coat of paint. She could see plush carpet hugging the floor and the double-hung window covered with a filmy white curtain.

She could actually live up here and work downstairs. Excitement buzzed through her veins. Pursuing this dream had always lit her fire, but never as much as now. Because now it felt real. It felt plausible. It felt like it was hers and hers alone.

She worked hard to keep her thoughts from her face. Pamela was a sweet Southern shark, and she'd listed this house for the owners.

"It's got potential. But I see a lot of effort and money to make it work as a business."

"Well, sure, but you could do a lot of it yourself. And the place has great bones."

Grace agreed. She hadn't noticed sloping floors or any cracks, leaks, or stains anywhere. The house was built seventy years ago and built well. "A lot of structural and cosmetic changes, though. When did you say the plumbing was updated?"

"Ten years ago. New roof three years ago, so you're all set there too."

Grace nodded, then started back down the attic stairs, trying to calm the rising tide of anticipation.

"And just wait'll you see the garage," Pamela said.

Since Grace arrived home an hour before her shift, she slipped into the kitchen to help Miss Della with supper prep. She cut carrots and onions and whipped up the house salad dressing while the other woman did the real cooking. They gabbed about everything and nothing as they worked side by side.

Lately Grace had been spending a lot of time here and there helping in the kitchen. But if Miss Della noticed the shift in her habits, she hadn't said so. Grace had stepped up her efforts at church also. She'd filled a slot that had been empty for months—the toddlers' class. She'd also helped an elderly woman to her car Sunday night. She wasn't sure if any of it was helping her with her issues, but maybe that would take time.

When she was due for her shift, she washed her hands, said goodbye to Miss Della, and made her way to the front desk. Levi caught her up on a few things that had happened on his watch.

"How was the property you looked at?" he asked before he took off.

"Really good. Definitely a possibility. But it's just on the market, and Pamela thinks it'll go fast."

Levi rolled his eyes. "You know she's just trying to hook you."

"Well, sure, but I really liked it. And I won't have the money to do anything until this place sells. Maybe I should wait to start looking."

She didn't want to get her hopes up for nothing, and she had a terrible feeling some other buyer would swoop in and buy the property. In fact, she'd been fretting about that since she'd left the house.

"The inn might not take that long to sell, and you need to be ready to go once it does."

"I listed it everywhere this morning." She stepped up to the computer and opened the email program. Her heart stuttered at the email from one of the realty sites.

"Someone's already reaching out." She opened the email and read it.

"What'd they say?"

"They want to take a look. It's a couple from Tennessee that wants to open a bed-and-breakfast—the Farnsworths. She managed a hotel for six years, and he manages a landscaping business. They're asking if they can come Wednesday."

"Wow, that was quick."

"Can you imagine if we sold it that fast?" Grace could buy that little house and finally be in business for herself. Buy more equipment, hire some employees, advertise. She was going to have the best outfitters business around.

"Slow down, sparky. Coming to look isn't the same as making an offer."

"I know, but look at this place. What more could anyone want?"

"It doesn't come cheap. We don't even know if they can really afford it. But you should check Molly's availability for Wednesday."

Definitely. Molly, with her positivity and gift of gab, not to mention her love of this place, was the right person for the tour-guide job.

"I'll do that."

Movement sounded overhead. Was it Wyatt? She'd been so deep in thought when she pulled up she didn't even check for his car. They'd only spent an hour or so together since their return, when they'd gone to the police station yesterday to file a police report. And after all the time they'd spent together this week, she found herself missing him.

"Is Wyatt still around?" she asked before Levi slipped out the front door on the way to some wedding errand.

"He left a while ago."

Her spirits sank a little. "Okay, thanks."

She hoped Wyatt hadn't already gone to the library. She wanted to help him with the map. She certainly knew the area better than the librarians did.

Oh, who was she kidding? She wanted to spend time with him and just needed a good excuse to do it.

Grace tracked down Molly upstairs folding towels in the laundry room. "Guess who's found us a potential buyer?"

"What? Already?"

"I posted the listings this morning, and we just got an email from a Tennessee couple. They seem legit and want to inspect the place this week."

Molly hugged the white towel to her stomach. "Wow. That was quick."

"They'd like to come in Wednesday afternoon and possibly stay the night if they like what they see."

"Oh . . . Wednesday? I kind of have a full day. Think you can put it off till the weekend?"

"Weekends are our busiest times."

"Exactly. It'd be great for them to see how successful this place is."

Grace saw her point, but weekends were all hands on deck.

"Oh, wait," Molly said. "This weekend we have that family reunion. It's going to be a zoo. Maybe the next weekend?"

Grace saw that little house slipping right through her fingers. "I don't think we should make them wait that long. What if they find someplace else in the meantime? If you're not free Wednesday, Levi or I can show them around."

Molly bit her lip. "No, no. It's fine. I can clear my schedule."

"Are you sure?"

"Absolutely. Tell them it's a go."

Chapter Twenty-Four

*G*race steadied the kayak, holding her breath as the middle-aged woman stepped into it. Her husband was already set to go and waiting just off the dock. They'd come in this evening after seeing her ad on the diner's place mat.

Once the woman was settled in the cockpit, Grace relaxed.

"This is a nice one," she said. "Very comfortable."

"Glad you like it." Grace handed her the paddle, failing to inform the woman that she was the first to take it out. "Have fun, you two. Just pull it up on the dock when you come back and stop up at the front desk."

The two were already off, efficiently paddling their way past the end of the dock. Grace headed back up the slope of the inn's lawn. These were the first customers in a week who'd come in off the street. Most of Grace's business originated from the inn's guests, which worried her a little. What would happen when she moved to her own location?

She caught sight of Wyatt coming toward her, hands tucked into his jeans pockets. What that man did to a black T-shirt should be considered illegal.

"There you are," he said.

Her heart gave an errant beat as she realized he was looking for her, then she gave herself a mental shake. He probably needed extra towels or something.

"Sorry. I had to abandon the front desk. A hazard of running two businesses at once."

When they met up he turned and walked alongside her. "Your face looks a lot better."

"Gee, thanks."

"I meant the bruising."

"Relax, Romeo, I knew what you meant. Just wanted to see you squirm a little."

He gave a wry huff, then shook his head.

She was relieved that after being apart since Saturday their camaraderie was still there. "Is there something you needed? Extra pillow? Afternoon snack? Guided tour of the lake?"

"That last one sounds intriguing. But I was actually hoping to enlist your help with that map at the library. I had a look at it today, but . . ."

"Yeah, it wouldn't be very helpful if you don't know the topography of the area."

"I tried to check it out, but the librarian seemed to have mistaken it for the Holy Grail."

"Hildy's a little protective of the library's assets. In her defense, it is a one-of-a kind map. But I could go with you tomorrow morning and have a look if you're free then."

"That'd be great. Thanks."

They reached the back of the inn, and he opened the door for her. "I've been resting my shoulder, but I'd like to get back out there later this week."

"We're expecting good weather." Grace wasn't sure if he was just mentioning his plans in passing or hinting for help. They reached the front desk and she turned. "Well, if you need any help, I'm off Thursday."

"I might do a little looking on my own till then, but I'd love your help if you're willing."

Grace met his steady gaze with one of her own. "I'll be ready to go bright and early." They set a time in the morning to leave for the library, and Grace tried not to stare as he slipped out the door and headed for supper.

ℓ

Wyatt spread the map on the same back table he'd used the day before. The smell of books permeated the air, the hush of the space broken only by the soft flutter of turning pages.

Beside him Grace leaned over the map, her shoulder brushing his.

"So I know this is the area we covered last time." He drew his finger along Lone Creek heading east. "But I'm not sure exactly where we cut over."

Grace leaned closer, her hair falling over her shoulder. He caught a whiff of her sweet shampoo.

"It's right here, Cut Away Road," she said. "And this is the bridge that was out. We backtracked here and took this road down the mountain. Do you feel we went far enough up Lone Creek, or do you think we should continue up into the mountains?"

"What's the topography like farther up the creek?"

"It's high land with lots of pine trees. It sounds like the type of terrain you described to me, but I don't know how far from town you want to go."

He thought back to the trip he'd taken with his mom. He wasn't sure where they'd started from exactly, and the trail had seemed cut back and easier, not like the last part of their hike. But his memory was unclear, and a lot could change over that many years.

"To be honest, I'm not sure we went far enough."

"Well, let's pick up from there then. We can drive up this road here, cut over to the creek, and start where we left off. If we don't find the spot we can tackle Pine Creek next. It's right here. There's a good path that runs all the way to here. And this area is much like the terrain you describe. You can see the tributaries running into it along the way, but most of those are very small, not likely to be the creek you remember."

Wyatt stared at the huge map with its miles of mountain range and creeks and tributaries that had in all likelihood changed over the years. The truth was he couldn't even be positive they'd gone east. It was just an impression he had. There were miles and miles of mountains around Bluebell. What if this was a lost cause? Maybe he'd never find the spot. Never get closure. Never feel okay about what he'd done.

Maybe he needed extensive mental health counseling, or maybe this was just his crutch to bear. But how could he deal? How could he sleep with all the nightmares? How could he maintain his job without sleep? He was so close to his dream job. Hopelessness rose inside him, dark and threatening, like a storm cloud.

Grace touched his arm. "Hey."

He blinked away his thoughts and focused on her clear blue eyes. On the whisper-soft touch of her hand.

"We'll find it, Wyatt. You know what you're looking for, and you'll know it when you see it."

"Grace . . . I can't even be sure it was east of town. I was just a kid, and I was following my mom."

"But you have a good sense of direction. Trust that. We're going to find it."

"I've been here a week already."

"And look, you've ruled out this entire area." She swept her hand over a small region. "We're making headway. Don't lose hope."

He soaked in the confidence behind her words. He was used to teamwork. His job required it. But he'd always carried this particular burden alone. It felt nice to have someone alongside him. It felt good to have Grace alongside him.

She was studying his reaction. "All right?"

She definitely wasn't the cheerleader type, though she looked the part. But she'd known just what to say to encourage him, and he appreciated that more than he could say. "All right."

Grace parted ways with Wyatt and headed back to the inn. Now that there was a showing tomorrow, it was all hands on deck. The grass needed mowing and the public areas needed a thorough cleaning, and that was on top of their regular duties.

When Grace walked into the inn, Levi was at the front desk, and she heard the vacuum running upstairs. "How's it going?"

"Guests are gone for the time being, and we almost have a full house tonight. It'd be nice to get some of the cleaning done while our guests are out."

"I'm on it." Grace gathered the cleaning supplies and went to work in the living room, polishing the furniture.

She and Molly had begged Levi to hire a once-a-week cleaning service, but even though they could afford it now, Levi wasn't quite reformed from his penny-pinching ways. The only thing that kept Grace from arguing the point was that the money they saved would eventually fall into their pockets—and into Grace's new business.

The floor needed a good shine, and the drapes needed washing, she noted as she dusted. They were going to get this place so pristine the Farnsworths would make an offer on the spot.

Molly should make sure the couple enjoyed at least one meal in the dining room. Miss Della had already said that if she was needed she'd like to stay on once the inn was sold. Her continued services were a huge selling point. The Farnsworths needed to know what a jewel she was.

In the dining room, the menus, salt and pepper shakers, and condiments needed to be wiped down. The wood tables were starting to show a little wear and tear. Maybe they should buy tablecloths. Class the place up a bit.

The inn's windows needed to be cleaned, inside and out. It was a little overwhelming. But once Molly was done cleaning the rooms upstairs, they'd make better headway.

Grace was polishing the coffee table legs when Molly trotted down the stairs. "All right, guys, the rooms are cleaned, so I'm off."

Grace straightened on her knees. "Wait. Aren't you going to help clean?"

Molly peeked through the open French doors. "I told Adam I'd proofread his chapters. But I have the front desk tonight. Maybe I can get some cleaning done then."

"There's a lot to do before tomorrow, Molly. All the windows need cleaning, inside and out."

"I'm sorry, but they're not coming till tomorrow afternoon. We still have time."

"We have to clean rooms in the morning, and Levi has the desk. When will we have time?"

"Grace, the place looks great. The windows aren't that bad." Molly cast Levi a glance. "If you really think it needs to be done, we could always hire a service."

"You know I don't like to do that."

"Jeez, Levi," Grace said. "It won't kill you to hire it out for once. We need to put our best foot forward here."

He looked between his sisters. "Fine, but just this once."

Chapter Twenty-Five

$\mathcal{G}$race walked along the sidewalk in front of the bungalow she hoped to buy soon. The For Sale sign was still propped proudly in the yard, and the house was locked up tight.

Please, God, if You could just keep people away till I have the money to buy it.

She checked her watch. Molly was showing the Farnsworths through the inn this very moment, and Levi was working the front desk. They'd agreed they shouldn't all be hanging over the Farnsworths' shoulders, so Grace had slipped out to run a few errands. And of course she visited her little house and did a little daydreaming.

And PS, God, if the Farnsworths are completely taken with the inn today, that would be terrific.

It was too early to return to the inn. They had it all planned. If the couple liked what they saw on the tour, Molly would take Levi's place at the desk, and he'd sit down with the couple and go over the inn's impressive financial statements. The couple would then have supper in the dining room—the coup de grâce, so to speak.

But that was at least another hour away. Grace turned away from her dream home and headed toward the coffee shop. A frappé would be a delicious way to pass the time. On her way she texted Sarah and told her about the bungalow. Her friend responded immediately with lots of enthusiasm.

Minutes later Grace approached Firehouse Coffee. The garage doors of the old fire station were up, and the patio tables were half filled. She opened the front door for a young mother with a baby, then breathed in the energizing aroma of freshly brewed coffee.

After receiving her vanilla bean frappé, Grace scanned the shop for a place to settle. Her eyes stopped on a familiar set of shoulders in the back corner, facing the patio.

She headed that way and slipped a hand over his eyes from behind. "Guess—?"

A hand clamped over her wrist as he whipped around.

She squealed, sloshing her drink.

He dropped her hand. "Sorry. Sorry."

Grace's heart was thumping like a bass drum. It had all happened so fast. She glanced around, but no one seemed to have noticed the commotion that was over almost before it had begun.

"You all right?" he asked.

Grace sank onto the seat across from him, resisting the urge to rub her wrist. "Remind me not to sneak up on you again."

"Sorry. Occupational hazard." He took her hand and rubbed his thumb across her wrist. "You okay? I didn't hurt you?"

Grace felt the brush of his finger all the way down to her toes. "I—I'm fine. You just startled me, so I guess we're even."

"I'm batting a thousand, huh? That's twice I've hurt you."

"You're a real hazard to my health."

He gave her that guilt-ridden look she was coming to love.

"You need to lighten up. You're on vacation. Sort of."

Wyatt's gaze swung up and past Grace, and he straightened as he stared at something behind her.

Grace turned just as her ex-boyfriend Nick reached their table. His brown hair was neatly clipped and swept to the side. He was in his usual uniform, a button-down and khakis. "Hi, Graceful. Fancy running into you here."

Grace winced at the nickname. "Hi, Nick. I didn't see you out there. How are you?"

"Not bad." Nick glanced at the center of the round table where Wyatt's hand still rested on her wrist. His eyes darted to Wyatt before returning to Grace. "I was taking a short break from work and saw you come in."

"Um, Nick, this is Wyatt," Grace said into the weird tension hovering over the table. "Wyatt, this is Nick, a friend of mine."

Nick stuck out his hand, forcing Wyatt to let go of Grace.

"Pleasure," Wyatt said, then placed his hand right back on Grace's.

Heat inched its way up her neck and into her face, but she kept her smile steady on Nick. "So, um, how's your mama? I didn't see her at church Sunday."

"Her lupus is flaring up, I'm afraid, so she hasn't gotten out much. She'd love to see you sometime."

"I'll have to visit her soon. I owe her a game of Scrabble."

"I could meet you over there, bring supper."

"Sure. That'd be great."

"How's your business going? I saw your ad in the *Bluebell Beacon*."

"It's going well. I'm actually hoping to move out on my own sometime soon. The inn's up for sale now."

"I saw the sign out front. I hope it goes fast. I'll help spread the word if you'd like. I could put up a flyer at the marina if you have one made up."

"Thanks. I'll print one out and get it over to you."

Nick's eyes flitted to Wyatt, who sat quietly, staring at Grace. A long, uncomfortable moment passed.

Grace sipped her frappé.

Nick shifted. "Well . . . I guess I'd better get back to work. It was good seeing you, Grace."

"You too, Nick."

"I'll check with my mom and give you a call."

"Okay, great."

He gave Wyatt a polite nod and slipped out the door.

Wyatt watched him leave, then turned back to her as the door swung shut. "*Graceful?*"

"I didn't pick it."

"I thought you said he works at the marina."

"He does." Grace took another sip. "Office manager."

"You run into him often?"

"Have you seen the size of this town?"

"Fair enough. Is it always that awkward?"

"Um . . ." She looked pointedly at his hand still on hers, then gave him a look. "It was only awkward because of you."

He pulled his hand away, drawing his mug to twitching lips. "I was just testing a theory."

"And what theory would that be?"

"You said the breakup was mutual—and I call baloney, Grace Bennett."

Warmth trickled into her cheeks. "Maybe I was the one who initiated the conversation, but he agreed with me."

"He was saving face. I don't know how to tell you this, but that man still has the hots for you."

"He does not."

"Did you see the look on his face when he saw our hands? Like someone killed his puppy."

"That's ridiculous."

"Please visit my mom so I can have an excuse to see you. Let me help sell your inn, Graceful. I'll call you soon. You're still on speed dial."

She chuckled. "Stop it."

"You know I'm right." He took another sip of his coffee. "Not that I can blame the poor guy. It's never fun being friend-zoned."

"Like you've had so much experience with that."

He let the comment pass, and the subject shifted to the goings-on around town. Then Wyatt caught her up on the areas he'd hiked this week. Grace told him about the little house she was hoping to purchase and about the prospective buyers now touring the inn.

The next time Grace glanced at her watch, over an hour had passed. The Farnsworths were probably sitting down to supper. It was possible they'd discuss things over the meal and have an offer tomorrow before they left—or even yet tonight.

"I should get home." Grace stood and grabbed her empty plastic cup. "I'm dying to see how it went."

"I hope there's good news waiting for you."

"Me too. It was nice chatting—even if you did attack me again."

He winced, making her laugh again.

"See you, Wyatt," she singsonged.

"See you, Grace," he singsonged right back.

She left with a smile and it lasted the whole way back to the inn. Wyatt was so easy to talk to. That guardedness he wore like a shield came down when it was just the two of them. She wished he'd ask her on a date, even though she knew nothing could come of it. Her life was here, and his was . . . wherever duty called him apparently.

She was eager for their hike tomorrow though. Her heart squeezed tight when she remembered the look that had come over his face yesterday at the library. He seemed so deflated as he stared at the hundreds of miles represented on the map. She would make it her mission to help him find the closure he needed, whatever it took.

When she reached the inn she opened the door to find Molly assisting an elderly couple with restaurant recommendations. Grace waited patiently while they went through virtually every Bluebell dining option. Finally they headed out the door.

Before Grace could blurt out the question, Levi came down the stairs toting his toolbox. "Hey," he greeted Grace, then turned to Molly. "The shelf in room five is officially fixed and ready for the Farnsworths. How'd the tour go? Are they having supper now?"

Molly bit her lip. "Um, no. They actually left already."

"They went out for supper?" Grace asked.

"No . . . they *left*, left. As in, back to Tennessee."

"What?" Grace frowned. "Why?"

Levi set the toolbox on the floor. "I thought they were spending the night."

"I did too. I don't know what happened. We did the tour, and I talked up the unique history and the inn's features, and they seemed interested. But when we were finished they just thanked me and said it wasn't quite what they'd had in mind and they were going to head home."

Gravity pulled at Grace's shoulders, her stomach deflating like a week-old party balloon. "You're kidding me. 'Not what they had in mind'? What does that even mean?"

"They didn't offer a better explanation."

"Maybe this is just a buyer's tactic," Levi said. "To make us think they're not interested, and then they come in with a lowball offer in a day or two."

Molly shook her head. "I didn't get that vibe. They were pretty straightforward people. And we definitely shouldn't take a lowball offer. It's priced fairly, and we're not in a huge rush. I did give them my card and told them if they changed their minds to give me a call."

Grace sighed. "That's not likely if they weren't even interested enough to spend a night. I thought for sure . . ."

"I told you not to get your hopes up," Levi said. "This is a huge financial investment. It might take a while to find the right buyer."

But she didn't have "a while." Not if she was going to snag that sweet little bungalow.

"Don't lose hope," Molly said. "We already have an email from another prospective buyer."

That news lightened the blow. "Well, that's something. When are they coming?"

"I haven't written them back yet. I was waiting to see how this couple panned out."

"Well, let's try to get them in right away," Grace said.

"Yes, let's. If they can come this weekend we could always get one of our part-time workers to assist." Even if Levi encouraged them to be patient, he had his own reasons for wanting a quick sale. He'd put his life on hold for four years, and he was ready to get on with it. Ready to move to LA and start a life with his soon-to-be bride.

Levi would head off to LA, and Molly and Adam would be leaving for Italy . . . The thought left Grace feeling more than a little lonely.

Chapter Twenty-Six

*H*e was running out of time. Wyatt stepped over a fallen tree, gave Grace a hand, then continued on the path alongside Pine Creek. The temperature was a balmy seventy-five today, and under the shade of the deciduous trees, it was downright pleasant. The air was filled with the loamy scent of earth. Birds tweeted from the leafy canopy overhead, and a squirrel nattered from the underbrush nearby.

They were high in the mountains now, having been hiking for almost six hours. They only had another hour or so before they'd need to cut over and head back, but he was hopeful because the terrain appeared just as he'd remembered. The only thing missing was the waterfall and stack of boulders. He kept his eyes peeled for them and knew Grace was doing the same.

There'd been a definite bounce in his step all day. He felt ridiculously buoyed to have Grace with him again. He didn't mind being alone. But hiking without her these past couple days had felt lonely after having her company last week.

Spending more time with her wasn't smart or sensible. And he could tell himself all he wanted that he needed her assistance, but the truth was, he couldn't seem to help himself.

"How's your shoulder holding up?"

"It's fine. The lighter pack helps."

"And how've you been sleeping lately?"

He opened his mouth with a quick reply, then closed it before he answered honestly. "About the same."

They hiked in silence a minute, then Wyatt held a branch aside for her.

"Molly has some tea she swears by," Grace said. "She says it knocks her out like a light."

"Wouldn't mind trying some." Maybe it would help ward off the nightmares too. Because knowing what was coming once he closed his eyes served as an effective deterrent. He tossed and turned for hours each night, and the lack of sleep made him less focused and alert than usual. What a disaster that would've been on protective detail if he hadn't been forced to take leave.

He had to resolve this and soon. The clock was ticking. He had to pass that psych eval.

Wyatt stopped when he came to a narrower creek that ran into Pine Creek, cutting off the trail. Water bubbled noisily over the rocks. "Which way?"

"Pine Creek continues that way." She pointed in the direction they'd been headed and eased her bag off her shoulders. "This is just a tributary, and it comes from the wrong direction, so we can rule it out."

"That's something, I guess." Wyatt dropped his pack and removed his boots and socks. There were lots of rocks, but the shallow stream was at least twenty feet wide, and the water was swift.

Once they'd rolled up their pants and stuffed their boots into the bags, they padded toward the creek's edge.

Wyatt stepped into the frigid water, testing the bottom as Grace stepped in beside him. "Careful, it's slippery."

They took their time, slowing down when they reached the stream's center. Water hit his calves with surprising force, and he carefully picked his way across, using large rocks as stepping-stones when he could.

"Want to break for a snack soon?" Grace asked.

"Sure. I'm pretty hungry."

"Me too. That apple tart is calling my—" Grace squealed as she slipped.

Wyatt grabbed her arm, preventing a complete dousing. "You okay?"

She got her feet under her. "I think so. So much for staying dry."

He kept a firm grip on her arm as they navigated the rest of the stream. When she stepped out of the water, he saw the bloody trail leading down from her knee. "You're bleeding. Sit down."

"It's nothing." But she sat on a rock on the shore's edge. "Just a scratch."

Wyatt unzipped his pack. "I've got a Band-Aid." He fished out the first-aid kit as Grace pulled out a baby wipe and cleaned off her shin.

He loved how low maintenance she was. None of the women he'd dated in the past would be caught dead on a hiking trail, much less sitting here so calmly while blood ran down her leg.

He opened the kit and fished out an alcohol wipe. Ripping it open, he sank down in front of her, getting his first look at the injury. She must've caught it on a jagged rock because it was torn open and raw looking. The water had washed it out, but it still needed to be disinfected.

"That looks pretty nasty, but you shouldn't need stitches." He unfolded the wipe. "Nonetheless, this is going to hurt."

"Go ahead."

He gently pressed the wipe to the wound.

A sharp intake of breath was her only sign of pain.

"Sorry," he said. "I'll try to make it fast."

ℓ

Grace gritted her teeth as he sterilized the scrape, her fingers tightening into a fist on her lap at the sharp sting. "I'm not usually so clumsy."

"Could've just as easily been me. At least you didn't get too wet." He finished the task as quickly as possible. Then he bowed over the wound, and Grace felt the cool, soothing breeze of his breath.

A shiver passed through her as he blew on it again. Goose bumps danced across her skin. The gesture was so unexpected. So nurturing. So . . . intimate.

She stilled, looking down at the top of his head, at the chips of leaves lost in his thick hair. At the masculine slash of his brows and the soft feather of his dark eyelashes brushing the tops of his cheeks.

As if sensing a shift in mood, he straightened, coming face-to-face with her. He was close. His gaze sharpened on her eyes, his face changing slowly as the moment morphed into something that electrified the space between them.

A heartbeat passed, or maybe it was longer. Maybe the sun stood still in the sky. She wasn't sure, because everything else ceased to exist. Everything except his eyes, fixed on her, laden with desire.

Kiss me.

He rose onto his knees, coming closer, and now she was looking up at him. Then, as if he'd read her mind, he took her face in his hands and pulled her to him.

His warm breath whispered against her lips, and Grace's eyelids fluttered shut. And then she lost all coherent thought. She was just feeling now. Feeling his firm touch. His bold mouth. His solid frame.

She felt the brush of his lips on hers, soft and confident and so, so good. She felt the warm squeeze of attraction deep inside and the wild beating of her heart.

And the intense need for this kiss to go on forever—she felt that too. Because really, how would she bear it when it ended?

Somebody whimpered. Maybe her. She roped her arms around his broad shoulders, plowed her fingers into the soft hair at his nape.

He responded with a moan.

She took everything he offered and gave back freely. Her stomach fluttered, her skin tingled. There wasn't a square inch of her unaffected. How was this possible? This was not her first kiss. Had she been doing it wrong all along? Or just doing it with the wrong person?

When the kiss ended she didn't have a clue how much time had passed. She was out of breath and out of thoughts and out of words.

What was . . . ? She'd never . . . This was . . .

His face slowly came into focus as if she'd blacked out or something. Maybe she had. She was delighted, at least, to see that he looked as flustered as she felt. His heavy-lidded gaze, flushed cheeks, and ardent expression made her want to grab some seconds.

But he was easing away, putting space between them. Only inches, but it felt like miles as cool air rushed between them. She instantly missed the feel of him against her.

The look on his face shifted, making her remember the way he'd kept her at a distance when they'd met—had it really only been ten days ago? Anxiety squirmed into her heart like a worm into an apple. Did he regret the kiss? He'd just turned her entire world upside down with his mouth.

"I didn't intend to do that."

"Don't you dare say you're sorry, Wyatt."

He stared at her for a long minute in that inscrutable way of his.

She steeled herself for his rejection. Braced herself for the hurt that would follow.

"Go out with me."

She blinked. Okay, she hadn't seen that coming. "You aren't seeing enough of me now?"

He drew his knuckle down her cheek, leaving a wake of warmth. "No."

She could point out that he was only visiting Bluebell. That he had a life that was far away. That she was tied up here. But she couldn't even think past the feel of his touch.

"So, on this proposed date . . . Where would you take me?" As if that would factor in at all.

His mouth twisted into a smirk. "Not putt-putting."

She tilted her head at him.

His gaze roamed over her face as if searching for something. "I think I'll surprise you."

"You seem to be very good at that so far."

"Are you free tomorrow night?"

"I have a dress fitting for my brother's wedding at three, but I'm free after that."

"When's the wedding?"

"A week from Saturday. Levi's fiancée flies into town tomorrow, and I should go ahead and warn you that it's Mia Emerson."

"Who's that?"

Grace blinked at him. "Mia Emerson, the actress."

He shook his head.

"*Into the Deep*? *Twelve Hours*? *Lesser Days*?"

"I'm more of a reader, I guess."

"But the wedding's top secret, because . . . paparazzi, so you have to keep it under your hat."

"Paparazzi, top secret, got it. You know, we're getting way off subject here. So, tomorrow night . . . Six o'clock work for you?"

"Tomorrow night, six o'clock."

"It's a date then." His lips lifted in a grin, then he eyed her wound. "Now we'd better get that knee patched up."

e

Darkness pressed in, the moonlight glowing dimly through the curtains in Wyatt's room. Somewhere on the lake a boat's motor hummed as it passed by. What were they doing on the water past midnight?

He turned on the mattress, the bed squeaking in a familiar way. Sleep wasn't coming again tonight, but this time the blame fell on Grace.

The hike had been unsuccessful in one sense but highly productive in another. He hadn't been lying when he told her he hadn't planned the kiss. Conversely, he'd had every intention of keeping their relationship platonic for all the reasons he'd focused on since his arrival.

But sometimes a man just had to go with his gut. It didn't make sense, Grace and him. But he'd never clicked with a woman the way he clicked with Grace.

And that kiss had all but sealed his fate.

He loved that she hadn't tried to hide what she felt. She was so responsive, so genuine. Her ragged breath. That needy little gasp. The way her fingers tightened in his hair until his scalp stung. Like she was as surprised as he, as helpless as he, against the rising tide of want.

How could he shut it down after that kiss? How could he give up something he hadn't known he'd needed until the moment his lips were on hers? He wasn't one to throw caution to the wind, but he was going to spend time with Grace. He was going to know what made her tick. And he was going to kiss her again.

After bandaging her knee they'd returned to the business of

hiking, and he hadn't kissed her again. As quickly as that first one had taken off, he decided he'd better slow things down.

Being with Grace soothed his soul. Thinking of Grace was like floating on water. Relaxing. Tranquil. Wyatt's weight sank into the mattress, his eyes growing heavy as thoughts of Grace consumed him. And when he finally fell asleep, the nightmares didn't come.

Chapter Twenty-Seven

$\mathcal{G}$ race and Molly hung back inside the inn while Levi went out to greet his fiancée. The sisters weren't above a little eavesdropping through the front window, however. Mia's flight had been delayed and, much to Levi's chagrin, she was arriving only an hour before the girls' dress fitting in Asheville. It had been three months since Levi and Mia had been together. She'd been on set in Vancouver filming her next movie.

Grace watched Mia unfold from the rental and get swept into Levi's arms. She wore her usual disguise, a baseball hat and sunglasses, but the hat soon fell off and Levi removed the sunglasses as he took the kiss deeper.

"Go, Levi," Molly said.

"I think I've seen enough." Grace went to straighten her outfitter brochures at the front desk.

"I remember those days," Molly said wistfully, still watching out the window.

Grace snorted. "You mean yesterday?" Molly and Adam might've been married for over a year now, but they were always touching. It was kind of sickening.

Molly dropped the curtain and gave Grace a sly grin. "You're right. We've still got it. You'll understand that kind of chemistry someday."

Grace straightened the other brochures in the rack, heat climbing her neck as she thought of Wyatt and that kiss they'd shared yesterday. Talk about chemistry. She'd reviewed that lip-lock about a hundred times and was still dumbfounded. The kisses in her past had not prepared her for Wyatt. Not even close.

Molly sometimes read Grace snippets of her favorite romance novels, which Grace barely tolerated without rolling her eyes. She viewed the fictitious kisses as fanciful hype, drivel for hopeless romantics like her sister. But yesterday had turned that kind of thinking on end.

Grace became aware that Molly was studying her, head tilted thoughtfully, a suspicious twinkle in her eyes.

Grace shifted. "What?"

"You're blushing."

"No, I'm not."

"What happened? Tell me everything."

"Nothing happened." But Grace's face was flooded with heat all the way to the tips of her ears.

Molly narrowed her eyes. "Did Wyatt kiss you?"

"What? No."

"Your voice went up two full octaves."

"I thought you didn't approve of Wyatt."

"I didn't say that. I was just suggesting you exercise caution. You've spent quite a bit of time with him, and if you trust him, I'll give him the benefit of the doubt. Now stop stalling and spill the details."

Grace shuffled more brochures. "He asked me out, that's all. We're going out tonight."

"*You're going out?*"

The door burst open, and Mia and Levi entered on a cloud of euphoria.

Ah, love to the rescue. Grace gave Molly a smug grin.

Molly's look said, *This subject is not yet closed.*

Levi let loose of Mia long enough for Molly to sweep her soon-to-be sister-in-law into a hug. "It's so good to see you! It's been too long. You have to tell us all about the filming."

"It was awesome. I can't wait to catch up."

Grace was next. "Hey, Mia."

Mia touched Grace's hair. "I love your hair. Are you doing something different with it?"

"She took it down from its perpetual ponytail," Molly said.

As they caught up, Grace's eyes fixed on her brother. He seemed happy and relaxed for the first time in weeks. Grace was glad Mia was finally here. She was so good for Levi.

Before they knew it, the time had come to leave for their dress fitting. Levi would've climbed right into the car, except someone had to stay and mind the inn.

An hour later Grace squirmed into the snug halter-style dress, pulling it down past her hips and legs where it flared out like a billowy cloud. The bridesmaid gown was a pretty blush color, and the style suited her. But Grace rarely wore dresses. They made her feel like a little girl playing dress-up.

Molly and Grace were serving as Mia's bridesmaids, and Mia's best friend from LA, Brooke, was her maid of honor. Mia probably could've had ten attendants, but smaller was better for keeping the shindig secret.

"How's it going in there?" Molly called from outside the dressing room. Mia had arranged for a private fitting, so they were alone in the shop today.

"Fine. I'm just . . . adjusting things a bit." Like her boobs, which seemed to have disappeared inside the material.

"Let's see."

Grace scanned her form in the floor-length mirror, turning side-ways. She was blessed to be tall and thin, but would a curve or two have killed anyone?

A knock rattled the louvered door. "Come on, Grace. I wanna see."

"Hold your horses."

A few minutes later she stepped quietly from the dressing room to see Molly on the pedestal in front of the three-way mirror. Mia was gazing approvingly at Molly's gown—same color but a slightly different style than Grace's.

Mia was fully made up and wearing a pretty sundress, her long, wavy blonde hair down around her shoulders. She looked, well, like a movie star.

Mia turned and her green eyes lit up at the sight of Grace. "Oh, Grace! You look amazing in that dress. Doesn't she, Molly?"

Her sister was already coming close to flitter around Grace. "It really does suit you."

"I think the chest needs to be taken in."

Molly fussed with Grace's bodice, and Grace swatted her hands away.

"You probably just need the right bra. But if it needs an altera-tion the seamstress can do it."

"She'll be right in," Mia said. "She had to take a phone call."

"Are you getting excited?" Molly asked Mia. "A week from to-morrow you'll be walking down the aisle!"

"I can't wait. But we have so much to do before the wedding. This week is a whirlwind of appointments and details. And honestly, I'm mostly just excited about starting our life together in LA." She winced. "I know that means taking Levi away from you, though, and I promise we'll make a point to get together as often as possible."

"It's a lot of change," Molly said, "but mostly good stuff. I'll be headed to Italy before we know it. And Grace is ready to give Blue Ridge Outfitters a permanent home."

"I'm excited for you both. Have you had any more interest in the inn?"

"We had a showing yesterday, but I don't think anything will come of it."

"What?" Grace said. "You didn't tell me that."

"You were hiking with Wyatt. It was an older gentleman from Hendersonville, and he didn't really seem like the inn type. I think he was just being nosy. We still have that couple from Charlotte coming tomorrow."

Mia's eyes sharpened on Grace. "Who's this Wyatt?"

Heat inched up Grace's neck. She faced the mirror and fussed with the bodice. "He's just a guest. I've taken him on a couple of guided treks."

Molly smirked. "He's midtwenties, very hot, and Grace has a date with him tonight."

Mia's eyes lit and she smiled wide. "That's super, Grace. What will you wear?"

"Um, I don't know. I guess I'll have to scrounge up a pair of dress pants or something. I don't even know where he's taking me. It's a surprise."

Mia beamed. "Ooh, a surprise."

"You should ask him what to wear," Molly said. "You can't assume he'll take you to a fancy restaurant or something."

They discussed where he might take her before the conversation flowed to Mia's upcoming film and all the things going on in Hollywood. They were laughing their heads off by the time the seamstress entered, measuring tape draped around her neck.

"All right, ladies, let's get you ready for this beautiful wedding!"

Chapter Twenty-Eight

*P*icking up a woman for a date had never been so easy. Wyatt checked the mirror one last time before he left his room. His heart was thudding as he walked down the hall. He wiped his palms down his jeans before he tapped on Grace's door. Did she have her own set of butterflies flittering around her stomach?

The door swept open, and all thoughts of nerves vanished at the sight of her. It wasn't her long blonde hair, full of waves and begging to be caught up in his hands. Or the easy, off-the-shoulder white top. It was her shy smile and the hint of anticipation lighting her blue eyes.

"You look amazing."

She gave a nervous laugh. "I guess anything beats T-shirts and hiking boots. Am I dressed okay for whatever you've got planned?"

He raked his gaze over her. "You're perfect."

She rubbed her lips together. "You look nice too."

He smiled as he took her hand and drew her out of the room. "Let's go."

"Do I get any hints at least?"

He loved the tension that crackled between them at mere eye contact. "You'll just have to trust me."

They took the steps, and once they reached the ground floor he was relieved to see that her brother was busy at the front desk with a customer. Levi had been cordial enough since he sucker punched

Wyatt, but he was clearly reserving judgment. Wyatt wasn't sure if Levi knew about this date, but now wasn't the optimal time for that revelation.

When Grace headed toward the front door, he tugged her hand. "Nope. This way."

"Okay . . ." She followed him down the hall and out the back door. Once the dock came into view it only took her a few seconds to spot the boat tied up there, an antique wooden Chris-Craft.

She gasped, looking at him. "Is that Adam's boat? How'd you pull that off? He won't even let *me* drive it."

"I gave him my extensive list of boating credentials and signed over my firstborn."

"This is so great. I've only been in it once."

He sensed her relaxing into the date. With another woman a fancy dinner and theater tickets might impress. Grace was different. She was comfortable outside, comfortable on the water. And, of course, he'd taken all that into account because he wanted her to relax and enjoy their evening.

They made their way down the grassy slope, no longer holding hands. She preceded him down the wooden dock, which shimmied under their weight.

When he pulled the keys out of his pocket and handed them over to her, her eyes widened. "What? I can drive it?"

"She's all yours for the evening. Got Adam's permission and everything."

She gawked at the boat, then back at him. "What kind of magician are you? How did you do this?"

"I enlisted your sister's help, that's all. Seems she has a lot of sway with her husband."

"She didn't say a word."

"We've been texting back and forth the past couple hours." Wyatt had planned to rent a boat for the night, but when he asked Molly what Grace's favorite type of boat was, she went on a mission to make the date a success. God bless her.

He helped Grace into the boat, untied the lines, and stepped aboard. As Grace sank onto the bench seat behind the wheel, her wide smile was contagious. Once he was seated she started the engine and it roared to life, making the boat vibrate beneath them.

Wyatt pointed across the lake. "Head that way, Captain."

Grace beamed at him. "Aye, aye, sir."

He'd thought it might take a while to arrive at their destination. Grace had obviously taken time with her hair, and he knew by now women didn't like having their hard work undone.

But once Grace cleared the no-wake zone, she went full throttle, her hair waving behind her like a flag. And Wyatt thought it might be the most beautiful sight he'd ever seen.

l

"That was so fun." Grace settled across from Wyatt at a patio table behind Clem's Lake Shack where they could keep a close eye on Adam's boat.

"She sure rides like a dream."

Grace used her fingers to unsnarl her hair. She probably looked all windblown, but it had been worth it. "And I love this restaurant. Have you been here before?"

"No, but I've heard great things. Some hikers were telling me I shouldn't miss it, and Molly confirmed that you liked it."

"I do. It's been a while though." The restaurant wasn't fancy, but it wasn't quite the "shack" it claimed to be either. The shaded outdoor patio overlooking the lake made it popular with tourists, and the tasty dishes made it one of the Bennetts' top restaurant recommendations.

The temperature was pleasant tonight, around seventy, and a light breeze blew in off the lake. All in all, a perfect night for patio dining.

"I have a confession to make," Grace said after the server took their drink order and left. "I don't usually like surprises."

"People who say that usually mean they fear the surprise will be a bad one."

"Hmm. That might be true. So you went out of your way to make sure this was a good surprise."

"It wasn't that much trouble." His eyes glinted with amusement. "You deserve better than putt-putt."

Though he said it lightly, she could tell he meant it. For someone who'd initially been so mysterious he was certainly up front with her. She'd expect a man like him, so good-looking and confident, to be a bit of a player. He was anything but.

"You're certainly full of surprises."

The server set their waters down. "I'll be right back to take your orders."

After she left Wyatt leaned his elbows on the white tablecloth. "How so?"

"Shall we start with the Secret Service job or go straight to our soul-baring camp conversations? Please. You've done nothing but surprise me since we met. It even surprised me that you asked me out."

"After that kiss?"

She cleared her throat and twisted her hands in her lap. "Yeah, well, that was a surprise too."

His eyes pierced hers, and the cord of tension pulled tight between them. "I think we can agree on that."

The server stopped to take their order, but they hadn't even opened their menus. They took a moment to peruse the options. Grace settled quickly on the pecan-crusted walleye, mainly because she wanted to get back to their conversation.

Moments later the server returned. Wyatt ordered a pulled pork dish she'd heard good things about. She might have to sample.

When the server left the table, Grace leaned forward. "So why did you finally ask me out?"

His brow cocked. "Finally, huh?"

Okay, maybe that had been telling. "You had your reasons for holding me at arm's length, I'm sure."

"I did that?"

"Admit it, you thought I was a mere child."

"Wouldn't put it quite that way."

"Then how would you put it?"

"Maybe I did recognize the gap between our ages and levels of life experience."

She took that in. Let it settle a bit and found herself unable to argue the point. "Fair enough. But I'm still twenty-one, you're still twenty-six, and my life experience has remained fairly stable since meeting you."

"That's true."

"So what else? We live in different cities . . ."

"An obvious obstacle."

"And still unchanged. Am I missing anything?"

"That about covers it."

"So before . . . when you alluded to the kiss as having been a factor in asking me out, what did it change exactly?"

His gaze sharpened on her. "You're very direct."

Jeez, Grace, lighten up. It's a first date. She was supposed to be telling him about her favorite food, sports team, and hobbies. Not interrogating him about why he'd asked her out.

"Sorry. I guess I'm a little nervous." She reached for her water.

He touched her wrist. "That wasn't a complaint. I like that about you, Grace. To a guy who's been around a lot of hardened, guarded people, you're pretty darned refreshing."

His fingers trailed away as he withdrew his hand, and Grace was still feeling the touch a full five seconds later.

"And that kiss," he continued. "Obviously it didn't negate all the obstacles. It just made me realize I cared too much to let them stand in the way."

Grace's lungs emptied even as his gaze captured hers, leaving her no means of escape. "And you say I'm direct."

His lips twitched. "Too much?"

"You've surprised me again."

"It's fun keeping you on your toes."

"My heels haven't touched the ground since we met."

He chuckled, that dimple making an appearance, and the warm, rich sound wove around her like a spell.

"I think I'd like to keep it that way," he said.

She imagined him literally lifting her heels off the ground, with his arms around her waist, lifting her into him, chest to chest, his mouth pressed to hers.

When the image cleared, there was Wyatt, studying her face, not missing a single thing. "What are you thinking about over there, Grace Bennett?"

"Nothing," she said, then grimaced because Molly was right. Two whole octaves.

He gave a lazy smile that made her think of sultry summer evenings and moonlit kisses.

"Hold that thought," he said.

Whew. Was it getting hot out here?

They talked nonstop as they waited for their food. He had a hundred questions about her family and growing up in Bluebell. She had plenty of her own about his summers here as a child and about his family—which consisted mostly of his father, stepmother, cousins, aunts, and uncles. He had two sets of grandparents who lived in Florida and Pennsylvania but didn't see them often.

Before she knew it the food arrived, and the aroma of his barbecue pork took first prize. On the trail they'd each prayed over their own meals, so she was surprised—pleasantly so—when he took her hand and offered a quick grace.

"Thank you," she said as he squeezed her hand, and they both dug into their meals.

He shared a bite of his pork with her, and she had a moment of regret until she tasted her own crispy fried fish. "Yum. Wanna try?"

When he agreed she offered him a bite on her own fork. He tasted it, then nodded in approval. "Good. Not at all fishy."

"I think fish is the only food that isn't supposed to taste like what it is. You never hear anyone complain of beef that's too beefy."

"Or chicken that's too chicken-y."

"Right? It's weird."

"So," he said after they'd enjoyed a bite or two in silence. "You basically opened a business straight out of high school? You didn't want to go to college?"

"Not really. Which is a little strange because I had good grades. Levi about had a conniption when he found out—the summer after I graduated high school. I got a lot of lectures about how many business start-ups fail."

"That was a bold, independent decision on your part."

She gave a wry chuckle. "That's not quite how he saw it. But he came around eventually. In all fairness, we were struggling to get the inn going at the time, and he was already overwhelmed."

"Seems to be working out now."

"It is. The inn's doing good business and will soon be sold, God willing. I'm really excited to branch out into my own building. Though I'm a little nervous about it too."

"Why's that?"

"Well, right now I have help from Levi and Molly. Whoever's working the front desk handles rentals. Once I'm on my own, I'll have to hire help. Plus a lot of my customers find out about the business because they're staying at the inn. I'm a little worried tourists won't find me so easily."

"Sounds like a good marketing plan will be the solution."

"Yes, but that takes money. The sale of the inn should leave me set to make a big push though." The problem was, tourists came and went, so the marketing had to be ongoing. She brushed her worry aside, not wanting anything negative to intrude on the night.

"So tell me how your brother ended up becoming engaged to a celebrity."

Grace chuckled, remembering the craziness from two summers ago. "Funny thing, Mia actually came to the inn on her honeymoon."

"Come again?"

"Well, to be fair, her wedding didn't exactly pan out, so she came alone. You didn't hear about this? It was all over social media and the gossip sites."

"I don't really follow those things."

"You don't read *People*?" she asked facetiously.

He gave her a *get real* grin.

"Yeah, so there was a lot going on in Mia's life that summer, including a huge scandal and paparazzi."

"Here?"

"Right here in little ol' Bluebell. And Levi came to her rescue." As Grace remembered her brother's fierce protectiveness and googly eyes, she laughed. "He fell for her hard and fast. It was fun to watch, let me tell you."

"He seems a little . . . tightly wound."

"Just because he sucker punched you at first chance?" she deadpanned.

"It factored in."

"Thank you for not laying him flat, by the way. But yes, he can be a little uptight. That's what made it so fun, watching him go down. You haven't seen him around Mia yet. It's like she calms him or something with just her presence."

"You and Molly get along with her? She's going to be part of the family soon."

"Oh yeah, she's great. Not at all full of herself or—as Miss Della says—'too big for her britches,' like you might expect a celebrity to be. She's kind and thoughtful and easy to talk to. Levi's ready to put an end to this long-distance dating though."

A while later the server was removing their plates just as the giant pink orb of the sun began melting into the horizon. Pink and purple clouds swathed the sky in a brilliant display of artistry, the colors reflecting off the water's smooth-as-glass surface.

"Look at that," Grace said. "You timed it perfectly." Wyatt's actions were strategic and precise. She'd never considered how sexy those traits were, especially when he used them to please her.

They declined dessert and watched the sun go down in quiet awe. Grace never got tired of the beautiful lake sunsets. Mostly, though, she was thinking how strategic and precise his kiss had been. But there'd been a wildness too, and with that wildness a measure of restraint. She hoped he'd get the chance to display all those traits a little later.

Chapter Twenty-Nine

*O*nce the sun was gone, darkness quickly closed in. Wyatt settled the bill and led Grace from the restaurant, taking her hand as they made their way across the lawn toward the pier. Her hand felt small and delicate in his. Her skin soft.

He'd enjoyed their conversation over supper. Grace was easy to talk to and witty with her dry sense of humor. She wasn't one to gush, but her love for her family was obvious. She was still younger and less experienced than he was, but instead of being repelled by her fresh outlook and naïveté, he found himself drawn to those qualities.

He hoped to extend the evening and was glad it was dark now so Grace couldn't jet them across the lake in ten seconds flat.

The dock shimmied as they walked down the length of it, and when they reached the boat he released her hand. Grace slid behind the wheel while Wyatt untied the lines. Once they were both aboard she started the boat and found the nav lights.

"Back to the house?" she asked.

"If you'd like. Or we could do a little stargazing out on the lake."

Overhead the stars shimmered like sequins in the autumn skies. She shot him a little smile as she pulled from the slip. "Stargazing it is."

A while later they drifted to a stop in the middle of the basin. Grace shut off the lights, and the night went dark around them. There was no room to spread out on the boat, which had only two bench seats, but at least it was comfortably padded.

The temperatures had cooled, so Wyatt grabbed the light blanket he'd brought from the backseat and wrapped it around Grace.

"Thanks. It is getting a little chilly. Fall is on its way."

They leaned back against the seats, their eyes having adjusted to the darkness. To the west, the sky was still deep blue, but overhead the black canvas showed off pinpricks of twinkling lights.

The boat bobbed gently, the water kissing its sides with quiet ripples. The scent of a campfire drifted past on a breeze.

Grace's arm rested against Wyatt's, and their thighs touched. He loved being close to her. He laced his fingers with hers, resting their hands on his leg. "I can teach you the constellations."

"I already know the constellations." A grin tinged her voice.

"Okay, smarty-pants." He pointed to the sky. "What's that one?"

She leaned closer to follow the direction of his finger. "Give me a break. It's Sagittarius. Everyone knows that."

"Okay, that was an easy one. How 'bout that one?"

"The one with the tail? Draco."

He shifted his finger a tiny bit. "That one?"

"Hercules. My turn to quiz you." She pointed into the sky. "That one—the one that looks like a graduation cap."

"Aquila?"

"Very good. And that one?"

He put his arm around her, leaning in closer, not necessarily because he needed to. He drew in a whiff of her flowery shampoo. "Which one?"

"Right there. The one shaped like a Christian fish symbol."

"That's not a constellation."

"Yes, it is. It's Pavo."

"You're making that up."

She chuckled, glancing at him. "No, I'm not."

"Somebody did do well in school."

"I may have been a bit of a perfectionist."

"What kind of grades are we talking about here?"

"Well, I wasn't valedictorian or anything."

"What was your GPA? I know you know it."

"It was 3.78," she admitted. "It was algebra that did me in."

"I liked algebra."

"You would."

He smiled to himself. "That's quite an achievement, Grace. Are you that much of a bookworm, or did your parents push you?"

"Not at all. And I'm not a bookworm. I just pushed myself and got very upset when I didn't do my best."

He thought about that a minute. "Do you think that might be related to the survivor's guilt you mentioned earlier?"

Her gaze burned into the side of his face. "That's very perceptive. And yes, I do. But I've been working on it, trying to manage my expectations."

His heart went out to her. He wished he could see more than just the gleam of her eyes in the dark. "You don't have to do anything to prove your value. You're worthy just as you are—just as God made you. I know you know that already. Just wanted you to hear it from someone else."

"Thank you."

They stared at each other, the moment drawing out. Liquid heat hummed through his veins from her nearness alone. She was the only woman who'd ever had that kind of power over him.

"I feel like we've known each other longer than ten days." She ducked her head.

If it had been any other woman he might've been put off that she'd counted the days. Instead he felt relieved. A little heady, actually. He hoped she never lost that sweet innocence. "Well, we've covered a lot of ground together."

"Literally."

"Quite literally."

She tilted her head up, looking at him. "I had a great time tonight, Wyatt."

He touched her face and leaned closer until their breaths mingled, because he had to have another taste of her. And soon.

"The best is yet to come," he said softly.

"You—you can beat the Chris-Craft? Clem's food? The autumn sky?"

His lips tipped upward. "Let's give it a whirl."

He took her mouth like a man starving. Because he *was* starving for her. Their kiss may have been only yesterday, but he wasn't counting in days. He was counting in hours, in minutes. And it had seemed like a million of each had passed since he'd claimed her lips.

He deepened the kiss, and she yielded to him, clutching his shirt, hanging on for dear life. He was doing the same. Already fighting for breath, zero to sixty in ten seconds. That's how it was with Grace. He was warm all over, tingling and buzzing and dizzy with want of her.

His hand moved to cup the back of her head. His fingers dove into the hair behind her ears, the silky strands threading between his fingers. Her feminine smell invaded his senses in the most wonderful way.

Her hands slid up his chest and around his neck, and she settled into his arms, into his chest . . .

Into his heart.

The tender thought made his breath catch. They were combustible together, was the problem—if one could consider that a problem. And yes, moving too fast would be a mistake. He wanted to be careful with Grace. She deserved that.

A little restraint was a good thing. He couldn't quite make himself believe it just now. Especially when she made that little mewling sound. *Sweet heaven.*

He gentled his hold. Slowed his pace. Managed—with the discipline of a saint—to dial it back a notch. He took small delicious nibbles, letting his mouth wander to the corners of her lips, each side. Then to her cheek, her jaw, the fragrant curve of her neck. She tilted her head to the side, the curtain of her hair falling aside as she made room for him.

He glided his nose back up her neck—that smell. He was already addicted. He straightened, brushing her nose with his, letting his heart settle in the silence. He gradually became aware of the gentle rocking of the boat, the whisper of the breeze, the distant ping of hardware on a flagpole.

Her fingers moved at the back of his neck, stirring every cell to life. "To be honest, I thought maybe last time was a fluke."

Her ragged voice made him want to make her breathless again. "Me too."

"It's all your fault," she said lightly.

"Mine? It's totally yours."

She held his gaze in the dark for a long moment. "What are we going to do?"

His lips inched upward. "More of that, I hope."

When their mouths met again, she was smiling against his lips.

Chapter Thirty

Saturday morning Grace was so distracted by thoughts of her date she'd completely forgotten that a prospective buyer was coming. She grabbed a stack of fresh towels from the cleaning cart when she heard Molly leading them up the stairs. Grace was glad she'd just finished cleaning the last vacated room.

"The Bluebell Inn has the distinction of being the town's very first inn," Molly said. "It was built in 1905 and featured ten bedrooms. Early on it was even a stagecoach stop. And starting in 1957, it housed the post office. We actually uncovered the old mail slot when we were renovating and found an old love letter—there's a long story there, but I'll spare you.

"The inn's been several things over the years, including a saloon, if you can believe it. In the sixties—the lake's real heyday—other hotels opened, but the Bluebell Inn remained *the* place to stay.

"In 1978 it was bought by Governor Jennings and turned into his family lake home. Then my parents purchased it, and my siblings and I had the pleasure of growing up here. Our parents dreamed of turning it back into an inn during their retirement. But sadly, that wasn't to be. They passed away unexpectedly four years ago. But my siblings and I took it upon ourselves to fulfill their dream."

"I'm sorry for your loss," a woman said.

"That's some mission you took on," a man said. "This place has quite the history."

"That's only the tip of the iceberg, I assure you."

They reached the top of the stairs and rounded the corner, and Grace smiled as the attractive middle-aged couple came into view.

"This is my sister, Grace," Molly said. "Grace, these are the Wellingtons—they're from Charlotte."

They exchanged greetings and made small talk for a moment, then Molly led them past the cart and continued the tour.

Grace put the towels in the room, closed the door, and pushed the cart up the hall toward the supply closet.

"This is our suite." Molly's voice carried down the hall as she unlocked the door and ushered them inside. "All of our rooms feature an en suite bathroom, but as you can see, the suite also features a sitting area, fireplace, and a generously sized walk-in shower. This room functions nicely as a honeymoon suite—we have a lot of destination weddings here in Bluebell."

"It's quite charming," Mrs. Wellington said. "I love the décor."

"This particular room was updated two years ago when we had a small flood."

Grace aimed a frown at the end of the hall even though her sister couldn't see her.

"A flood?" Mr. Wellington asked. "What happened?"

"Well, we had an old pipe burst, unfortunately. But no worries. We got it all cleaned up and had all the piping replaced."

"How extensive was the damage?" Mrs. Wellington asked.

"The water covered most of the upstairs, but we cleaned it up quickly, cut away the drywall, sanitized . . . You know the drill."

The floor squeaked as they moved across the hall to another room. "This is the last vacant room I can show you, but the others are very much like this one. As you can see, each room is equipped with a mini-split to heat and cool the rooms. We like their high efficiency, and the guests enjoy the ability to control the temperature. Each room also comes with a large closet, a top-of-the-line mattress, luxury bedding, a thirty-two-inch flat-screen TV, a Keurig machine, and plush robes."

Grace finished stowing the cleaning cart and slipped across the hall into her room. She left the door cracked so she could eavesdrop.

"It sounds like you've done a lot of work to the place, getting it up to code and all," the man said. "But the house is quite old. How's the foundation?"

"We did discover some foundation issues when we renovated, but we had those fixed."

"What kinds of issues?" he asked.

"Well . . . you'd have to talk to my brother. He's the one who handled that part of the renovation. He previously worked as a commercial building contractor in Denver, so he's knowledgeable and very thorough."

"He decided not to update the plumbing though?" the woman asked.

Grace winced. Why was Molly sharing so much?

"Oh, well, yes, he thought we'd get by with the plumbing for a while. But one of the pipes had enough, I guess." She gave a nervous chuckle. "It was just one of those things. All new plumbing now though, so you don't have to worry about that."

They were making their way down the hall now, Molly mentioning some of the area's natural attractions.

"I didn't see any other hotels around town," the woman said.

"There are a lot of homes for rent around here, but we're the only inn in Bluebell. So far anyway . . ."

"Are you aware of another one coming?" Mr. Wellington asked.

"Well, no, not really. There are rumors that a chain hotel is interested in a property on the lake, but that probably won't happen."

As her voice faded, Grace glared at Molly through the door. She was supposed to be selling the inn's positive features, not pointing out all the negatives! This wasn't like her Pollyanna sister at all. There wasn't a thing wrong with the inn, and business rumors swirled around town all the time. Ninety percent of them never panned out.

Grace could almost see her perfect little house on the edge of town getting snatched up from beneath her. She paced her room, checking out the window as she waited for the couple to leave. Finally, after about fifteen long minutes, the couple got into their car and drove away.

Grace left her room and traipsed down the stairs, hoping to catch Molly before she left. When Grace reached the bottom her sister was talking to Levi in the lobby.

"Yeah, unfortunately, I don't think they're all that serious," Molly said.

"What makes you say that?" Levi asked.

Grace folded her arms over her chest. "Possibly because she was pointing out all the inn's flaws."

"I was not!"

Levi looked between them. "What are you talking about?"

"You told them about the flood. You told them we had foundation issues. You told them a chain hotel might be coming to town."

Levi gave Molly a look. "Seriously?"

"I didn't say that. Well, okay, I said some of that, but I didn't— I said we had a flood, but we cleaned it all up. I said we *used* to have a foundation issue, but we fixed it. I told them there was a *rumor* about a hotel chain."

"Well, why bring up any of that?" Grace asked.

"And I said a ton of other things. Positive things. Glowing things!

You didn't hear all that. I told them how busy we are, how satisfied the guests are, how supportive the community is."

"Still, Molly," Levi said. "Why mention all those other things? There's nothing wrong with the inn. Why make them question that?"

Molly's face gave away every thought. "Okay, fine. Maybe I shouldn't have brought it up. I was just trying to be honest."

"When people hear *flood* they imagine ongoing mold issues," Levi said. "Expensive mold issues. They weren't here to see our meticulous cleanup. We know there's no mold problem, but they don't, so we don't need to mention it."

"Fine. I won't bring it up."

"Did you mention that stuff to all the other people who came through too?" Grace asked.

"No . . ." Molly shifted, her gaze darting around restlessly. "Well, maybe some of it."

Grace threw her hands up. "Great. No wonder no one is interested. We've had Eeyore giving the grand tour!"

Molly gasped. "*You're* calling *me* Eeyore?"

"No one is more surprised by that than me."

"Settle down, you two. We'll have plenty more interested parties."

The front door opened and Wyatt entered wearing gym clothes. He glanced between the siblings, obviously catching the tense vibe.

His gaze zeroed in on Grace. "Everything all right?"

Grace calmed instantly at the sight of him. "Fine. Just sibling stuff. Good workout?"

"Very good."

Mia came down the stairs, greeted them, then went straight to the front desk and leaned in, giving Levi a kiss. "Good morning, sweetheart."

"Morning." Levi went from stressed to smitten in ten seconds flat.

Grace introduced Wyatt to Mia, further dispelling the tension in the room. Then Grace agreed to take the desk while Levi and Mia ran some wedding errands. Molly, looking like a dog with its tail between its legs, slinked out the front door, leaving Grace alone with Wyatt.

After the door shut, Wyatt looked at Grace. "Not to sound narcissistic, but that wasn't about me, was it?"

"What?"

"That wall of tension I walked into."

Grace took her place behind the front desk. "That was about the inn. I overheard Molly not doing such a great job with the prospective buyers. I think she might've scared them away."

"Maybe she's not the right person for the job. You'd be great at giving a tour."

She smiled at him. "Thanks, but Molly really is the right person. We had a talk with her, and she promised to straighten up. It'll be fine."

He ambled over to the desk, something shifting on his face with each step. He was staring at her in a way that stirred up those butterflies.

"I had a nice time last night, Grace."

"Me too." She'd been so full of adrenaline when she turned in last night, she couldn't sleep. She kept reviewing that kiss—those kisses. Yum.

He looked at her mouth like he was doing that right now. Then his gaze swung back to her eyes, holding them captive for a long, delicious moment.

She'd been toying with an idea all morning but was afraid it was too soon. They'd only had one date, and he hadn't yet mentioned a second. But those kisses. She was positive he'd enjoyed them as much as she had. And the warmth in his eyes gave her the courage to ask the question.

"I was wondering—"

"What are you—?"

They spoke at the same time.

He smiled. "Ladies first."

This was the first time she'd considered that standard a disadvantage. She straightened the brochures. "Right. Okay. So I'm hesitant to ask you this because we've only gone out once. But it appears there's a wedding coming up in our family, and I have a plus one. It's next Saturday—and I don't even know if you're still going to be around—but I'd like to bring a date. And I know weddings have all kinds of heavy implications, real and imagined, and guys get nervous about that kind of thing. But really, I'm just looking for a friendly date, someone to—"

"A friendly date . . ."

"—dance with. I was actually thinking of asking Nick, you know, just as friends, but—"

"You are not asking Nick."

She crossed her arms and lifted her chin. "You're a little bossy." Funny how it was so much more annoying when Levi did it.

"Are you trying to ask me on a date, Grace?"

Her face warmed, and heat prickled under her arms. He was always throwing her off balance. And from the cocky look on his face, he didn't mind it one bit.

"I guess I am," she said, flustered. "If you're still going to be around and everything."

"I am going to be around. And I'd love to be your plus one." He set his palms on the counter, leaning in and coming within a foot of her. Giving her that intense look that made her knees go all wobbly.

"But that's a whole week away, Gracie. And I'm not waiting that long to kiss you again. Go out with me tonight."

Chapter Thirty-One

$\mathcal{G}$race followed the path down the peninsula, better known as Pawley Park. Maple trees cast long shadows on the well-manicured lawn as the filmy sun sank behind the mountains. Folks were out enjoying the mild evening weather: kids on the swing set, a young couple pulling ashore in a rowboat, and a couple of guys fishing off the pier.

Grace headed toward the white gazebo where Molly and Adam had gotten married. There'd been another wedding earlier today—the podium still stood beneath the pavilion, and white chairs were lined up across the lawn like a sheet of postage stamps. Grace spotted an empty picnic table around the bend and headed toward it.

She'd had some errands to run in town after work, so she and Wyatt had agreed to meet here. He was bringing food. She was early, but she'd sent him a text, telling him where she'd be.

As she neared the picnic table, one of the guys on the dock gave a whoop. He grabbed the fish that flopped around on the end of his line and began removing the hook from its mouth. She was about to look away when the man turned.

At the sight of his silhouette she stopped, her heart crashing into her ribs. It was the guy who'd grabbed her up by the creek. The tall, dark-haired one. His fishing buddy was the bearded blond.

Grace's heartbeat reverberated in her ears. Her lungs struggled to keep pace. She darted behind the nearest covering, a tree twice as wide as she was.

You're fine, you're fine. Settle down. It's a public park. It's daylight.

Not comforting, since the biggest fright of her life had happened in broad daylight.

She leaned against the trunk, letting the solid feel of it ground her. She glanced around the park, the bark snagging her hair. No one else was around that she could see.

Her legs were numb, but she forced herself to remain standing. She didn't want to be caught unaware. She was being paranoid. They hadn't even seen her, and they weren't drunk this time. They might not even remember her or what had happened.

But all those reassurances did nothing to quell the fear and sense of doom that hit her like a tidal wave. She breathed through the panic, afraid to close her eyes for even a moment.

It'll pass. Nothing is going to happen. God, help me. Because it sure felt like something was going to happen. Something bad. Something inescapable.

The seconds dragged on, each one an eternity. She had no idea how much time passed. She didn't hear the men anymore, but she was afraid to look.

A hand touched her shoulder.

She yelped and spun around, ready to scratch and claw and scream her head off.

But it was only Wyatt.

He held up his hands. "Hey, hey. It's all right. It's just me."

Grace clutched her chest to make sure her heart didn't leap out onto the ground.

Wyatt had stiffened, his gaze darting around the park. Hand on the gun at his waist. "What's wrong?" he asked without looking at her.

"Those guys." Grace breathed though the panic. "The ones fishing off the pier."

"Where?"

She found the courage to peek around the tree. "Over there. The man who attacked me at the creek and the other one. The drunk guys."

His brows pinched together. "Did they bother you?"

"I don't think they even saw me. I'm probably overreacting."

His eyes narrowed on the men. "That's not them, Grace. Look."

She studied the guys who were baiting their hooks. Wyatt was right. The tall guy was lankier than the one at the campground. And his blond friend had a beard, but it was too long to be the guy she remembered.

What had she been thinking? "You're right."

Wyatt's hand fell from his hip. His body lost some of that rigid alertness as he assessed her. "You're white as a sheet." He took her hand and gave a tug.

That was all it took. She wrapped her arms around his middle and buried her face in his chest. "What's wrong with me? I'm losing it. My heart's beating so fast."

"You're fine." Without letting her go he lifted her wrist and took her pulse, holding her hand almost as if they were dancing.

"Purse your lips," he said against her temple. "Breathe through your mouth real slow. You're all right. Nothing bad is going to happen."

She'd forgotten about that little breathing trick. It helped. As did knowing Wyatt was here and would protect her. Since when had she been so dependent on a man? But right now, security meant more to her than independence.

The panic was subsiding, embarrassment creeping in. This was the second time he'd found her like this. And this time she'd freaked out over nothing. He probably thought she was a real nut job.

He let go of her wrist and rubbed her back. "Better?"

"Yes, I'm sorry."

"Don't be sorry."

"I feel stupid."

He leaned back, taking her face in his hands, searching her eyes. "Does this happen often?"

She gave a wry laugh. "What, seeing things or flipping out?"

He waited silently for her response.

"It's a new thing. You're just lucky enough to be around when it does happen."

"I think you're having panic attacks, Grace. You should see a doctor."

"You're probably right. But I feel much better now."

He held her gaze for another moment, as if appraising her assertion. Then he dropped a soft kiss on her lips and let her go.

When he knelt she saw he'd dropped the bags.

"Our food." She bent down to help.

"No harm. It's well packaged." When it was all collected and put back in the bags, they stood.

"Do you want to go somewhere else?"

Grace surveyed the park. It was private and quiet and beautiful. But the peace had been ruined for her. "Would you mind?"

Wyatt gave her a little smile. "I know just the place."

e

Wyatt pulled his car into the turnout at Summit Ridge and turned off his car. He'd found the overlook this weekend when he was out driving. It had a pavilion, much like the one they'd spent the night in, and several picnic tables, all of them empty now.

"This is perfect," Grace said. "My favorite vista in the whole area. We'll get to watch the sunset again."

He helped her from the car. She seemed a lot steadier. Her face had lost that ghostly pallor, her eyes no longer wide and frightened. He hated seeing her like that. Would do anything in his power to keep it from happening again.

As far as the food went, he'd asked Della if he could order something off the menu for their picnic.

"I can do better than that." She'd proceeded to make all Grace's favorites and refused to charge him a dime.

Wyatt spread a tablecloth—Della again—on the rough-hewn table, and they sat across from each other. Grace raved over the chicken salad sandwiches, potato salad, and fresh fruit heaped on her plate. He liked that she had an appetite. He suspected she had a killer metabolism. She was active and in good physical condition.

They talked about the upcoming wedding and the dress she was required to wear. They talked about his love of science and math and her dislike for the financial side of her business. Her knack for bowling, his incompetence at anything requiring artistic skill.

"But you play the guitar. That's artistic."

"But it's not visual. There's a difference—I'm living proof."

"I'm tone deaf."

"Let me hear you sing something."

She laughed. "Um, no. Some people are tone deaf, and they don't know it. I know it."

Then the conversation moved on to his training, some of the dignitaries he'd protected, some of his friends from the field office. She listened intently while he went on longer than he usually did about his work. She was a good listener. Not demanding or pressing. Just letting him say what he wanted.

"So . . ." Grace shifted in her seat. "About your work. I've been meaning to ask you something."

"Hit me." He took a bite of the peach cobbler and pushed the container toward Grace, giving her his full attention.

"Would you mind if I told Levi and Molly what you do for a living? I kind of feel like I'm keeping something important from them."

Wyatt felt a twinge of guilt. After all, he had secrets of his own. He hadn't shared that the inn used to be his family's summer home. If he did, then Grace would figure out who his mom was and how she'd met her end. He didn't want to bring Grace into the middle of that horrible event. Their relationship was new and fresh and happy and he liked it that way.

"Wyatt?" she nudged when he was quiet for too long. "I'll understand if you don't want me to."

He leaned forward on the table, quirking a brow. "Will your brother stop giving me the stink eye?"

"Probably."

"Can they keep it to themselves?"

"They have their flaws, but they do know how to be discreet."

"All right."

"Just like that?"

"It's the Secret Service, not the Top-Secret Service," he said with a smile.

"You're quiet about it though."

He lifted a shoulder. "I don't broadcast it. That doesn't mean I can't tell people what I do. I don't exactly want to be the talk of the town, that's all."

"Are you allowed to tell friends and family where you're going, how long you'll be gone?"

"Sometimes—and sometimes not. There are times I'm sent on assignments with little notice. I have to drop my life and do my job. I had to miss my dad's wedding, and I was his best man—that was the worst. I've missed Christmas and birthday parties and anniversaries."

"Family or girlfriend?" she asked.

"Both."

"I can see where that might be a problem."

"It's a sacrifice. Not just mine, either. But people's lives are at stake, and I'm one of the people they depend on to make sure nothing happens."

Grace closed the lid to the peach cobbler and propped her chin on her palm. "I bet you're really good at what you do. You took a bullet for someone."

"Part of the job."

"Well, it's admirable." She gave a self-conscious chuckle. "You've seen how I handle danger. You don't want me around in an emergency."

"I bet you can handle more than you give yourself credit for." He studied her face for a beat. "Been meaning to ask you something ever since that idiot assaulted you up by the creek. But after today at the park . . . Would you be open to learning some self-defense? You're a strong woman, but I'd feel better knowing you can protect yourself in a dangerous situation."

"Would I be able to take down a full-grown man?"

She looked a little too delighted by the idea. "It's a possibility—eventually. But first we'll focus on buying a little time so you can get away with your life."

She sobered a little at the thought, then gave a nod. "All right. You're on."

Chapter Thirty-Two

$\mathcal{T}$he next morning Grace pulled Levi and Molly into the library. Molly had front desk duty, and Levi and Grace were dressed and ready for church. Wyatt was going with them this morning. The thought put a little spring in Grace's step, even if she did have the toddler class this week.

"We're going to have guests checking out," Levi said.

"This'll only take a minute."

"What's all the secrecy about?" Molly asked as Grace pushed the door shut behind them. "Tell me—my lips are sealed."

"I just wanted to let you guys know something. It's about Wyatt, and it's sensitive information."

"He's a convict," Levi guessed with a straight face. "A felon. He has a rap sheet a mile long."

"Someone's been watching too many cop shows. No, Levi, he's not a convict." Grace drilled him with a look. "He's a Secret Service agent."

Molly gasped. "He guards the president of the United States?"

"He's not on presidential detail—it takes time to rise in the ranks apparently. But he does guard other people, politicians and dignitaries and such."

Molly clutched her chest, letting out a swoony sigh. "He puts his life on the line to protect people. How sexy is that?"

"I know, right? I've seen him in action too—he's amazing."

Levi rolled his eyes. "If it's true, then I guess I'm relieved."

"It is true, Captain Dubious. He showed me his badge and everything. Would you like to call his superior?"

"He has a badge," Molly said giddily. "When you said he was in security, I was thinking police officer or sheriff or—"

"Mall cop?" Levi said.

Grace scowled at her brother. He was really getting on her nerves.

Molly looked at Levi and burst out laughing. "And you *assaulted* him! You're lucky Grace stepped in. He would've kicked your butt."

"Ha-ha. I'm not exactly a wimp, you know. I can hold my own."

Grace quirked a brow at Levi. "What she said."

"I sure never imagined this," Molly said. "I mean, how safe are we right now?"

"Yeah, well, he doesn't broadcast it, so keep it under your hats." Grace gave Molly a look. "And try not to lose your cool the next time you see him."

Molly's eyes widened, blinking. "Who, me?"

e

Wyatt faced off with Grace on the yoga mat she'd borrowed from Molly. It was spread out in the inn's backyard, just off the patio. The sun was high in the sky, the lake starting to get busy with boats. The sweet scent of some flower hung heavily in the air, mingling with the smell of pine and fresh water.

Grace looked adorable in a T-shirt and leggings. She'd worn a pair of tennis shoes, as he'd suggested, and had her hair back in a ponytail.

She stood with her feet shoulder-width apart and shifted her weight from one foot to the other like she was a prizefighter.

"Okay, bring it on, big guy."

He smiled patiently. "Settle down there, Gracie. We'll just be walking through a few moves today. Proper preparation will take more than one lesson. You'll need to rehearse the moves I show you a few times a week. Muscle memory is everything. You need to know them so well you perform automatically in a threatening situation. I checked with Jim's Gym, and they have protective padding. So once you have the moves down we should go there and practice a full-on assault."

"Yeow. That sounds painful."

"It's the only way to prepare you for a real threat. I wouldn't be doing you any favors by treating you like you're made of glass—an attacker sure won't."

Her playful expression fell away. She was probably remembering how she'd felt when that idiot had assaulted her.

"There's no reason to be afraid. I won't hurt you, and by the time I'm finished, you'll be a lot more prepared. A lot more confident."

"All right. Where do we start?"

"This is a pretty basic move. Let's do it in slow motion. An attacker grabs your wrist—"

"That's what that guy did to me. I tried to pull away, but he was too strong."

"A natural reaction. Try this instead." He took her wrist in a firm hold. "Here's what you're going to do. Make a fist with that hand, then grab it with your opposite hand. Good. Now with the arm he grabbed, point your elbow up. Higher. That's right. Now slice down as you twist away from him, using the strength of both arms."

Grace did as he directed.

"That's it. When you make that twist in real time, use your core—

that's where the real strength comes from. Your purpose is to get loose and run. Let's do it again. When you complete the move, take a few steps to get into the habit of making a break for it."

They went through the move again. And again and again. Grace's motions became more natural and confident each time. "Wow, that seems so easy."

"Let's try it in real time. I won't grab you hard—we'll wait for the padding for that. Ready?"

She nodded.

He took her wrist.

Grace went through the motions, but her feet got a little tripped up as she turned to run.

"Let's talk about feet. Whichever side he grabs, put that foot forward. When you twist, you'll pivot on that foot. Once you have this down, we'll practice with the other hand."

While they went through the motions again, Levi and Mia exited the house and stepped onto the patio.

Grace finished the move perfectly this time.

"Good job," Wyatt said.

"I'm afraid to ask." Levi's gaze slid down to the mat. "And you're flattening the grass."

"I'm taking him down—that's what I'm doing—and you're next."

"What'd *I* do?"

"You're a Groomzilla."

"Not since Mia arrived."

"I'll give you that."

"Aw." Mia snuggled into Levi's side, clipboard and all. "Have I tamed you, honey?"

His face softened as he looked down at his fiancée and whispered something in her ear.

Mia smiled, a pretty blush blooming on her cheeks.

While the lovebirds talked over the details of the backyard wedding, Grace and Wyatt went through the moves he'd just shown her, practicing them with the other hand in slow motion until she had the hang of it.

A few minutes later Levi led Mia away. As he opened the door, he looked back at Wyatt. "Try not to break her. She has to walk down the aisle in six days."

"Your concern is overwhelming," Grace said.

She and Wyatt took a quick breather as the couple disappeared inside.

Grace appraised the yard. "Hard to believe there's going to be a wedding here this weekend."

"Will it be very big?"

Grace shook her head. "It's only family and a few close friends. Mia's best friend is flying in Friday and her dad, stepmom, and their kids are coming Saturday—Mia only reunited with her dad a couple years ago."

"And her mom?"

"She passed away."

"That's too bad."

"Everyone who's flying in is being picked up at the airport by Skeeter—our resident floatplane guy—and flown straight to our dock. Hopefully we can keep this under wraps through the wedding. We'd like to avoid hovering helicopters."

"They'd do that?"

"You have no idea. They could turn this place into a media circus."

After they regrouped Wyatt squared up with Grace.

"This one's a grab from behind. You're going to incapacitate the attacker this time before you run. Turn around and face the other direction." After she did as he asked, he stepped close and wrapped his arms around her waist, bringing him flush against her.

She softened in his arms, and it took every bit of his discipline to block out the feel of her body against his, the delicious scent of her hair. "Okay, this one involves some punches and knees to the groin, so we're going to be very careful. We're just going to simulate those until we have pads."

"Trying to preserve future generations of Jennings?"

"Among other things. Grab my arms. Good." He instructed her to pull herself in at the waist, swing her hips to the side, make a fist, and strike the groin.

After she completed this he said, "Now pivot and reach around my neck, interlocking your hands."

She did as he asked, peering up at him. They were inches apart. His hands clenched at her sides.

"This is nice right now," she said. "But it's the last thing I'd feel like doing in the middle of an attack."

"It goes against instinct to get closer to the threat, but it works. Now's when you drive your knee upward into the groin once or twice. You'll want to do all this quickly, catch him off guard. An attacker won't be expecting this—that gives you the element of surprise."

They went through the motions. There were more moves to this one, but she was a fast learner, so it didn't take long. In a short time she had two defensive moves down pretty solidly. It was rewarding, teaching her to protect herself.

He thought back to his conversation with the gym owner. Jim had asked if Wyatt would be interested in teaching a course, but he wouldn't be around long enough to do so. Too bad, because that was something he'd always wanted to do. Teaching women to defend themselves was a worthy cause. His schedule just didn't allow for it.

"I think that's enough for today," he said as she drank from her water bottle.

"Just one more?"

"You need to work on the ones I just showed you. Practice them for a few minutes every day if you can. Maybe midweek we can go to the gym and spar for real—if you have time with all the wedding stuff you've got going on."

"Now that Mia's here, she's taken all that on. But what about your search? I have Thursday off. And I get off Wednesday at three—that's a little late in the day to get started, I know."

Wyatt had been giving that some thought the last few days.

"About that . . ." He stepped closer and took her hand, running his thumb along the soft skin on the back of it. "I'd like to have you along, but I don't know about the nights, Gracie. The camping."

Understanding dawned on her face. "Things have changed a little since last time."

"We've definitely crossed a certain line. And as much as I might want to share a sleeping bag with you, it's probably not the smartest idea."

"Did I say you could share my sleeping bag?" she teased. "But yeah, you're right. We'll have to work around that somehow, the overnight part."

He stepped closer and set his hands gently at her waist. "Let's practice the frontal hold."

"Is that a thing?"

"It's a very good thing." He pulled her closer until their faces were inches apart. He took in the beautiful planes, the perfect little nose, the lush lips, slightly parted and ready for him.

"Would now be a good time for me to practice that knee move?"

"Only if you want me to stop."

"Hmm." Grace stretched toward him like a flower toward the sun. "Never mind."

Chapter Thirty-Three

The next week passed in a blur. It was a good thing they'd hired Miss Della's granddaughter, Jada, to help out around the inn because the wedding preparations ended up absorbing extra time. The bridal party had one more dress fitting. There were extra errands and last-minute glitches. Grace and Molly pitched in wherever they could to take the stress off Levi and Mia.

On Tuesday evening Grace slipped away to practice the defense moves with Wyatt at the gym. As promised, he didn't take it easy on her. He was formidably strong and difficult to escape. She was worried about hurting his shoulder, but he insisted he was fine. As they executed the moves he was very encouraging, always praising her efforts.

She had the moves down, and he continually pushed her to use all her strength, to be bold and aggressive. He even had her shouting as she went through the motions. She felt silly at first, but something about using her voice freed her up to be more forceful. Their demonstration gathered a small crowd, and afterward several people expressed interest in learning self-defense.

Unfortunately, due to the wedding preparations, Grace had to call off the hike with Wyatt on Thursday. He went on without her, leaving Wednesday morning. She spent the day transporting tables and chairs from the church and stringing white twinkle lights on the back patio with Mia and Molly.

Mia and Levi could've easily afforded to hire out the grunt work, but the more people involved in the wedding, the likelier that the news would leak. Grace didn't really mind. They were used to pulling their own weight around here, and their small circle of friends were pitching in.

They'd had some good news this week. Two brothers from Chicago were interested in seeing the inn. Grace had been emailing them all week, answering questions. One of them was an accountant, so Levi sent them the financials. After they had a couple days to review them, they wanted a tour as soon as possible. There would be no time before the wedding, so Grace had set it up for next week.

On Friday, they turned on the No Vacancy sign. They'd blocked out Friday through Sunday to give them privacy for the wedding—Wyatt being the sole exception.

Mia's best friend, Brooke, arrived on Friday, and that night they went through a brief rehearsal. Miss Della topped it off with a big dinner, complete with all of Levi's favorite foods and Mia's favorite dessert—crème brûlée. There was much love and laughter as they gathered around the table to celebrate the upcoming nuptials.

Saturday dawned clear and sunny. The weather forecasted a beautiful day with a high temperature of seventy-eight. Levi and Mia decided to shun the tradition of the groom not seeing the bride on the day of the wedding. The logistics were too difficult, given the secrecy and need for all hands on deck.

They waited until afternoon to set up the backyard, as the property was visible from the lake. Throughout the afternoon Levi and Mia could be found off to the side, whispering into each other's ears or canoodling in various nooks and crannies in the house and backyard.

"Get a room," Grace called as she passed with another armful of chairs. "Or better yet, grab a few chairs."

They didn't even respond.

Mia's family arrived by floatplane midafternoon, and by four o'clock the girls were upstairs getting ready, a trusted photographer documenting the occasion. Their nails had been done earlier, and they had three hours to get ready for the sunset service.

The bridal party took over the suite, and the men crammed into Levi's room downstairs. Brooke had worked as a makeup artist, so she had the very easy task of making Mia beautiful.

Molly dressed early and hovered around Mia, bringing drinks, adjusting the room temperature, and otherwise fluttering about like a fairy godmother. Grace's dress fit her perfectly, and her heels didn't even squeeze her toes.

"It's a mystery to me why you don't wear dresses every day," Molly said when Grace emerged from the bathroom.

"There are women in Hollywood who'd kill for those legs," Mia said. "The single men are going to be all over you tonight."

"They won't be able to take their eyes off you long enough to notice anyone else," Grace said.

"Besides," Molly offered, "I don't think Wyatt'll let anyone else near her."

A moment later Brooke brought the gown to Mia. "Time for the big moment."

Mia stood in her slip, and Brooke helped her into the gown while Molly stood back, hands folded as if in prayer.

Mia's long blonde hair was worn in a loose updo with artfully arranged curls framing her face. She was gorgeous. And she was just as beautiful on the inside.

Even Grace's breath caught as Brooke slid the bodice into place. The dress was as elegant as the bride with a halter neckline that showed off her square shoulders and slender arms. Once Brooke buttoned up the bodice, the gown fit like a dream. Delicate sequins sparkled under the lights, and the gently flaring skirt swirled around Mia's legs as she turned to look in the full-length mirror.

Molly clapped, her eyes shiny. "You look amazing. Levi's going to faint dead away at the sight of you."

"I hope not. He has some vows to get through first."

Grace wasn't one to cry at weddings. She really wasn't much of a crier at all. But seeing the two empty front-row chairs in honor of their parents challenged that quality. As did seeing Mia's long-lost father escort her proudly down the aisle.

And watching Levi's expression shift as his bride walked toward him . . .

He looked so happy. So in love. He'd sacrificed a lot for Grace and Molly. He'd given up his job, his apartment, his whole life in Denver to come here and run this inn. And then he'd stuck with them for four years while they'd made a go of it. Yeah, he was annoying sometimes. Bossy. Intrusive. But he'd gotten better about that. And Grace didn't know many brothers who'd have done what he had. She loved the big lug, and he deserved happiness more than anyone she knew.

And these thoughts were doing nothing to help with the teary situation. When she blinked a tear streamed down her face, probably wrecking all of Brooke's hard work.

Grace looked away from her brother, seeking distraction, and her gaze collided with Wyatt's. He was sitting in the third row, watching her intently. Saying a thousand things with just his eyes. His dark hair was neatly combed, his jaw freshly shaven. He looked so handsome in the black suit and crisp white shirt. He must've gone shopping. Worth every dime.

His lips tipped up just then, and her heart stuttered. Literally, a chest palpitation. She almost clutched her heart.

Grace swallowed hard and looked back at Mia, who was joining Levi at the front. But all Grace could think of was Wyatt and the feelings that had just zipped through her. She'd never felt this way before—not even close. Was she falling in love with him? Had she already fallen in love? Impossible. It hadn't even been three weeks.

Did Wyatt feel the same? Or was this some little fling to fill the time? He had so much more experience in this area.

Maybe it was just the wedding. Maybe she was having one of those ridiculous girly moments. A flight of fantasy where as she watched the celebration of true love, she wished it into being for herself. That was so uncharacteristic of her though.

She wanted to seek out Wyatt's gaze again, try to determine if she'd seen love in his eyes or maybe just affection. But she was afraid her feelings were written all over her face right now.

She forced herself to pay attention as the pastor prayed, then segued into a beautiful explanation of married love. The ceremony was brief and poignant, the love the couple shared so apparent in the looks they exchanged, in the words they shared. There were no songs, no poems, just a heartfelt message by the pastor and the quiet exchange of vows.

Throughout the ceremony Grace periodically checked the skies and the lake, fearful they'd have unwelcome guests. But it appeared all their work had paid off. The twenty-seven guests and all those who'd helped make this day happen had managed to pull off a quiet celebrity wedding.

In no time at all the pastor pronounced them husband and wife. Levi took Mia into his arms and placed a loving kiss on her lips. When they broke apart the smiles on their faces could've lit an entire city.

ℓ

It was taking forever to get to the part Wyatt was most anticipating—the dancing. Not because he'd been blessed with great rhythm, but because he couldn't wait to get his arms around Grace.

He'd hardly been able to take his eyes off her tonight, from the time she'd walked out the back door until now, as she watched Levi and Mia share their first dance on the makeshift dance floor.

The sun had set during the ceremony, and darkness had slowly fallen. The small crowd gathered on the large patio where round tables were set up. Now the meal was finished, and the bride and groom swayed together under the twinkling lights to the soft strains of a string quartet.

"It was a beautiful wedding, wasn't it?" Grace's chin was propped on her palm as she watched the couple. A wayward curl had fallen from her updo and kissed the curve of her cheek.

"Beautiful," he said.

"The weather sure cooperated. And the sunset was—"

"Perfect."

She must've caught the tone of his voice, because she turned his way.

"Did I tell you that you look amazing tonight?" he asked.

"At least three times, not that I don't appreciate it. And you should know it's a real rarity to see me in a dress. Like sighting an American coot or something—that's a bird."

"As beautiful as you are right now, you're also pretty cute in a ponytail and that big purple T-shirt. I like how it falls off your shoulder."

She blushed prettily. "You're especially handsome in your suit tonight."

"I caught you staring at me earlier, from up front."

Something drifted across her face. Something uncertain. "You were staring at me too."

"I *was*."

She fiddled with the edge of the tablecloth. "And what were you thinking, Mr. Jennings?"

The final note of the song played out, and Levi swept Mia into a dramatic dip to the applause of the delighted crowd. The quartet struck up another tune, and guests were invited to join the couple on the dance floor.

Finally. He held out his hand to Grace. "I've been waiting all night for this."

The dancing went on a long while—almost long enough for Wyatt to get his fill. Finally the bride and groom tossed the bouquet and garter, then cut the cake. It wasn't even ten o'clock yet, but Wyatt sensed their eagerness to be off and away.

A short while later they disappeared inside the house to change. Grace went inside with Molly to say their private good-byes while the rest of the party lined up outside the back door.

Soon the crowd cheered as the couple exited the house in their travel clothes and ran down the lawn hand in hand. They continued all the way to the end of the pier where they slipped into the waiting floatplane. Moments later they took off across the water and lifted into the dark sky. They were headed to Charlotte where they'd catch a flight in the morning and set off for a romantic week in Paris.

The crowd slowly dispersed after that, and Wyatt helped their friends and neighbors clean up. It wasn't quite midnight when he was walking Grace to her door.

She looked satisfied but tired as she turned at her door and wrapped her arms around his neck. "Thank you for being my plus one tonight. It was a lot of fun."

"Thank you for inviting me. You're a good dance partner."

"Is it awful that I'm glad to have the wedding behind us? It'll be good to get back to some normalcy and focus on finding a buyer for the inn."

"Normalcy is good. You're excited about that bungalow, aren't you?"

"And afraid I'm going to lose it. Pamela's having an open house tomorrow. Pray that nobody puts in an offer?"

"Of course. But have a little faith. If it's meant to be, it'll be." Wyatt took her face in his hands and pressed a soft kiss to her lips.

Grace gave a contented sigh.

He didn't let the kiss go on and on but made proper use of the time. Then he pulled away and brushed her cheek with his thumb. "You're tired. I'll let you get to bed."

"I'm so sleeping in tomorrow."

"Late service?"

"Deal."

"I'll plan on hiking afterward." He was running out of time and starting to feel a little desperate. His leave was officially up in a week and two days, and he was no closer to a resolution.

"I wish I could go with you."

"I know." He set a kiss on her brow and said good night.

It was only as he closed his own door that he realized he'd never answered Grace's question about what he'd been thinking earlier. That was just as well, because he'd been thinking that he might be falling in love with the woman.

A pleasant sensation spread throughout him at the thought. He'd never felt this way, as if he were floating. Who knew it would take a woman like Grace to reach a place so deep inside him?

But even as he enjoyed the heady feeling, an ache pressed in, bringing his feet back down to the ground. Because his and Grace's lives were not compatible, and no amount of wishing would make it otherwise.

Chapter Thirty-Four

$\mathcal{M}$olly led the Johnson brothers down the inn's staircase. They'd spent almost two hours poring over every inch of the place, and she'd been very careful to avoid the subjects that had gotten her in trouble with her siblings.

John and Jake were nice guys in their midtwenties. They seemed slightly out of place in their city-slicker suits and trendy haircuts, but they were from Chicago after all. They were so young to be buying an inn, but Molly had gathered from their conversation that they were trust fund babies.

John was an accountant and all about the details. Jake was all business and married to a woman who was interested in running the restaurant portion of the business. How would Miss Della feel about that?

There was nothing wrong with them per se. They were polite and very interested. They asked good questions and made positive re marks. They just seemed so . . . business oriented, using words like *assets* and *investments*. They didn't ask about the guests who chose to stay here or remark on the outstanding hospitality they offered. And that's what the inn business was really all about—hospitality.

When they reached the lobby, John turned and thanked her for her time. "We'll be in touch in the next few days, Molly."

"You have a wonderful business here," Jake said.

Molly let them out the door, feeling a leaden weight in her stomach as they said good-bye.

"Everything all right, Molly?" Jada asked from the front desk after the brothers had left.

Molly dredged up a smile, wondering why it took so much effort. "Everything's fine. I'm just going to go see if your grandmother needs help with cleanup."

Molly didn't have to wait a few days to hear from the brothers. Jake called that very evening when she was helping Adam clear the supper table.

"John and I have talked it over, and we'd like to make an offer on your inn."

Molly turned away from the sink and leaned back against the counter. "Oh! I didn't expect to hear from you so soon."

From the dining room Adam gave her an inquisitive look.

"The numbers look great, and the inn seems like just the investment we've been searching for. It needs a little updating, but that's just cosmetics."

Updating? The inn was in exquisite shape.

"We'll put in a formal offer through our attorney, of course, but I wanted to let you know we're offering the asking price. It's a fair price, and there's no need to waste time. We'd like to get going on this venture as soon as possible."

"Oh. Oh, that—that's great, Jake. I'll have to talk to my siblings, but . . . asking price. I can't imagine they're going to have a problem."

When she disconnected the call, Adam joined her in the kitchen.

He poked his glasses into place. "They're making an offer?"

"Asking price."

"That's great." He studied her a moment, then his eyes narrowed. "Isn't it?"

"Of course it is!" Molly turned around and began rinsing a plate. "Now we can all move on. This is definitely a best-case scenario. Who knew it would sell so quickly—and for the asking price! Levi and Grace will be thrilled to pieces, and I won't even have to move out of the inn because I already live here! With you! Grace already found a place for her business, and of course Levi is eager to move to LA with Mia. I think he even has a couple of job prospects already. This is perfect!"

Adam pried the wet plate from her grip—she must have been scrubbing it awhile—and set it in the dishwasher.

She picked up the other one. "It would've been difficult to sell in the winter, you know. If it hadn't sold in the fall, it probably wouldn't have sold till spring, and then Grace would've lost her little house, and that would've put Levi and Mia in a real fix too."

Adam took the other plate, and Molly went to work on the pan. "They're going to be so excited. I wonder if I should wait until Levi gets home though. He's on his honeymoon after all. That's what I'll do. I can't bother him with this. So maybe I shouldn't tell Grace yet either. For that matter, until I have an offer in hand there's probably no point getting anyone's hopes up. What if it falls through? I'll just wait for the offer, and then we'll need to have an attorney read it, of course."

"Of course."

She gave the pan some elbow grease as she tried to imagine the brothers fluffing the bed pillows, folding the towels just so, and setting out fresh cookies every afternoon. But she just couldn't. They probably wouldn't do any of that. They probably wouldn't even give the historical tour to their guests!

"Who names their son John Johnson anyway?"

"Molly . . ."

"That doesn't matter. They're very nice people, and I'm sure they'll do a good job. They're even siblings—I told you that, right? That's kind of perfect. We're passing the inn from one set of siblings to another."

But that was about all the siblings had in common. She'd even heard John mention painting the woodwork that their parents had so lovingly restored to its original condition. Her heart was about to jump out of her chest at the thought of all the changes they might make. They'd talked about adding a fancy spa too, and while there was nothing wrong with that exactly, it just sounded so . . . commercial.

"Didn't even care about the history," she muttered.

"Molly."

"But they really know their stuff. Did I mention John's an accountant? They're young but they have a lot of business experience. They'll have no trouble keeping it in the black. Listen to me—I sound like Levi!" Her laugh sounded a little manic, even to her.

He took the pan from her, set it in the dishwasher, then turned her around before she could go at the silverware.

Water dripped from her hands as she met Adam's concerned gaze.

"All right, Molly. What's going on here?"

"What do you mean?"

"You're acting very strange. You're babbling. You're almost giddy, but something's not quite right."

"Of course I'm giddy. We just got asking price on our inn, and very soon now we'll be free to move to Italy and start a bed-and-breakfast. This is perfect."

"That's your third use of that word in two minutes."

Well, it is perfect!

Molly beat back the automatic denial and accompanying irritation. Instead she stared into Adam's faded blue eyes. Her heart was kicking her rib cage, and a weird ache settled in the back of her throat.

She had to give consideration to his assessment. Her husband knew her better than anyone, and he was easily the most intelligent person she knew. Not just book smart either. She suspected his emotional intelligence was off the charts.

She grabbed a towel and dried her hands. "Okay. All right. This isn't easy. Of course it isn't. This is our parents' legacy we're talking about. There's bound to be some . . . difficulty letting go. Selling the inn will be a little sad, like losing a piece of them. And yes, it's the only piece of them we have left, save the memories, but it has to be done. We all have dreams and plans that don't include the inn, and selling it was part of those plans from the beginning."

Adam cupped her neck, brushing her pulse with his thumb. "Sometimes plans change, and that's all right too."

Molly shook her head despite the leaden weight in her gut. "I'm just feeling a natural reluctance to let go. Change is hard. I'll be fine. And now that I think of it, I should probably go ahead and tell Grace about the offer so she can put an offer in on her house, contingent upon the sale of the inn, of course. She's really excited about it, and I don't want her to lose it. There was an open house there Sunday and Pamela said one of the couples was interested."

Adam's eyes searched hers for a long moment. "Are you sure this is what you want, sweetheart?"

He was so good to her. Even willing to move to a foreign country to make her dreams come true. She palmed his face, the bristle of his jaw pleasantly scratchy against the sensitive flesh. Then she leaned in and pressed a kiss to his lips.

"I'm sure. Once the official offer comes in, I'll tell Grace. And shoot, might as well tell Levi too. It'll be good cause for celebration on their honeymoon."

Chapter Thirty-Five

$\mathcal{G}$race pushed the cleaning cart into the closet and started the last load of sheets. They only had three rooms filled, so cleaning didn't take as long as it usually did. She sent Wyatt a text, asking if he wanted to get some hiking in today. He responded affirmatively and said he'd get supplies from Della and meet Grace in the lobby.

Grace dashed into her room and changed clothes. She'd only seen Wyatt here and there since church Sunday. He'd done a fair amount of hiking on his own, and she had extra work with Levi gone.

They'd snatched a bit of time together last night. They watched a movie in the living room, munching on popcorn and sneaking kisses here and there. Very nice kisses.

When she caught her reflection in the mirror, she was wearing one of those goofy grins. And for some reason, she was just fine with that.

When she was dressed, she shouldered her backpack and made her way down the staircase, already planning ahead. They'd drive up to Lost Creek, to the place where Wyatt had last left off. It was only eleven, so they'd have hours to search. Maybe today would be the day. She longed to give Wyatt the closure he needed.

At the front desk Molly was frowning at the computer.

"Something wrong?"

Molly looked at Grace, her face instantly brightening. "Nothing at all. In fact, everything is perf—great! The Johnson brothers made an offer. I just got it via email."

Grace blinked. "Are you kidding me? What'd they offer?"

"Get this—they're giving us asking price!"

Grace never dreamed they'd get asking price. "That's great. That's awesome."

"I need to read through the details, and of course we'll need to hire a lawyer to review it."

"How long will all this take? I can put an offer in on the house now." The sellers hadn't been willing to tie up the sale with a contingency offer until the Bennetts at least had an offer on the inn.

"I'm not sure. But you should probably make that offer soon. I wouldn't want you to miss out."

"I'll text Pamela right now."

Grace got an immediate and enthusiastic response. Pamela suggested they meet at the coffee shop at three o'clock to write it up. Grace paused.

Molly was still chattering about the offer.

Wyatt entered the lobby, carrying his pack. "You got an offer on the inn?"

Grace turned to him, smiling. "Asking price, can you believe it?"

"That's great. You should call your Realtor and get an offer in."

"I texted her and she can meet at three, but . . ."

He squeezed her arm. "Grace. Tell her yes. We can hike later. You don't want to miss out on that property."

She nearly melted at the concern on his face. "Are you sure?"

"I can go on my own today."

"He's right," Molly said. "And I'll send Levi a message."

Grace widened her smile at Wyatt. "All right. But let's plan on a long day of hiking Thursday."

"You're on."

Chapter Thirty-Six

*G*race and Wyatt had been hiking for hours. Wyatt set the pace, walking in front of her, holding back limbs and helping her over fallen trees. The smell of decayed earth filled her nostrils, and fallen leaves softened their footfalls. Lost Creek rippled past them, its wide body narrowing as they went higher into the mountains.

The day was sunny and in the low seventies, and under the leafy treetops, it was several degrees cooler. October had ushered in the beginning of fall in the mountains surrounding Bluebell. The trees had already begun turning in the higher elevations. Soon that color would trickle downhill until the entire valley was a riot of color, stretched out beneath the autumn skies and reflected in the glassy waters of Bluebell Lake.

Next year this time Grace would be running Blue Ridge Outfitters out of her own building—the owners had accepted her offer yesterday. Grace had been so eager to buy the little house there'd been little room for panic. But that had set in soon after the call from Pamela.

What if the business couldn't survive outside the inn? What if she fell flat on her face? She'd do anything to keep that from happening, to her own detriment, she knew. Look at how demanding she'd been of herself in high school from academics to athletics! She'd insisted on perfection and continually fell short, which led to her berating herself. The old adage "Aim for perfection, settle for excellence" sounded great, but she'd found she couldn't quite accept the second part of the phrase. She would have to work on that. Perfection was unattainable and striving for it was exhausting.

As they climbed, the deciduous trees gradually gave way to evergreens. Wyatt had grown quiet, but so had she. The uphill climb stole her breath as even the minor change in altitude affected air pressure.

Wyatt had taught her more self-defense moves yesterday at Jim's Gym, and she used the hiking time to mentally rehearse them. The ground began leveling off a bit, allowing Grace to catch her breath. It was about time for a break. It was late afternoon, and her rumbling stomach notified her that she'd worked off the apple and nuts they'd eaten a few hours ago.

A movement in the sky drew her attention to a red-tailed hawk, soaring over the treetops. They'd seen all manner of wildlife today: a bullfrog, a deer, a groundhog, to say nothing of the numerous squirrels and songbirds.

She was still searching the sky when she crashed into Wyatt, who'd stopped without warning.

"Whoa there," she said after she'd found her balance again. "Forget your blinker, mister?"

Wyatt was still as a stone, staring into the distance.

Her first thought was that they'd stumbled upon a bear, but she didn't see any animal, and his hands were hanging loose at his sides, not reaching for his gun.

"Wyatt?"

Her eyes caught on a small waterfall just ahead. About fifty yards beyond it a stack of boulders reached for the sky. Was this the spot he'd been searching for? A quick scan of the area turned up a hilly plateau replete with towering evergreens.

Wyatt hadn't yet moved.

Grace came to his side where she could see his face. He seemed to be taking in the area with all of his senses. His pulse throbbed in his neck. His Adam's apple bobbed as he swallowed, his chest rising and falling quickly.

She touched his arm softly, not wanting to startle him. "Is this it?"

"Yes," he said without looking at her.

She waited for him to make the next move. What was going through his mind? What emotions were flooding to the surface? They'd just entered a very private area of his life. Did she have the capacity to help him deal with whatever he'd be facing?

He started walking again, toward the boulders. Grace whispered a prayer for him. A prayer that she'd know how to help him. *This is a good thing. He'll finally find closure.*

Once at the tower of boulders, he stopped and looked around. Turned to face the south. He stared into the sparsely wooded forest, its floor carpeted with pine needles.

"We camped over that way." He strode that direction.

"Do you want me to stay here?"

"No."

She traipsed after him, relieved. She wasn't sure what he'd need from her, but she didn't want him to be alone. "Do you remember how far it was?"

"Not far."

He was walking faster now, on a mission, seemingly confident of the direction he'd chosen.

Grace hurried to keep up with him, the scent of pine filling her every breath. They ascended a small incline, dodging red spruce and Fraser firs and moss-covered rocks. A squirrel scuttled across their path, jumped onto a tree trunk, and scampered up it.

l

Wyatt stared straight ahead as he strode up the incline. It was just over this ridge. He knew it like he knew his own birthday. Like he'd known they were entering the area before he even saw the tower of rocks. He'd felt it in his bones.

He'd planned to leave Grace there and continue on alone. Wasn't sure what he'd feel when he returned to the spot that had changed his life forever. But when she'd asked in that soft, careful voice, he realized he wanted her there. He wanted her calming presence and her soothing touch. He was going to need it. His racing, erratic heartbeat and spinning thoughts were proof of that.

He reached the small rise and stared down into a shallow basin where the evergreens soared overhead. The area didn't look much different than what they'd just traipsed across, but he knew without a doubt—this was it.

He walked down the small incline and toward the spot where they'd camped. He'd forgotten about the smell of decay. Forgotten the gnarly tree roots poking up through the forest floor and the fallen tree trunks covered in moss.

He remembered now.

He could only approximate the spot where they'd pitched their tent, but that didn't matter. This was the last place his mother had laughed. The last place she'd spoken to him. The last place she'd drawn breath.

"This is it."

Grace's fingers slowly laced with his, and he was grateful for the touch. For the connection. The area was so peaceful and beautiful in its own rugged way, the sunlight breaking through in spots. "Hard to believe something so awful happened here."

She pressed into his side. "You must've been so frightened."

She had no idea—because he'd told her very little. But he was finished holding back. It was time to bring down the wall. He braced himself for the memories, the feelings, the helplessness that would crowd in, trampling the illusion of confidence he'd built over the years. He knew he needed to face this once and for all. Face his inadequate response. And somehow learn to live with it.

"My mom didn't just die out here, Grace." The rush of blood in his ears nearly drowned out his own voice. "She was killed."

Chapter Thirty-Seven

*G*race stared at Wyatt, his shocking words still registering in her brain. A bird cried from a nearby tree as a cloud moved over the sun, cloaking the forest in shadow.

"Your mom was killed?" She didn't want to press him. He almost seemed as if he wasn't here at all. Maybe he wasn't. Maybe he was back there, back then, revisiting his worst nightmare.

"We were camping." His tone was devoid of all emotion. "Spent a few days every summer doing that, me and my mom. Dad wasn't much for the outdoors, but my mom . . . She loved it out here. We set up camp at sunset as usual. I gathered wood and helped her build a campfire. We ate beans and cornbread, and later we roasted marshmallows."

Grace braced herself for what was coming next, her mind spinning with *who* and *how* and *why*, feeling that if she knew the answers she could somehow change the outcome.

"We talked a lot that night by the fire. I wish I could remember what we talked about. Wish I'd known that was the last time I'd get the chance."

Grace grasped his arm, holding on to him tightly.

"We settled into our sleeping bags as usual. I don't even remember falling asleep. But the next thing I knew I woke up, and my mom was screaming. I saw a big shadow in the tent. I was so scared, I scurried into the corner. My mom was telling me to run, but I—I couldn't move. I was frozen.

"The man was trying to take my mom—she was fighting him. But he had a gun. I heard the click when he cocked the hammer. He threatened to shoot me if she didn't go with him . . . so she did. I tried to scream, but nothing came out. Wouldn't have done any good anyway, I guess. Once he had her outside I could hear him dragging her deeper into the forest." His words wobbled with emotion. "And then I couldn't hear anything at all."

Something in his story pricked some distant memory in Grace, but the urge to comfort him superseded it.

She gathered him close, pressed her face into the curve between his neck and shoulder. "Oh, Wyatt. How awful."

"I just . . . sat there, Grace. In the tent. Safe in my little corner while that monster killed my mom."

She leaned back to look at him, her throat aching. "You were just a little boy, Wyatt."

Pain resided in the tightness of his face, in the road map of blood vessels in his eyes. "She needed my help and I did nothing."

The words came reluctantly. As if it had taken everything in him to say them aloud. Had he ever said them to anyone before?

Oh, the poor baby. Grace took his face in her hands. "Wyatt, your mom loved you, and she wanted you safe. You did exactly what she wanted you to do."

"I was a coward."

She gave his head a shake. "No. You were smart. How would your mother have felt if you'd died trying to save her? And you surely would have—he was an adult male with a gun. There's nothing you could've done that would've saved your mom."

Her words didn't seem to give him the solace she longed for him to have. "I understand guilt, Wyatt, and this kind of guilt is useless. It sucks the life out of you and gives nothing back. You need to let go of it. Ask God to take it away from you. It serves no good purpose, and He doesn't want you carrying this burden."

"It's not that easy."

"I know." They were all the words she needed to hear herself, but she had been so inept at implementing them. "I know it's not. But we both need to work on believing it, because it's the truth."

"I sat there for so long in the dark. At first light I left the tent and called for my mom, but no one answered. I thought maybe he'd kidnapped her. I went for help. I went back to the creek—to those boulders, and I followed the creek all the way back to town. I don't even remember that walk back."

He stared off into the woods. "They found the spot later that day—someone knew where those boulders were. They found my mom. He'd strangled her."

A vise tightened around her heart. "I'm so sorry, Wyatt."

"They caught him, at least, put him behind bars where he belonged. I later learned he'd been up this way and just happened to see our campfire. A crime of opportunity. He'd had an abusive mother and developed a real hatred for women. When his mom passed away he flipped out. He was quoted as saying, 'I was going to kill the first female I saw, didn't matter who.'"

The quote sent chills down Grace's spine. She'd heard those words before. They were cemented in her memory because they were said by the man who'd nearly abducted her.

That meant Wyatt's mother was Janet Jennings—the governor's wife. The woman who'd been killed instead of Grace.

Her hands dropped to her sides, and she stepped away from Wyatt. She needed to think. Needed some distance. He was watching her closely, so she turned before he could read every thought in her mind. She took a few steps, pretended to observe the area while she tried to make sense of it all.

"Grace?"

His family had owned the inn—the governor's summer home. Wyatt had never mentioned that, but it had to be true. His last name bore it out. Gordon Kimball had tried to abduct Grace on her way home from school that day. And when he'd failed, he hid in the woods where he'd stumbled upon another victim—a woman with a boy too young to protect her.

Grace's gut churned with the revelation. If she hadn't managed to evade the man, Janet Jennings's life would've been spared. Wyatt would've been spared all these years of grief and guilt.

Culpability rose inside, swamping her. She knew it was unreasonable. She didn't have to know Mrs. Jennings to believe she wouldn't have wanted a seven-year-old girl to suffer at that monster's hands. This wasn't Grace's fault any more than it was Wyatt's, but still . . .

The weight of it was crushing. The self-loathing she hadn't fully felt since she was a girl flared up like a fuel-induced fire.

"Grace, what is it?" Wyatt was close behind her now.

She couldn't breathe. Someone had sucked all the oxygen from the forest.

He turned her around to face him, but she couldn't look him in the eye.

He tipped her chin up until she met his eyes, and she knew he'd see all the emotions roiling inside. She was helpless to hide them.

"Tell me."

She would. She had to. This awful event connected them, and he deserved to know the truth. The whole truth.

"You're Governor Jennings's son." She started there because she prayed she was somehow mistaken about all this.

"I'm sorry I didn't tell you earlier. I just didn't want to get into all this . . ."

No easy out. Okay. She had to tell him then. Grace braced herself for his reaction. He might hate her. He probably had a right to. At the very least he would resent her, wouldn't he? How could he not?

"Wyatt . . ." She swallowed past the lump in her throat and gathered her courage. "I'm the girl who got away."

l

Wyatt stared at her as the words sank in. He wasn't thinking very clearly right now. Or she wasn't making any sense.

"The girl who got away?"

She continued to look at him, as if hoping he might figure it out on his own. When he didn't she said, "Earlier in the day . . . Gordon Kimball tried to abduct a little girl. Did you know that?"

His thoughts spun. It had been a part of the articles he'd skimmed over. Some lucky girl had gotten away. His mother hadn't.

His hand dropped from her chin. "It was you? You're the girl?"

Silence filled the space between them, expanding, thickening, making the air hard to breathe.

"I—I was walking home from school, and he was following me in a van. I ran away. When I got home, my parents reported it, but the man disappeared into the mountains and they lost track of him. It was the thing I told you about the night we played that first conversation game—the guilt I was carrying."

Somewhere from the recesses of his memory her words surfaced. *"Someone died and I didn't, and deep down I feel like it should've been me."* He'd recognized it as survivor's guilt. He just hadn't known his mother was part of the equation.

This couldn't be happening. He couldn't think. It was too much. He turned and paced a few steps away, sightless. He was grateful Grace had escaped the monster. Of course he was. But if she hadn't . . .

No, he couldn't think like that. He would never wish any harm on Grace. He loved her. But he'd loved his mom too.

"I'm so sorry, Wyatt."

"There's nothing to be sorry for." The words sounded like lip service, but he knew they were right. "I just—I'm a little overwhelmed right now."

"Of course you are. I—I don't blame you."

He hated how tentative she sounded. But he couldn't deal with her emotions right now when his own were crashing into him like a tidal wave.

"I—I think maybe I should wait for you back by the creek," she said. "Give you a minute alone?"

He needed space to process this. Didn't want to say something he'd regret later or hurt her unintentionally.

He nodded. "All right."

"Take all the time you need."

He heard her quiet footfalls receding until the sounds of nature were all that was left. How was he supposed to deal with this new insight? How was he supposed to digest that his mom had been taken instead of Grace? How was he ever supposed to heal?

He'd come here for answers but had only gotten more questions.

Chapter Thirty-Eight

Thirty minutes later when Wyatt returned to the creek, he didn't look any better. His eyes were still bloodshot, his face slightly flushed, his shoulders set. But otherwise, the poker face was back.

He offered a bland smile, which seemed to require great effort. "We should probably find that road to cut back on. It's getting late."

She didn't know what she'd expected. Absolution was too much to ask for. Rejection or blame maybe? But somehow this hard-fought effort at civility was even worse.

Grace was happy to lead the way because it allowed her to hide her tears. She was also grateful for the rippling creek, which disguised her sniffles.

The hike back to town was eerily quiet and gave her plenty of time to think. She wished she knew what was going on in Wyatt's head, but she was afraid to ask. All she knew was that she felt less worthy with each step.

So this was it, she thought as they finally reached the rutted road and started the winding way downhill. He'd done what he'd come to accomplish. Well, no, not really. He'd come to heal an old wound, and Grace had managed to rip off the scab.

Now he had more to digest. More to heal from. And she wasn't doing so swell on that front either. Her eyes filled with tears, her vision going blurry again. It was a wonder she hadn't tripped over something yet and fallen flat on her face.

Wyatt had come here to find the spot where his mother had passed, though, and found it he had. Maybe it hadn't had the intended effect, but there was no reason for him to stay in Bluebell now, was there?

She'd wondered what would happen when they reached the end of his stay. Where could they possibly go from here? The answer was obvious now. Nowhere.

God, why did You bring him into my life only to take him away again? Why is this happening? I wanted to help him, and instead I've only found another way to hurt him. A tear leaked out, finding a familiar path to trickle down.

Stop it, Grace. He doesn't need your self-pity.

She blinked back the tears crowding her eyes. The creek and its camouflaging sounds were long behind them. Wyatt was dealing with enough without having to worry about her feelings too.

She covertly dried her tears. She needed to hold it together. Needed to look normal by the time they got to the car. Once she reached the safety of her room she could unleash the flood of tears.

He was so quiet behind her. She couldn't even hear his footfalls. But she knew he was back there. She could feel his presence.

A few cars passed them on the road as they neared the parking lot, and Grace gave them halfhearted waves. When they reached the car, Wyatt slipped into the driver's seat. She sneaked a peek at his face, but his expression gave nothing away. His silence, on the other hand, said plenty.

Being crammed into the small car made the drive back seem to take even longer than the hike back. The sun was dropping behind the mountains, and a chill was setting in—from her bones outward. She wanted to say something, but she didn't know what. Didn't know where he was in his processing or what she could possibly say to make it better.

There's nothing you can say. You're alive and his mother isn't.

The tension in the car swelled with each mile. Grace's throat felt achy and raw, her emotions ready to burst through the makeshift dam she'd built to hold them back.

When she sighted the inn she felt only relief. He pulled into a slot at the curb, and before he could turn off the ignition she reached for the door handle.

"Wait."

She paused, her hand clenched around the handle, her breaths coming too fast.

"I need to say something, Grace."

She braced for his anger. For blame and rejection. And she just needed to absorb it all. Suck it up. He needed to get this off his chest, and maybe then he'd feel better. Maybe then he'd find closure.

"Grace, look at me."

She turned toward him and raised her eyes but couldn't seem to lift them past the ribbed collar of his T-shirt.

He touched her chin, tipping it up until her eyes met his. She couldn't read his expression. But what else was new?

"I'm sorry. I'm not handling this well."

"You don't owe me an apology, Wyatt."

"Yes, I do." He pulled her into his arms, resting his head on top of hers.

She held herself stiffly, unwilling to accept his affection. It was unwarranted. Undeserved. Her breath felt stuffed into her lungs, and her heart knocked against her rib cage.

"I'm so thankful you got away," he whispered. "That should've been the first thing I said."

But if I hadn't, your mom would've lived, she wanted to say. But the pressure was building up in her throat, and she pressed her lips together to keep it from escaping.

"It's not your fault," he whispered into her hair.

She blinked back tears. A squeak escaped.

"It's not your fault, Grace."

She couldn't hold back the floodgates anymore. They cracked open and a sob escaped. And once it was out, another followed. Tears flowed like a river down her face and into the soft cotton folds of his shirt. Her body shuddered under the weight of her burden.

"Oh, honey." He tightened his hold on her. "Let it all out."

"But you're the one—"

"Shhhh. Let go of the guilt. If you do, I will too. There's only one person responsible for our pain—and it's neither one of us."

"But . . . what if I hadn't gotten away?"

"Don't play the what-if game, Grace. You'll lose every time."

She pulled herself together. Drew away far enough that she could meet his gaze. See if he really believed what he was saying.

He thumbed away her tears, and she could've melted into the warmth of his eyes.

"Remember what you said to me earlier?" he asked. "That I was just a child? You were right. And so were you, Grace. We have to remember God's sovereignty in all this. He allowed this to happen—your escape and my mom's death. I don't know why. Even our meeting like this . . . But maybe this is what was necessary for healing to take place. For both of us."

A reflective look came over his face. "It's weird, this feeling I have inside right now. I've been praying for peace for a long time, and I think He's finally giving it to me. Or maybe I'm only now in a receiving frame of mind. But since we started walking it's been slowly swelling, getting bigger by the minute. And I want that for you too, Grace."

How could he be thinking about her right now? "But . . . if I hadn't gotten away from him—"

He placed his finger over her lips. "Stop. I can't even bear to think about that. Don't you know how much I've come to care for you?"

"But your mom . . ."

"In a perfect world, none of that would've happened. But it's not a perfect world, and we need to accept what happened. We need to trust that God has a plan for each of us. We both need to let go of this."

Another tear trickled down her cheek. "I don't know how."

"I don't either, honey. But we'll figure it out one day at a time, okay? We have to. I can't live with this anymore, and I don't want you to either." He framed her face, his eyes piercing hers. "You're deserving of good things, Grace."

She wanted to believe that. Wanted to believe it so badly. And if Wyatt, of all people, thought so . . . maybe, just maybe, it was true.

Chapter Thirty-Nine

From the car Wyatt watched Grace mount the porch steps. They'd talked until the sun set. Until Grace calmed down. Then when the conversation tapered off and he sensed she needed time alone, he sent her inside with a soft kiss.

He wished he'd handled himself better on the mountain. He hadn't realized she'd been beating herself up all the way down the hill. He hated that she thought he'd resent her for surviving. Didn't she know he loved her? Maybe he hadn't verbalized it, but he thought he'd shown her.

During their talk they hadn't even touched on their relationship. There were too many other things to resolve. But there'd be time to talk that through tomorrow after they'd processed today's revelation.

For now, he needed to call the one person who understood what he'd been through. His dad had been in his corner every step of the way. He'd allowed Wyatt to grieve as a young boy even though he must've been falling apart himself.

And though Wyatt had never admitted to having ongoing issues related to his mother's death, his dad was no fool. Wyatt knew he worried about his son, but his mother's death was a subject that neither brought up these days for fear of hurting the other. Wyatt felt compelled to talk to him about it now, however.

He placed the call, wondering belatedly if his dad was at some political event or fund-raiser. But his dad picked up on the second ring, greeting him with the same warm, robust manner that had gotten him elected again and again.

"Hey, Dad, it's me."

"Wyatt. It's good to hear your voice. How are you doing? How's your shoulder?"

"It's good. Really good. Listen, are you alone? You have a minute to talk?"

"I can be. Just a second."

Wyatt heard his dad's muffled voice as he spoke with someone, then a little shuffling around. A door clicked shut.

"I just finished supper with Valerie. She made her scrumptious chicken and dumplings, and now I'll have to jog an extra two miles tomorrow. So what's going on with you, Son? I hear something in your voice, and I don't know if I should be worried or excited."

"You don't need to worry, Dad. Not anymore."

Wyatt told him about the troubles he'd been having on the job. About the nightmares that the shooting had resurrected. He told his dad where he was now—where he was staying. He told him why he'd come to Bluebell, what he'd been looking for, who he'd found. *What* he'd finally found.

"I came here searching for something, Dad. I didn't find what I'd expected, but I found what I needed: peace. I needed peace."

His dad was quiet a long moment, and Wyatt could feel his dad's emotion vibrating through the phone.

"Oh, Son." Dad's voice wobbled. "You don't know how long I've prayed for this."

"I can't tell you how much lighter I feel. I thought facing this would be hard and painful. But I feel like my legs are full of helium. Like I can draw a free breath for the first time in a long time."

He might even make it through the night without a nightmare.

Which would mean he was fit for work again. The thought brought mixed emotions. He was eager to get back to work, but that would also mean leaving Grace.

"I'm so glad, Wyatt. You could've told me where you'd gone. I would've tried to get away."

"I think this was something I needed to do alone, Dad. Besides, I didn't want to worry you."

His dad gave a little chuckle. "That's what dads do. But I'm so relieved you're finding closure."

"About time, huh?"

"And this woman you met . . . Grace. She's going to be all right too?"

Wyatt remembered the mess she was in his arms earlier. "She will be." He believed that. God was going to do something really amazing with her.

"She's special, this woman? I hear it in your voice when you talk about her."

"She is special, but . . . there are obstacles."

His dad was quiet for a beat. "Well, if it's meant to be, you'll work it out, I guess."

But Wyatt didn't want to think about that right now. He wasn't seeing a solution at the moment, and he wanted to enjoy the wonderful freedom for a while longer.

"I'll give it some thought," he said.

Chapter Forty

Grace lifted the Surly touring bike onto the pegs in the garage. Her rental merchandise had gotten a little out of hand as of late. Kayaks lay haphazardly on the cement floor. Bikes leaned, pedals tangled with wheel spokes, and life jackets draped randomly from various objects.

Levi and Molly didn't necessarily return everything to its place when tourists returned rentals. To be fair, sometimes it got a little crazy trying to run the front desk and dole out equipment. But Grace needed the space to be organized, everything in its place.

She grabbed a bike and guided it into the proper slot in the rack. Darkness had fallen some time ago, but she needed time to think, and she did that best when she was busy.

A moment later the side door squeaked open and Molly peeked inside. "Oh, hi. I was on my way home and saw the light on. I thought I might've left it on earlier."

"Nope. Just straightening things up."

Molly gave Grace a hangdog look. "Sorry about the bike I left out earlier. And the kayak. I did manage to hang up the wet life jackets—not necessarily in the right place though."

Grace wheeled a Trek into the rack. "No worries."

A scratch on the bike's frame made her wince a little. These bikes were expensive. But they were rentals, and wear and tear was going to happen.

"Okay, what's wrong? I gave you the perfect opportunity to give me a hard time, and you completely passed it up."

Grace shrugged. "A lot on my mind, I guess."

Molly stepped inside and grabbed a bike, kicking up the stand. She wheeled it over. "Would it, perhaps, be the same thing that was on Wyatt's mind earlier? He walked right past the front desk without a word. I don't think he even saw me."

"Yeah. Probably the same thing." She got the bike into the slot and looked at Molly. "Guess I may as well tell you. You're going to get it out of me anyway."

"Smart girl."

So Grace told her sister why Wyatt had come to Bluebell, what Wyatt had been looking for in the mountains, that his mother not only died out there years ago but had been killed. Then she told Molly about the connection between Grace's abduction and Wyatt's mom.

Molly gasped. "His mom was Janet Jennings?"

"Yes."

Molly stared wide-eyed at Grace. "He's Governor Jennings's son then. This was his summer home. The same man who tried to abduct you killed his mom?"

"Yes."

Molly grabbed Grace's hand. "Oh, honey. Are you all right? That must've really thrown you for a loop."

"Not gonna lie—it kind of freaked me out."

"Of course it freaked you out! Did Wyatt know who you were the whole time he's been here?"

"He was as caught off guard as I was. He'd only told me his mother had died up there—not that she'd been murdered. I didn't put it together until we were at the actual scene of the crime. Molly, he was there when she was killed—just twelve years old. He must've felt so helpless."

Molly placed a hand to her chest. "Oh, the poor dear."

"He's had a difficult time finding closure. And when I found out who he was, who his mom was, all I could think was . . . if I hadn't gotten away his mom would still be alive."

Molly's brows drew together as her eyes searched Grace's. "He didn't make you feel that way, did he? Grace, that was in no way your fault."

She thought of those moments in the car earlier, Wyatt's tender words and gentle touches. He'd been so loving, so careful.

Her eyes filled with tears as she remembered. "Oh, Molly . . . he was so incredibly kind. He was . . . amazing." His words were too private to share. She wanted to hold them close to her heart and savor them instead.

"Okay, well, good. This whole thing is just so crazy, him coming here and meeting you. Maybe God brought him to this inn—to you—to bring him healing."

"I think you might be right. He didn't even have a reservation when he came to town. He just drove by the inn because he wanted to see his old summer house. When he saw it had been turned into an inn, he decided to stay here." That must've taken a great deal of courage. Must've stirred up a million memories, both good and bad.

"God at work. That's so cool."

It was kind of cool. That God cared so much about both of them. That He took two hurts and spread His healing touch over both of them with one simple stroke.

"So . . . ," Molly said, "I can't help but wonder, where does that leave the two of you?"

Grace considered the question, wishing for some miraculous

solution to appear. "I don't know. I guess in the same place we were in before. He has a life somewhere else doing something he loves. And I . . ." She looked around the garage at all the merchandise she'd so lovingly selected. "My dreams are here. I just bought a house, and Bluebell is my home. The thought of moving away from here—it would tear me up inside." Though losing Wyatt wouldn't exactly feel great either.

Molly squeezed her hand. "I'm sorry."

"To be honest, Molly, Wyatt's not the only one who needed closure. I've kind of been struggling lately."

"Struggling how?"

She gave Molly a sheepish look. "I might've had a panic attack or two."

"Grace! Why didn't you say something? We need to get you to the doctor. Panic attacks are nothing to mess around with, and you probably need to have some blood work—"

"I've only had two, and I really think it's about what I went through as a kid. Maybe the stress of starting my own business brought it on. I don't know. I probably need a little therapy or something."

Those words of Wyatt's replayed in her mind. *"It's not your fault, Grace."* She closed her eyes as a feeling of peace moved in like an autumn fog. She allowed it to roll over her. Allowed it to soothe her spirit. It wasn't quite forgiveness he'd granted. It was the complete absence of blame. However she defined it, it was freeing.

"Well, I'm here whenever you need to talk."

"Thanks." Grace glanced around the shed. "Right now I think I just want to get this space back in order."

Molly moved toward the life jacket hanging from an oar. "Well, I guess the least I can do is stay and help."

l

It was nine o'clock by the time Molly made her way home. She'd texted Adam earlier to let him know to eat supper without her.

Her mind was still spinning with the fact that the governor's son had been under their roof for more than three weeks. He'd been a regular mystery man since his arrival. But when she thought of what he'd suffered as a child, she couldn't blame him for keeping secrets. Also, it came as no surprise that a child who'd been unable to defend his mother had chosen a career in which he protected people.

As they'd put the garage to order, Grace hadn't said anything more about Wyatt. Unlike Molly, she wasn't one to process things verbally. Instead they'd talked mostly about the sale of the inn and Grace's plans for her new house.

Boy, a lot sure happened when Levi left town. In two days, when he and Mia returned from their honeymoon, they'd have a lot of catching up to do. Molly would be glad for things to settle back to normal.

But then, things would never really settle back to the way they were, would they? The inn was selling. Levi was moving to LA. Molly and Adam were moving to Italy. And Grace would be here alone, trying to make a go of her business.

The realization put a pinch in Molly's chest.

When she pulled into the driveway she parked beside Adam's car and entered the house through the side door. Adam was in the living room reading the *New York Post* on the sofa.

"Hi, honey, I'm home."

"Hi, sweetheart." Adam lowered the paper, and Molly leaned down and placed a kiss on his lips before she plopped down beside him. "Wow, what a day. How was yours? Did you get through that chapter that was giving you fits? I was right, wasn't I? The protagonist needed to get on her motorcycle and let her hair down. Or was it the hero's motorcycle? I can't remember. So what'd you decide to do, huh?"

Adam folded up the newspaper, set it on the coffee table, then sat back, searching her eyes for a long moment. "Did something happen today?"

Molly turned fully toward him. "Oh, Adam, wait'll I tell you." She spilled Grace's story, all of it somehow taking three times as long as it had taken her sister to tell. He listened quietly, nodding and frowning at all the appropriate moments.

When she was finally finished he said, "That is a lot. Is Grace all right?"

"She's a little shaken, but I really fear what's going to happen when Wyatt leaves. I think she's in love with him. She didn't say so—she might not even realize it yet. This is all new to her, and I think Wyatt loves her too, but he has a life somewhere else. It's all so sad."

Molly was surprised that she was getting teary. A lump swelled in her throat, and those tears . . . Despite her best efforts one of them spilled over.

"Honey . . . what's wrong?"

"I'm—I'm just worried about Grace, that's all. She's having panic attacks and she's about to lose her first love!"

"That is hard." Adam brushed the tear away. "But are you sure that's all it is?"

"What else would it be?" The tears just kept coming, one after the other. Her lips trembled.

"You tell me." Adam gazed at her with those knowing eyes.

Molly searched her heart and latched on to the one thing that had weighed heaviest on her mind. "You know what's wrong with me? Everything's changing, that's what."

"Tell me what's changing."

"Everything! Levi's moving to LA, we're moving to Italy, and Grace is buying a house and staying here all by herself."

Adam's gaze turned thoughtful. "I thought that's what everyone wanted."

"It was. It *is!*" So why was she so conflicted about it? "Argh! I'm not making any sense."

He gave her a patient smile. "Honey, when's the last time you researched places for your bed-and-breakfast in Italy?"

What did that have to do with anything? "What? I don't know. Maybe a few weeks ago? I've been busy."

"You were searching every day there for a while, until the wee hours of the morning—right up until you put the inn up for sale. Honey . . . maybe you don't want to move to Italy anymore."

Molly bristled. "Yes, I do. I've always wanted this. It's my dream. I took three years of Italian in preparation for this. You're having second thoughts! You're backing out."

"No. No, that's not it at all."

Molly crossed her arms, her foot ticking off time. "Sure sounds like it to me. You want to stay in the States. You don't want to be that far from your family. You don't want to travel to a different continent for your book tours. You love this house. You want *this* to be our home."

"Molly, look at me."

She was too upset to meet his gaze. Too afraid what she'd find there. Her stomach was in knots and her throat ached.

Adam took her chin, forcing eye contact. "If you want to move to Italy, I'm 100 percent behind you, honey. I don't care where we live because *you* are my home."

Her heart melted at his words. At the love written across his face with all the eloquence of a romantic poem.

"Oh, Adam." The tears kept coming.

"What's really bothering you?"

She sniffled and made herself verbalize her feelings. "The inn's going to change and not for the better. I should be grateful. I mean, we have a buyer and they're paying full price, but . . ."

Adam pulled her into his arms and set his chin on her head. "But what?"

"The *Johnson brothers* are going to open a spa! They're going to change the inn's name! They're going to get rid of Miss Della and cook city food in her kitchen! They're not going to pass along the inn's history or pamper the guests with all the little extras. They're going to charge for Wi-Fi! They may as well just put up a Marriott sign!"

He rubbed her back in long, soothing strokes for a full minute while she let the tears come.

"Molly," he said finally. "Hear me out, okay? I'm just listening to you and trying to assimilate everything you're saying, everything you've said lately. And it sounds to me as if maybe you don't want to sell the inn at all. It sounds as though you might want to keep it for yourself."

Molly opened her mouth to refute the words. But before they could escape, the notion took hold. She closed her mouth long enough to let the idea marinate for a minute.

And it felt . . . right.

She pushed away from Adam, far enough away that she could look into his eyes. But she wasn't really seeing him. She was seeing herself running the inn. Seeing herself giving that historical tour as she'd done hundreds of times. Seeing herself chatting with Miss Della in the kitchen over a plate of cookies during the slow periods. Adrenaline seeped into her bloodstream. Her heart shimmied in her chest. Her face flushed with heat.

She pictured the inn without Levi or Grace—and surprisingly, that didn't break her heart as she'd thought it would. Because the inn would be the place they could return to. It could be their *home*.

They'd all set out to fulfill their parents' dream—but somewhere along the way the dream had become her own.

But there were obstacles. She only owned one-third of the inn, and her siblings wanted to sell it.

"Tell me what you're thinking."

Molly blinked, seeing the concern in those faded blue eyes. She tried to collect her thoughts, but they were zinging through her mind at warp speed. All this thinking had at least caused the tears to abate.

"I'm thinking it's too late, Adam. We've already sold the inn. And I can't run the business without Levi—he's the financial wizard behind its success, and he wants to be done with it. Who can blame him? He's already sacrificed so much for us. I can't ask him to give up any more.

"And Grace needs the money from the inn for her new location, and she's already signed papers on the house! I don't even have the money to buy them out. Yes, yes, I know you'd be happy to do that for me, but I can't let you. This is my problem. No, it's not feasible. I can't do this to them."

Adam tucked a strand of her hair behind her ear, his eyes sharpening on hers. "But is it what you want, Molly?"

How very like Adam to get right to the heart of the matter. She could do nothing but give him—give herself—a completely honest answer. "Yes. Yes, I would love to stay here and run the inn on my own, but—"

He put his finger over her lips. "That's the only part I need to hear. Let's break down what you just said. The inn is already sold? You haven't signed the papers yet; you were waiting for Levi's return. And yes, he's great with numbers, but you can learn to do it yourself or hire it out. The inn's profitable enough to afford the expense. And Grace doesn't have to give up her house because . . ." He took her chin and searched her eyes. "Your problem is my problem, and my money is your money. We're a team, Molly Bradford, ever since I put that ring on your finger. If I needed something you'd move heaven and earth to get it for me. How could you think I'd do any less?"

Her eyes prickled with new tears because what he said was absolutely true. Adam proved his love for her every day in big and small ways. And she could tell by his tone that her statement to the contrary had stung.

She touched his face. "I'm sorry. I didn't mean to hurt you. And yes, I would do anything for you. You know I get on a tangent sometimes and say stupid things. I love you so much, Adam."

"I know you do, honey. I love you too."

She pressed a kiss to his lips, savoring his familiar taste and feel.

Everything had already been set into motion with the sale of the inn. She didn't know how to bring the machine to a screeching halt. "They might want to sell the inn regardless. They might want to close this chapter of their lives. It's been a long, hard road."

"Well, there's only one way to find out."

Chapter Forty-One

$\mathcal{W}$yatt's first thought when he opened his eyes the next morning was that he didn't remember a single dream. He'd slept right through the night for the first time in days.

His second thought was of Grace. He needed to talk with her. See how she was doing. The memory of her distress in the car yesterday made his chest ache. He hoped she hadn't tossed and turned all night. He hoped she'd find a way to shed the guilt. He hoped she'd find the same peace he had.

He rushed through his shower and dressed in the only clean outfit he had left. He needed to make some calls today—particularly the one to his boss. His leave was up in four days, and he needed to confirm that he was ready to get back to work.

He needed to call Ethan and catch up. His friend had texted yesterday while he'd been out of range, and Wyatt hadn't had a chance to reply.

It wasn't yet nine o'clock when Wyatt made his way down the stairs. He said hello to Jada, the new girl at the front desk, and followed the delicious aroma of frying bacon to the dining room.

He caught a glimpse of couples and small families before he saw Grace. She was sitting at a table for two by the window, tapping her laptop keys, a half-eaten muffin on a plate at her side. Her hair was up in a ponytail, exposing her graceful neck and the delicate shells of her ears.

She didn't notice him until he was lowering himself into the chair across from her.

"Good morning," he said.

"Morning." She stared at him tentatively, probably trying to work out how to behave after all that had happened yesterday.

He reached across the table and took her hand. "How are you feeling this morning? Yesterday was . . . a lot."

Her face softened, shoulders relaxing at the direct question. "No kidding. I'm better, I think. How'd you sleep?"

"Like a baby."

"I'm so glad to hear that, Wyatt. You look good—well rested."

One of the servers came to take his order, then retreated to the kitchen. A silence fell over the table. Wyatt dreaded the coming conversation. He'd turned this situation every which way, and it never ended well. He was the older, more experienced one here. He needed to be strong and do what was right for Grace. But when he thought about leaving her, he didn't feel strong at all. He felt like a bowl of quivering Jell-O.

Grace cleared her throat. "Wyatt, I—I wanted to thank you for everything you said yesterday."

"I meant every word."

"I know you did—that's why it meant so much to me."

"I called my dad last night, told him everything. He was relieved I'll finally be able to put all this behind me. I've tried to shield him from what I've been going through—it was a dark time in his life too. I think he's been more worried about me than he's let on."

"I'm happy for you. You deserve to have closure."

"So do you, Grace." It might take time, but he hoped eventually she would fully embrace that.

She gave him a wan smile. "I'm just starting to believe that."

"Do you realize we've both been dealing with the same thing for years? We both have survivor's guilt."

"We've dealt with it in different ways though."

"I made a career out of helping people."

"And I've been trying to justify my place in the world."

"And even though we're both Lone Rangers, it took us coming together to arrive at a place of healing."

Their eyes connected, a moment of silence passing between them, the weight of this discovery needing no words of explanation.

Grace looked down at her half-eaten muffin, then back up at him. "So . . . you found what you were looking for. I guess you'll be leaving soon."

He studied her eyes, noting the way the corners drooped in sadness. The way she rubbed her lips together.

"I have to get back to work Monday. I was a bit of a mess when I left, and unfortunately I have a psychological evaluation to pass before I can return to work."

Grace's brows hitched. "Are you worried about that?"

"Not anymore. The good news is I'll be getting promoted soon—to presidential detail." His face split into a grin. "I was reluctant to say that out loud until now."

"Wyatt—that's amazing. Your dream job."

"It's been a long, hard road. I'll need a couple days to sort things out at home before Monday. I've been gone awhile."

"Of course."

"I wanted to make sure you were going to be all right before I left."

She blinked. "Oh. Yeah, I'll be fine. Don't let me keep you."

Didn't she know? If anything at all could keep him, it was her. She deserved more than talking around the important topic of their relationship. He wanted to be up front about it.

He gathered his courage and squeezed her hand. "Grace, I wish I could stay. I wish . . ." He clenched his jaws together, keeping the words in. He wished he could tell her he loved her. Because he did. She'd become a part of him so quickly. So easily.

But telling her that seemed cruel when he was about to leave.

"I wish things were different," he said.

"It's okay, Wyatt. You have an important job, and I know it means a lot to you."

"And I could never ask you to give up your dreams. Your business is important to you, and you're going to do great. You're going to have the best outfitters business in the Blue Ridge Mountains, I have no doubt."

The smile she gave him seemed hard fought. "I hope so."

"Better believe it." He let his gaze rove over her face, memorizing the shape of her eyes, the gentle taper of her nose, the sweet curve of her lips. He only wished he could bottle up this feeling he had when he was with her. "This is going to be hard, parting ways. You've become someone I can confide in, someone I can trust."

"I feel the same. It happened so quickly."

"I keep telling myself we could keep up a long-distance relationship. I could come see you when I'm at the field office, weekends. But I travel so much, Grace. Communication is difficult when I'm on assignment, and there would be no end in sight. That's no life for you. You deserve so much better."

His job had never cost him so much; it was costing him the woman he loved. For a moment he was tempted to throw it all away—his training, his hard work, his promotion—and just tell her he was staying. He could be happy here in Bluebell with Grace. His heart pounded at the thought, and his chest tightened.

But protecting people was his way of life. His calling. He didn't even know what else he'd do that would bring him the same sense of satisfaction.

"I want you to be happy, Grace. I want that above all else." And he knew from experience, absence did not make a woman happy.

She opened her mouth, and he could tell she was about to refute the statement. Maybe say that *he* made her happy. But when she closed her mouth again a tiny bubble burst inside.

"You're right," she said, a catch in her throat. "I don't like it, but you're right."

They stared at each other across the table, linked by their hands, hopelessness weighting the air between them. He'd finally found a woman who felt like home, and he couldn't have her.

Why, God?

The server came and set his food on the table. But his appetite was gone. His stomach was in knots, and the pungent smell of bacon was an affront to his senses.

When the server left, Grace closed her laptop and checked the time.

"Are you headed out now?" he asked.

"The sellers are letting me into the house for a couple hours this morning to measure and stuff. I was just making a list of everything I need to do while I'm there."

He studied her for a long moment. "I was thinking of leaving today, Grace. Drawing this out will only make it more difficult for both of us."

"Is this it, then? Are we saying good-bye now?"

"I still have to pack up my stuff and check out. And I'd like to see your new place. How about if I stop by on my way out of town?"

Her lips turned up, but there was no smile behind those blue eyes. "I'd like that."

l

At the new house Pamela let Grace in and promised to return in a couple hours to lock up. Once inside Grace forced herself to work through her list. First she opened the windows to let the cool breeze in, then she took measurements for the windows and the checkout counter she was having made.

A friend of Levi's stopped by to talk about the walls that would need to come down and additional structural support. Once he left she went up to the attic and checked out her soon-to-be digs, getting excited at the thought of having her own place, despite the ache of impending heartbreak.

She made a list of all the things she'd need to make the house into her business. It was long and detailed, but it kept her mind off the realization that she was about to say good-bye to the love of her life.

It seemed absurd that she could say that about a man she'd only known three weeks. But she knew in her heart it was true. They'd been through so much together. She felt as if she'd known him for years. Or maybe that she'd always known him. Maybe this was how it always felt, falling in love. As if you couldn't fathom how you'd even existed before then. The thought made her heart palpitate, made her palms sweat.

But Wyatt had important things to do. He had a calling—his dream job awaited. And she loved him enough not to stand in his way.

He was an amazing man. Despite what he'd been through, he was confident but humble. Not feeling as though he was undeserving of good things. Just clearly seeing his place in the world and being content with that. She was striving for that. He'd shown her what that looked like.

She was coming down the attic steps when she heard the front door open.

"Grace?" Wyatt called.

"Right here," she called as she walked down the short hall.

In the entryway he took off his sunglasses, and with the light behind him silhouetting his frame, he surveyed the space with those keen eyes.

He looked so much like he had that first day he'd walked into the inn. Into her life. She thought he'd shaken her up good, but that had only been the beginning. He'd turned her inside out and upside down. In all the best ways.

"This is going to be perfect," he said as she joined him in what would be her store. "You were right about the location, and I can already see this space in my mind's eye. You have good instincts."

Joy swelled inside at his words. "You think so?"

He smiled at her and took her hand. "I know so. Give me the grand tour."

She took him around, pointing out the house's features and everything she was planning to change. Though she maintained a cheerful countenance, his impending departure was background music, a mournful playlist, its volume increasing with each passing moment.

By the time they were back downstairs and headed toward the front door, Grace's chest felt weighted.

"It's going to be great, Grace. *You're* going to be great."

When she reached the spot where her checkout counter would go, she turned to him. The tour was over, and she was almost out of time. Pamela was going to be here soon, and she still had a few items on her list to complete. She couldn't bring herself to care, however.

"Hope you're right." She'd tried for cheerful, but that playlist was getting to her, and her voice caught on the last word.

"Come here, honey." He took her hand and pulled her into his arms.

She gratefully pressed into the hard planes of his chest and buried her face in the warm curve of his neck. She inhaled his clean, masculine smell, wishing she could bottle it. She memorized the feel of his arms wrapped tight around her. The delicious rasp of his unshaven jaw against her forehead. The warm wisp of breath at her temple.

"I'm so glad I met you, Grace Bennett," he whispered, then dropped a soft kiss on her forehead. "And I'm so glad you survived."

Her eyes stung with tears because she knew what her survival had cost him. Her throat ached with his kindness. She tightened her arms around him.

"I want you to find that peace, Grace. If that's all that comes of what happened here, it would be worth it to me."

She couldn't speak past the lump in her throat, so she just held him and let him hold her. She tried to remember what this felt like so when she lay upstairs in her bed on lonely nights, she could call it all back up. So she could comfort herself with the memory of what it had felt like to be so fully loved.

A tear trickled down her cheek just as he drew back enough to look at her.

He kissed the tear away. "Know what I thought when I first laid eyes on you?"

She shook her head, gazing into eyes she adored.

"I thought, 'Now here's a very special woman.'"

She gave a wry laugh. "No, you didn't."

"Yes, I did. God has big plans for you, Gracie. This place, this house, is only the beginning of what He's going to do through you. You're here for a purpose. Don't ever forget that."

Another tear leaked out. She pressed her face to his shoulder, and he wrapped his arms around her again. How in the world did he always know exactly what she needed to hear? And what would she do when he wasn't here to say those things?

Maybe she'd have to start saying them to herself.

They clung to each other for a time, seconds bleeding into minutes. Pamela would be here soon, and she didn't want the Realtor walking in on their last moments.

As if reading her mind, Wyatt drew back. "I should go."

She gave him a wobbly smile. "I'll walk you out."

"No." His hands framed her face. "I want to remember you just like this. Here in your new place, living your dream."

Her eyes stung again, and she swallowed around the achy lump in her throat.

"I'll miss you, Grace. You have no idea how much."

"Yes, I do."

He pressed a slow, soft kiss to her lips. It was too brief. But it could've gone on forever and still not been long enough.

He stepped away, turned to open the door. On the threshold he looked back one last time, gave her that enigmatic smile, and then he was gone.

Chapter Forty-Two

After Grace said good-bye to Wyatt she returned home and wept in the privacy of her shower. Later Molly tried to pry her feelings out of her, and when Grace shut her out, Molly switched to sympathetic looks. But Grace just put on a brave face and tried to keep busy.

On Saturday Mia and Levi returned from their honeymoon, a nice distraction from Grace's heartbreak. She'd always found that word to be so overwrought and sappy. Who knew that the actual experience caused a literal ache in the chest right where the heart resided?

After sleeping off their jet lag on Saturday, Mia and Levi awakened refreshed and ready to gush about their time abroad. They'd strolled the streets of Paris, visited the Louvre, floated down the Seine River, and taken the elevator up the Eiffel Tower.

As Mia spoke she wore a beautiful flush, and Levi watched her with affection. Every once in a while they traded private little smiles that made Grace happy for them even while she was sad for herself. She despaired of ever finding someone she could love as much as she loved Wyatt.

The whole family went to church on Sunday, leaving Jada in charge of the inn. Molly shifted and twitched beside her until Grace was ready to put an elbow in her ribs. After church they went back home and had lunch in the dining room.

Levi and Mia were flying to LA tomorrow with as much of Levi's belongings as he could stash in his suitcases. There'd be a press release and interviews about their wedding, which had still gone unnoticed.

They feasted on Miss Della's fried chicken and potato salad until they were stuffed. Lunch was slowly winding down, and the other guests had already finished and gone on about their day, leaving the dining room to the family.

Grace glanced around the table, acutely aware that her siblings were now coupled up, making her the proverbial fifth wheel. Would it always be this way?

Mia pushed back her empty plate. "I'm not ready to get back on a plane tomorrow."

"Or travel across three more time zones," Levi said.

"And I don't even want to get on the scale. I ate my body weight in baguettes."

"You look great. Please tell me I'm not going to be subsisting on tofu and seaweed once we get to LA."

Mia shrugged and gave him a *you'll just have to wait and see* look.

"Well," Grace said, "I know you're excited about moving, but don't forget to sign the Johnsons' offer before you leave."

"Did the attorney review it?" Levi asked. "Everything's on the up-and-up?"

"Um . . ." Molly cleared her throat and traded a peculiar look with Adam. "I wanted to talk to you guys about that . . ."

A niggle of anxiety wormed into Grace's heart. If that offer fell through she'd lose her house—and her earnest money. "What? Everything's all right with the offer, isn't it? They didn't back out or something?"

"No, no," Molly said. "That's not it."

"Then what's wrong?" Tension threaded Levi's words.

259

Mia had also come to attention.

Molly shifted her weight, giving Adam a nervous look, and he slipped his arm around her shoulders.

"I was just thinking . . . ," Molly began. "What if we didn't sell the inn after all?"

"What?" Levi said.

Grace threw down her napkin. "You've got to be kidding me."

"Wait, wait, give me a chance to explain."

"I have a house on the line here, Molly."

"In case you forgot, I'm moving to LA."

"Seriously," Grace said. "Hasn't he done enough for us?"

Levi looked at her in surprise, and she gave a sheepish shrug. So she usually took Molly's side.

"Hear her out, guys," Adam broke in with that quiet but firm voice of his.

Grace took a deep breath, as did Levi. The room was as quiet as the lake at daybreak, every eye on Molly, waiting for her to explain herself.

"None of that has to change." Molly looked at Grace. "I know what that house and your business mean to you. And Levi, you have done so much for us. I'd never ask you to stay longer than you already have. You and Mia deserve a chance to start your lives in LA together. I'd never suggest derailing your plans, any of you."

"Then what are you suggesting?" Levi asked, somewhat mollified.

Molly sat up straight and met each of their eyes, one by one. "I want to stay here and run the inn myself."

Grace blinked at her sister.

Levi seemed to be equally surprised, but he was the first to recover. "Okay . . . What about Italy?"

"No." Grace shook her head. "I know you guys are financially set here, but some of us need the money from the sale. Molly, you know I don't have the resources to refurbish that house and get my business off the—"

"You wouldn't have to." She traded a look with Adam. "We want to buy the inn, Adam and me. We'll pay each of you your shares, and I'll run the inn myself—with hired help, of course. I'll hire a bookkeeper; we can afford it. And I promise, I won't bother either of you for anything. I won't beg you to keep the books, Levi. And Grace, I won't ask you to clean rooms or work the desk. I know you're both ready to move on, and you deserve that. And I know you have your heart set on that house, Grace . . . but if you wanted to, you could even keep your business here."

Grace let the idea sink in a moment. It would be cheaper by a long shot. And easier since she'd have free help. But was that the right thing to do? Would Molly's plan to keep the inn even work?

"So . . . ?" Molly's gaze toggled between Grace and Levi. "What do you think? Would you be willing to consider it?"

"Molly," Levi said, "are you sure this is what you want? You've dreamed of Italy forever."

"I know I have. It took me a while to see it, but—it was just really bothering me, the thought of those guys, of anybody else, really, running this place, changing things. I think I was actually trying to sabotage the sale—subconsciously, of course." She gave them a guilty look. "Sorry. It took Adam to help me see that my dreams have changed. We've been talking about this since Thursday and I'm certain. Nothing would make me happier than to stay here in Bluebell and run this place. I love it so much." She blinked away the tears that gathered in her eyes.

"I know you do," Levi said. "To be honest, I was kind of dreading letting go of our home. It kind of felt like giving up another piece of Mom and Dad."

"I have to admit I love the idea of you staying here with me. And keeping the house in the family." Grace gave her sister a wry grin. "And I can totally see you bossing around a full staff and mothering the guests well into your golden years."

Molly sniffled. "You know me so well."

"You were born to run this place, Molly," Grace said.

Adam gave his wife a side hug. "So we're all agreed? We buy you guys out?"

Grace's eyes connected with Levi's. They exchanged an entire conversation in a five-second span.

And then they said simultaneously, "We're in."

Chapter Forty-Three

Wyatt stood guard beside Ethan inside the opulent dining room in Kuala Lumpur, Malaysia. He kept watch over the men in the room, but the real danger was outside where the other agents stood guard.

Around a long, oval table sat the US secretary of state, Malaysian officials, and interpreters. At the other end of the table some kind of golden seal was inlaid in the wall and flanked by the two countries' flags. The conversation went in one of Wyatt's ears and out the other as he watched for potential threats to the secretary of state.

The delicious aroma wafting Wyatt's way made his stomach give a hard growl. He was going on seventeen hours without a meal and twenty-four hours without sleep. But he took it all in stride; they'd been trained for deprivation.

They'd been on this mission for twenty-eight days, traveling across Asia on a foreign-policy mission. Wyatt had been coping well since he'd returned to work. He'd passed his psych eval with flying colors. He slept soundly when he was able to. He had his mojo back. Even Ethan had commented on it. He'd opened up to his friend about Bluebell and his revelations there.

It had taken Wyatt an additional two weeks, but over a game of pool back home, he'd also opened up about Grace. Ethan listened patiently, taking shots across the table without comment. Wyatt finished his story with, "So . . . I left. What else could I do?"

Ethan had been conspicuously silent on the matter.

How could his friend even relate? He was happily married with two little girls. He had the love of his life. Wyatt hadn't brought up Grace again.

The meal with the Malaysian officials dragged on and on. He was grateful to be posted in here rather than outside though. Being on high alert for so many hours was stressful, and nobody was at his best when he'd gone so long without sleep.

He fought a yawn. He'd catch a nap and, hopefully, a meal on the plane ride to Singapore.

Finally the meeting seemed to be winding up. A Malaysian official stood, followed by another. Greetings were exchanged and others stood, their movements putting Wyatt on high alert. He watched each man's body language, looking for hands in pockets or other suspicious actions.

It wasn't until he was inside the plane that he was finally able to let down his guard.

Wyatt awakened forty minutes after he closed his eyes, groggy and still hungry, even after the tray of food he'd scarfed down. Beside him, Ethan was staring out the window at the landscape.

"Didn't you sleep?" Wyatt asked.

"Little bit."

His friend had been quiet on this mission. Wyatt wondered if something was going on at home but couldn't imagine what. Ethan and Megan were regular lovebirds, and their daughters were the apples of his eye. He talked about them constantly. Missed them so much when he was away.

Unfortunately, it wasn't uncommon for married agents to cheat on their wives. Assignments could be long, and women were sometimes fascinated with the mystique of the Secret Service. Ethan, though, was true blue to Megan. Wyatt had never seen his head so much as turn at another woman.

Wyatt rubbed his eyes, the thought of two more weeks of travel making him nothing but weary. He'd missed his dad's fiftieth birthday party and his favorite cousin's wedding. He was eager to get back to the field office—a surprising thought. He'd never been a desk job kind of guy, but he was tired of missing meals and getting by on forty winks. What he'd give right now for a mattress and eight solid hours.

He'd found himself having a lot of those thoughts during the last month. He'd done his job as scrupulously as ever, but . . . somehow his heart just wasn't in it. He kept asking himself why he was even doing this, then wondering why he was having these thoughts about a job that had always felt like a calling. Something was missing. But surely when he was moved to PPD all that would change.

"Megan's divorcing me."

Ethan's announcement startled Wyatt. "What?"

"She told me before I left."

"She can't mean that. You guys are great together."

"You know the old argument. She wants to be married to someone who's actually around for her. For the kids."

"So quit, Ethan. No job is worth losing your family over."

Ethan gave a droll smile. "I finally offered, and know what she said? She said, 'It's too late.' Saddest words I ever heard, man."

Tears gathered in his buddy's eyes, and Wyatt wished he had words that would fix this. He'd known Megan complained about Ethan's schedule. Who wouldn't? But he thought she loved Ethan enough to muddle through.

"Maybe if you quit she'll come around. See you're serious about saving your marriage."

Ethan shook his head slowly. "I think there's someone else. There've been some red flags. I didn't want to see them. Besides, she's already filed. Wants me to move out when I get back."

"What about the girls?"

"We'll work out a schedule—as much as I can with this job." His voice was flat and lifeless. He looked at Wyatt. "This is a single man's job, buddy. There's no way to balance it with a family. You better know that if you ever plan to have one."

An announcement came over the speaker asking them to prepare for landing.

Wyatt's heart went out to the guy. "Whatever you need, I'm here, man."

"Thanks." Ethan leaned back and closed his eyes.

Wyatt buckled up and settled back in his seat, his friend's words playing over in his mind. The feelings he'd had over the past month settled over him like a blanket on a cold winter's night.

He'd known in his heart what his mind was only beginning to realize: This would be his last assignment.

This job produced adrenaline that—he was only beginning to see—he'd used as a tool to avoid dealing with his past. But he'd unpacked the trauma and had begun working through it. He didn't need the adrenaline anymore. He didn't need this job anymore. Not even the one he'd been gunning for.

The thought brought a few heart palpitations and activated the sweat glands in his palms. Would he regret the decision? He'd waited his whole life for an opportunity that was now within his grasp. But PPD would be just like his current job, just with a more prestigious protectee. And he'd officially had enough of this lifestyle.

That question answered, he moved on to the next: What would he do with his life if not this?

He could always get a job in investigations—every agent had a mandatory two years investigating financial crimes, cyberattacks, and the like before he could move on to protective detail. It was the direction most of the married agents went as it kept them closer to home. Wyatt had performed these tasks well enough. However, he hadn't found it fulfilling. Investigations had just been another hurdle on his way to his dream job.

He wasn't sure what he was going to do moving forward, but the skills he'd acquired were highly sought. All he knew was that this wasn't the life he wanted anymore. This job would never facilitate the kind of life he wanted—a life that included a wife and a family and kids.

A life that included Grace.

A strange feeling swelled in his chest. A wanting, a yearning for her. It filled him so full his lungs could hardly expand. He'd missed her every day, every hour since he left. Few things he'd ever done felt as wrong as driving away from Grace had felt.

And now he knew why. The question was, what was he going to do about it?

Chapter Forty-Four

October bled into November, and Grace hardly noticed the changing of the trees in the valley or the shedding of leaves. Thanksgiving weekend had just passed. Mia and Levi had flown in, and it had been good to have the whole family together for a few days.

The inn had officially been deeded to Molly and Adam, and Levi and Grace had walked away with their share of the buyout. Despite Molly's gracious offer to continue housing Blue Ridge Outfitters, Grace had decided she needed to do this on her own.

She hadn't heard from Wyatt since he'd left, but they had decided on a clean break after all. That realization did nothing to soothe the achy spot in her heart, however. How long would that feeling last? How long did it take a broken heart to mend? She supposed she was going to find out.

Whenever she found herself getting down, she reminded herself it had been worth it. She'd lose him all over again just to have him for a little while. Just to help him find closure.

Staying busy helped. Over the past six weeks she'd poured herself into renovating her new store. The walls had been knocked down, opening up the room. The garish shade of green had been covered with a fresh coat of greige, and the wood floor sparkled with new polish. Her tidy office in the back was all set up, but her attic space would have to wait until after she opened.

Grace hung the bells she'd purchased on the entry door and turned to survey the space. Her grand opening was three days away, just in time for the Christmas season. There were boxes of new merchandise everywhere, and racks waiting to hold it all.

She'd been working hard to get out the word about the opening. Levi had helped her with marketing ideas. Once the holidays passed, the off-season would be slow, but even after renovations she had a nice cushion in the bank to carry her through.

Grace moved behind the checkout desk, drawing her hand over the surface of her new glossy countertop. The desk was gorgeous, made from repurposed wood and facing the entryway. She could hardly wait till customers wandered in, looking for a sled or a pair of cross-country skis.

She squatted down and opened the box of Blue Ridge Outfitters T-shirts she'd ordered for her employees to wear—because yes, she'd hired two people to help run the shop. The front of the light-blue shirts sported the small, tasteful logo she'd designed. The back simply said, *The Outdoors Is Calling*.

She already had a great rapport with her staff and had begun forming relationships with other business owners in the community. Maybe Grace wasn't the people person Molly was, but she was finding that she was good with people in her own way.

The new bells above the door jingled. Probably Molly or even Pamela, who stopped in occasionally to check on her progress. Grace stuffed the box under the counter and stood.

But the visitor wasn't Molly or Pamela.

Grace froze at the sight of the man standing just inside her door.

The man who'd featured in every daydream she'd had since he'd left. His eyes fixed on her with that magnetic pull she'd begun to wonder if she'd only imagined.

The corner of his mouth kicked up. "Saw your sign as I was passing by."

He looked just the same as the first time she'd seen him, standing in the inn's lobby, saying those same words. Her heart went pitter-patter again, but this time it was because its owner had returned.

"Wyatt." Her brain couldn't seem to manufacture anything more.

His gaze left her to take in her new store, and she took the opportunity to scan him tip-to-toe, reveling in the sight of him. His crisp black button-up stretched taut across those broad shoulders. He wore jeans—and he wore them well.

"It looks amazing," he said.

"What?"

He gave her a bemused look. "Your store. It looks great. Just the way you described it."

"I—uh, I open in three days."

"I know. I may have stalked you online."

He took a couple steps closer, and as he neared, those brown eyes captured her. She told her heart to settle down. Told her nerves to get a grip. It didn't work.

"What—what are you doing here, Wyatt?"

"I quit my job."

Grace blinked. "What? What happened?"

"Nothing. And everything. Long story. But once I went back to work, I was on this assignment overseas that dragged on and on, and all I could think about was . . . you, Grace."

"Me?" she squeaked.

He came around the counter, his eyes smoldering. "Yes, you."

"But your job . . . It's your calling."

"It *was* my calling. I don't need it anymore." He kept coming.

The intense look in his eyes had her backstepping. "Um, why not?"

"Something has settled inside me—that peace I told you about before. I hope you've found some of that too." He was so close she could smell his clean, masculine scent.

"I did." Her back hit the wall. "Actually, I'm seeing someone."

He froze, inches away, his eyes sharpening as he searched her.

"I mean a professional," she added quickly. "Oh, jeez, a counselor. Not—you know, a man. Well, he is a man, but—"

Then his lips were on hers and Grace immediately lost all train of thought. The kiss was needy and demanding, and she yielded to him gladly. Oh, how she'd missed him. Missed his touch, missed his mouth, missed the way he commandeered her every thought, every breath when he touched her.

He placed his hands on the wall near her head, leaning in. She pressed her hands to the taut muscles of his obliques. She knew there was plenty more to talk about—she just couldn't remember what exactly. She'd despaired of ever being in his arms again, and here he was kissing her. Wanting her. She sent up a prayer of gratitude as she clutched his shirt.

She wasn't sure how long the kiss went on. There were some mewls and groans and one or two very sexy growls before Wyatt drew away. Their breaths were ragged as his eyes opened lazily.

"I missed you," he whispered with a love-drugged gaze.

It was addicting. "I missed you too."

He pressed another kiss to her mouth, this one soft and measured and over too quickly. "We have a lot to catch up on."

"Fifty-five days' worth."

He arched a brow.

Her face warmed. "What? I told you I missed you."

"Well . . ." He brushed her cheek. "There will be no more of that. I'm moving to Bluebell, Grace. Today."

"Today? What about your apartment? What about a job?"

"I subleased my apartment to Ethan, and I've rented a place here in town. It seems Chief Dalton was looking for a new cop." He gave her a crooked smile. "Meet the new cop."

Grace gaped at him. This was so unexpected, so great. She imagined him in uniform, a badge on his chest. She could see it so clearly—oh boy, could she.

"Wyatt, that's great." She huffed. "But talk about overqualified . . ."

He put his arms around her waist. "It's the life I want, right here in Bluebell. If that's all right with you."

"Well, I guess I wouldn't try to kick you out. You know, you being the new police officer and all."

"Don't make me regret those moves I taught you. And speaking of that—I've been talking with the owner of the gym the past few weeks. It appears I'll also be teaching an ongoing self-defense course there."

"You know you'll have every single woman within a fifty-mile radius signing up." She caressed his arm, remembering his devotion to his job. All that training, all that work, getting where he'd wanted to be. "Are you sure, though? You're giving up so much, Wyatt. Won't you miss the travel? The excitement?"

"I won't miss the travel, and being on high alert for days on end is exhausting, not exhilarating. I'm sure being a cop will have its own challenges, but they won't include the same level of sacrifice. Being an agent—it's just not for me anymore, Grace. I don't need it. I need . . . you."

She was starting to see a common thread. They both wanted the same things. And they seemed to be right there for the taking.

Wyatt grasped her face in his hands and gazed at her with such tender affection, her insides went liquid. "In case my actions aren't clear enough . . . I'm totally and completely in love with you, Grace Bennett."

Her heart gave a hard flop, and she couldn't stop the smile that lifted her lips. "I love you too, Wyatt. And I'm so glad to have you back in my life."

"I'm not going anywhere, Gracie. Just try and chase me away."

And then he pulled her into his arms and—nope—she had not one single urge to chase the man away.

Epilogue

$\mathcal{E}$veryone had told Grace that her wedding day would feel surreal. That she'd feel as if she were watching from outside her body. That she'd be so distracted by all the details she'd fail to remember or even enjoy the small moments.

She couldn't speak for the memory part just yet, but as she entered the sanctuary and her eyes connected with Wyatt's, she felt more present than she'd ever felt in her life. She forgot the people, forgot her simple white gown, forgot the details, which she'd handed off to Molly anyway.

All she could think about was walking down that aisle, getting closer to the man who was staring at her like she was the best thing to ever happen to him. In her rush to be near him she may have walked too fast, may have failed to hold her bouquet just so.

Levi, who walked her down the aisle, let her set the pace, God love him. And when they reached the front, she tore her eyes from her handsome groom to give him a grateful smile.

The pastor welcomed the crowd—half the town had turned out as well as Wyatt's large extended family. A prayer was offered. She joined hands with Wyatt. Words were said, and a song was sung by a friend of the family.

Wyatt had proposed in April following a picnic at Pawley Park. Today was the one-year anniversary of the day they'd met. Molly had freaked about the short engagement period, but Grace and Wyatt just wanted a simple wedding. She had to repeat the word *simple* to her sister at least twenty thousand times, and even so they'd wound up with a botanical garden and a tiered wedding cake of skyscraper proportions.

When it was time for the vows Wyatt's voice rang out confident and clear, his eyes never wavering. Grace soaked in every detail of him, committing them to memory. The crisp white of his shirt, the smoothly shaved planes of his face, the rough texture of his voice.

It was her turn next. She'd never been surer of anything than she was of the promises she was making today. As she finished she was only vaguely aware of Molly sniffling behind her.

Next, the pastor led them in the exchange of rings. Wyatt's band slid smoothly over his knuckle. Then her own band settled into place on her finger. They exchanged broad smiles as the pastor proclaimed them husband and wife.

Wyatt didn't wait for permission to kiss his bride, to the amusement of the crowd. He just gathered her in his arms and took her mouth in a loving kiss that went on about as long as was publicly acceptable. As he drew away he brushed her nose with his then whispered, "I love you."

What followed the ceremony was the promised whirlwind of activity. Grace and Wyatt posed for pictures with their wedding party. They were presented as husband and wife in the church's reception hall and made their rounds as everyone enjoyed the buffet Miss Della had organized.

As the meal wound up Molly made a long, sentimental toast, blubbering her way through some very nice words. Ethan's toast had been short in length but long in sincerity. His warm wishes touched a place deep in Grace's heart, especially since he'd just come through his own heartbreaking divorce.

Their first dance was next. Grace had chosen her parents' song: "When a Man Loves a Woman." As she swayed in Wyatt's arms she felt their presence, their approval. She hoped they were looking down from heaven, seeing how happy she was. How loved she was.

She pulled back from Wyatt to look him in the eye, feeling uncharacteristically sentimental. "My parents would've loved you, you know."

His eyes softened. "I wish I could've met them. But I kind of feel like I have, through you and Molly and Levi."

"Their legacy lives on."

"It really does, in so many ways. It's cool that we kind of grew up in the same house."

He'd been thrilled to find out they were keeping the inn in the family. It was his home, too, after all. "How many husbands and wives can say that?" she said as the last strains of the song played out.

"Husband and wife . . ." His eyes pierced hers as he lowered his head until his breath was a whisper on her lips. "That has such a nice ring to it."

Just as things were getting good, Molly tore Grace away for the bouquet toss. One beautiful arc-throw later, it was caught by Molly's friend Skye, who seemed rather pleased to find it in her grasp. After the toss Grace and Wyatt fed each other delicate slices of silky white cake to the applause of the guests.

Molly had hired a local band, so they danced until Grace's feet— even encased in her favorite sneakers—were pinched and aching.

When Wyatt slipped away to see Ethan off, Grace took the opportunity to plop into a corner chair and rest her feet. They were going away to Gatlinburg for a few days. It was barely off-season for her business, and it was still busy. She had a staff of four now, but she didn't feel comfortable leaving for a whole week.

Wyatt had settled into his position as a police officer. It meant working some unpredictable hours and being on call a lot, but the job suited him. And she'd been right about his self-defense course; he had a crowd each week—and some of them were even interested in learning self-defense. Grace often helped him by playing the "victim." He called her his star pupil.

The party went on, the band kicking up a rousing Luke Bryan song that had everyone crowding the dance floor. Grace scanned the happy gathering, a feeling of contentment rising. This was her place. These were her people. And now they were her husband's people too.

Her friend Sarah was dancing with Skeeter. He spun her around several times until she fell into his arms, laughing.

Adam was watching Molly affectionately from the sidelines as she dragged Miss Della away from the refreshment table and spun her around on the dance floor. Grace was glad to see them letting their hair down. Jada had taken a full-time position at the inn, and Molly had hired out the cleaning. She was thriving in her role as sole proprietor of the Bluebell Inn.

As Molly turned, Grace caught sight of her profile and the slight swell of her stomach under the snug dress. Two months ago Molly and Adam had announced that they were expecting. Molly's first trimester had been a little bumpy with morning sickness, but she was feeling great now that she was in her fourth month. They were going to be the best parents.

On the dance floor Molly stopped dancing as Adam approached, holding out a bottled water. Molly humored him, taking a long drink before handing it back. Grace loved the way Adam doted on her sister, even more so now that she was pregnant.

Just steps away from Molly, Levi and Mia were slow dancing, despite the up-tempo song, their foreheads pressed together. Levi was loving his new job at a commercial construction company, and Mia had just released a new film to critical praise. Levi was a handsome, quiet escort for her Hollywood shindigs. Sometimes Grace caught a glimpse of him in an entertainment rag and couldn't help but laugh. For someone so unsuited to Hollywood, Levi seemed awfully happy in his new life.

Wyatt had come back inside and was talking to his dad and step-mom over by the refreshment table. Her husband looked so handsome in his dark suit. He wore a single magnolia on his lapel in memory of his mother. He'd had some therapy of his own since his return to Bluebell. Grace was so proud of the progress he'd made. She was proud of her own progress too. She'd come to peace with survival. She hadn't realized what a weight she'd been carrying until she began to let go of it.

Grace had gotten to spend some time with Wyatt's family over the holidays and again in March. Governor Jennings was charming and kind, and his wife, Valerie, seemed happy for Wyatt's new course in life. His extended family—cousins, aunts, and uncles—were fun and loud, and Grace felt right at home among them.

Molly flopped into a chair beside Grace. "Whew! That's a workout. Taking a break?"

"Yeah, just taking it all in. You leave Miss Della to fend for herself?"

Molly pointed toward the dance floor, and Grace caught sight of Miss Della boogying with Darius Brown, the new landscaper Molly had hired.

Molly waggled her eyebrows. "They make a cute couple, huh?"

"You little matchmaker."

Wyatt turned just then and made eye contact with Grace, his gaze sharpening on her. His dad was still talking, but Grace was pretty sure he wasn't hearing a word. The corner of his lips made a slow curl upward, and Grace's heart stuttered. She was already thinking ahead to their first night alone. To the final part of "two becoming one." To waking up beside him in the morning and every morning after that.

Wyatt said something to his dad, not taking his gaze from Grace, and headed her way.

"Somebody's smitten," Molly teased.

Grace wasn't sure which of them she was referring to, but it didn't matter. All she could do was admire Wyatt's masculine form, his fluid stride, his laser-like stare as he approached.

"Sooo . . ." Molly stood, straightening the skirt of her dress. "Yeah, I'm out of here."

A moment later Wyatt lowered himself into the seat Molly had just vacated and put his arm around Grace. She leaned into him, accepting the slow, delicious kiss he placed on her mouth.

When he had her all melty and helpless, he whispered into her ear, "What do you say we get out of here?"

"Has—has it been long enough?"

"It's been a little over three thousand hours."

Grace chuckled. "They went by so fast."

"I want to be alone with my wife."

Ah, she did love it when he called her that.

"Let's just sneak out the back," he coaxed. "No one will notice."

She nudged him. "Everyone will notice. We can't do that. There's an exit and bubbles. Everyone has to line up outside the church, and we have to charge through a million bubbles. They look nice in pictures and represent our effervescent future. Or something."

His face fell. "More pictures?"

"It's a small price to pay. We can run all the way to the car though . . ."

Smiling, he stood and held out his hand to her. They tracked down Molly, and in record time her sister had everyone in place just outside the church doors.

Alone for the first time all day in the church vestibule, Wyatt tugged Grace into his arms. "Ready, Mrs. Jennings?"

Ready to go away with her husband? Ready to become his wife in every possible way? Ready for their amazing future together?

She beamed a smile that she felt all the way to her bones. "I am so ready."

Acknowledgments

*B*ringing a book to market takes a lot of effort from many different people. I'm so incredibly blessed to partner with the fabulous team at HarperCollins Christian Fiction, led by publisher Amanda Bostic: Jocelyn Bailey, Matt Bray, Kim Carlton, Paul Fisher, Jodi Hughes, Margaret Kercher, Becky Monds, Kerri Potts, Savannah Summers, Marcee Wardell, and Laura Wheeler.

Not to mention all the wonderful sales reps and amazing people in the rights department—special shout-out to Robert Downs!

Thanks especially to my editor Kim Carlton for her incredible insight and inspiration. You not only help me take the story deeper but also make the process enjoyable, and for that I am so grateful! Thanks also to my line editor, Julee Schwarzburg, whose attention to detail makes me look like a better writer than I really am.

Author Colleen Coble is my first reader and sister of my heart. Thank you, friend! This writing journey has been ever so much more fun because of you!

I'm grateful to my agent, Karen Solem, who's able to somehow make sense of the legal garble of contracts and, even more amazing, help me understand it.

The town of Bluebell was inspired by the little town of Lake Lure, North Carolina. Don and Kim Cason, innkeepers of the beautiful historic Esmeralda Inn, were so kind to host my husband and me for a few days and answer all my pesky questions. If you're looking to visit Chimney Rock and Lake Lure, I highly recommend it! https://theesmeralda.com

To my husband, Kevin, who has supported my dreams in every way possible—I'm so grateful! To all our kiddos: Chad, Trevor and Babette, and Justin and Hannah, who have favored us with a beautiful granddaughter. Every stage of parenthood has been a grand adventure, and I look forward to all the wonderful memories we have yet to make!

A hearty thank you to all the booksellers who make room on their shelves for my books—I'm deeply indebted! And to all the book bloggers and reviewers, whose passion for fiction is contagious—thank you!

Lastly, thank you, friends, for letting me share this story with you. I wouldn't be doing this without you! Your notes, posts, and reviews keep me going on the days when writing doesn't flow so easily. I appreciate your support more than you know.

I enjoy connecting with friends on my Facebook page, www.facebook.com/authordenisehunter. Please pop over and say hello. Visit my website at the link www.DeniseHunterBooks.com or just drop me a note at Deniseahunter@comcast.net. I'd love to hear from you!

Discussion Questions

1. Who was your favorite character in *Autumn Skies*? Why?
2. What was your favorite scene in the book? Why? Did it make you laugh? Bring you to tears?
3. Due to a traumatic childhood event, Grace felt unworthy to live. Have you ever experienced survivor's guilt or known someone who has? What advice would you give them?
4. Grace tried to eradicate her guilt by doing good deeds. Have you ever dealt with guilt in the past? How did you handle it? Discuss the difference between healthy and unhealthy guilt.
5. Wyatt's perceived uselessness as a child produced an adult who was driven to protect others. Do you feel this is a healthy or unhealthy response?
6. Both Wyatt and Grace struggled with guilt from a childhood event. Do you think this bonded them? Helped them heal? Have you ever found a friend through a shared experience?
7. Grace admired that Wyatt was confident yet humble. Unlike her, even though he also experienced guilt, he seemed to know his place in the world. Who has been a mentor to you—someone you can look to as an example? What qualities do you admire in them?
8. Discuss the parallels between Wyatt's journey for closure and his journey through the mountains.

9. In the story, God used a crisis in Wyatt's life to bring Grace and him together for the purpose of healing them both. Do you think God has ever allowed a crisis in your life to bring about good? Discuss.

10. If you've read all three books in the series, whose story did you most relate to—Molly and Adam's from *Lake Season*? Mia and Levi's from *Carolina Breeze*? Or Grace and Wyatt's from *Autumn Skies*? Why do you think that is?

An excerpt from

summer *by* the tides

Chapter 1

Maddy Monroe was cowering behind a ficus tree near the hostess station when her cell phone rang. Her hands shook as she silenced the phone before it drew the attention of the staff.

She jabbed the elevator button for the third time. "Come on, come on." A star could be born in interstellar space, a polar valley carved by a glacier in the time it took the elevator to reach this floor. Stairs were not an option, as she was on the twentieth floor of the Waterford building and sporting heels.

She sniffled. Drat. She seemed to be crying. She swiped a hand under her eyes, heedless of her makeup.

She heard voices, Nick's boisterous laugh. Maddy shrank deeper into the ficus and finally, finally, the elevator dinged its arrival.

"Maddy?" Noelle's concerned voice tunneled down the hall. "Maddy, wait."

"Oh, come on," she muttered, tapping her fingers against her leg until the gold doors crept open. As soon as she could fit, she squeezed inside and punched the ground-floor button.

She didn't draw a breath until the doors sealed and the elevator began to drop. She placed a palm over a heart that was threatening to beat its way out of her chest. Her white blouse clung to her back, and her skin prickled beneath her arms.

She closed her eyes, the scene that had just transpired playing out in fast-forward in her mind. And then, as if that montage weren't painful enough, the image of Nick's face appeared. The look on his face just before he'd kissed her good-bye last night.

Nick. She clamped her teeth together until her jaw ached.

There had been signs. Many of them, really, she was realizing now. They ranged from whisper-subtle to neon-sign obvious. But like so many other walking clichés before her, she was only seeing them in retrospect.

Maddy opened her eyes to the buttery sunlight streaming through her blinds. She scrambled for her iPhone to check the time. But as she did so, the events of yesterday washed over her like a tsunami. She didn't have to get up at all, because she didn't have a job anymore.

Her cell buzzed with an incoming call, and she squinted bleary-eyed at the unfamiliar number on the screen before declining it.

She drooped against her pillow, only now aware of how fat and swollen her eyes felt. Of the persistent achy lump pushing at the back of her throat. Her heartbeat made the bed quake. Her eyes burned with tears. Yesterday's anger had faded, and something worse had filled its spot.

Yesterday she'd come home, changed into yoga pants, and worked in her little garden until she was too exhausted to do anything but flop on the sofa. She hadn't fallen asleep until after three o'clock in the morning.

She didn't want to talk to anyone, didn't want to see anyone. She didn't even want to be awake today. She pulled the covers over her head and prayed for oblivion.

A steady pounding pulled Maddy awake. She turned her face into the pillow. Sleep. She just wanted to sleep. But the noise was relentless. Someone was pounding at her apartment door.

"Go away," she mumbled.

She wondered if it was Nick, coming with some lame apology. As if "sorry" could make up for what he'd done.

Her phone buzzed an incoming call on her nightstand. Why couldn't everyone just let her be? When the buzzing stopped the pounding resumed.

"Argh!" She tossed back the covers and checked her phone as a text buzzed in. Her best friend, Holly: Open the door.

Before she could put down the phone it buzzed again. I know you're in there.

Maddy let loose a sigh that had been building awhile. She pushed off the mattress, realizing she'd fallen into bed in the same yoga pants and T-shirt she'd gardened in. *Gardened* was such a tame word to describe her treatment of those poor weeds. She hated to think of the sight she must've made, tearing through her zinnias like a crazy woman.

A glance at the hall mirror also told a sad tale. A bedraggled ponytail captured only half of her hair, and dark smudges underlined puffy eyes.

She walked to the door and pulled it open, interrupting the loud banging. "All right already. Jeez."

Holly's brown eyes widened in surprise, whether at Maddy's sudden materialization or her disheveled appearance, she didn't know.

Leaving the door open, Maddy retreated into her living room, seeking the comforting embrace of her overstuffed sofa. She grabbed a fluffy yellow pillow and pulled it into her stomach.

Holly dropped beside her, the smell of fresh soil and flowers emanating off her. They'd met three years ago at the nursery where Holly worked, bonding over their love of all things green and growing.

"What happened yesterday?" Holly asked. "Noelle said there was some squabble at the restaurant and you tore off."

Yesterday's scene at Pirouette played out yet again in Maddy's mind, making her eyes sting.

Holly set her hand over Maddy's. "Honey, what's going on? Did you lose the promotion? It's not the end of the world. You're still assistant manager of Charlotte's most prestigious restaurant. There'll be other opportunities for—"

"I caught Nick and Evangeline together."

Holly blinked. "Evangeline, the owner? What do you mean, 'together'?"

"I mean exactly what you think I mean. They were all over each other." The image of it made her heart crumple up like a wad of trash.

Holly's eyes narrowed and her nostrils flared. "That jerk."

"But it's worse than that. I heard him accepting the promotion."

"What?" The indignation on Holly's face was like salve on a raw wound.

But his words still haunted her. *You made the right decision . . . Maddy's a terrific girl, but she gets frazzled . . . Wouldn't be able to handle more responsibility . . .*

Was there a nugget of truth in what he'd said? Had she been deluding herself all along?

"Did they see you?"

Maddy gave a harsh laugh. "Oh yes, they saw me. I stood there like a guppy, my mouth just working."

"Who could blame you? You were blindsided, you poor thing." Holly's eyes pierced hers. "How long do you think it's been going on?"

"I don't know, but when I saw them together . . . I ran. I just ran away. Oh, Holly, he planned this, didn't he? He played me like a fiddle." Tears seeped out the corners of her eyes.

"I could just throttle him."

It almost brought a smile to her face, trying to envision petite, pacifist Holly doing any such thing. She'd never cared for Nick, not that she'd said as much, but Maddy could tell. She should've trusted her friend's instincts since, apparently, she couldn't trust her own.

"I thought I was a shoo-in for that job." Pirouette's general manager was retiring and, as assistant manager, Maddy was next in line. "I feel so stupid."

Nick, the restaurant's beverage manager, had pursued her for months before Maddy finally went out with him. Holly had been encouraging her to put herself out there, and six months ago Maddy decided to give Nick a chance.

One date led to another. He was easy to talk to, he shared her faith, and since they were both passionate about the restaurant industry they found plenty to talk about.

"Let's keep it professional at work," he'd said as their relationship progressed beyond casual. It had seemed like a wise idea. But now she realized she may have played right into his plans.

Holly squeezed her hand. "I'm so sorry, Maddy. You don't deserve this."

"I'm not gonna lie, losing the promotion is bad, and losing my job is even worse. But having Nick betray me like this . . . You know how hard it was for me to take a leap of faith like that."

"Aw, honey." She drew Maddy into an embrace. "I just hate this. It won't always be this way, Mads. Someday you'll find the right man to love, and it'll all be worth it. I promise."

"Was this his plan all along? To keep me out of the way while he sucked up to Evangeline? Did he ever care for me? I thought he did, but what do I know?" Maddy's throat constricted around her words.

Holly rubbed her back. "Would it help if I told you he's not worth the lint on this old, smelly T-shirt you're wearing?"

"I feel like such an idiot. I keep remembering little things he said and did. I must've had blinders on."

"Hey." Holly pulled back and gave Maddy one of her stern looks. "Don't you be putting this on yourself. You trusted him. You gave him the benefit of the doubt. Nick's the idiot. Anyone who tosses you over like that needs his head examined."

Maddy absorbed the warmth from Holly's eyes. "I don't know what I should do now."

"You should tell Evangeline, that's what you should do. Tell her you and Nick have been dating for six months and he was cheating on the both of you."

"I'd love nothing more, believe you me." She gave Holly a guilty look. "But I told Nick about my résumé."

The air escaped Holly, deflating her posture. "Oh, Maddy."

Four years ago when Maddy applied for the assistant manager job, she'd falsified her experience. It was only one job. She'd been at a low point and overly ambitious—not that that was an excuse. She wasn't proud of it. She'd never done anything like that before or since, and she'd nearly come clean to Evangeline a dozen times over the years. She wished now that she had.

"Even if I go to Evangeline I won't get my job back. And that's on me. I knew what I was doing was wrong, and I did it anyway. That *is* my fault."

Holly studied her thoughtfully. "What are you going to do, honey?"

"Eat an entire package of Oreos."

Holly gave her a look. "After that."

"Look for another job, I guess. At least I've got money in the bank. I'm not flat broke or anything. I just feel so . . . ruined."

"You are not ruined."

Maddy's phone buzzed against her palm, and Holly uncurled her fingers and took it. "It's Noelle. She's worried about you. I'll let her know I'm here and you're okay."

"Nice of her to check up on me," Maddy mumbled, feeling numb after letting out her feelings.

She thought of all the people she was leaving behind at Pirouette. They weren't friends exactly. She was their boss—used to be their boss. She thought of everything she'd put into her job. All the over-time, all the energy. She'd lived and breathed that place. It was the reason she'd gotten to the ripe old age of thirty-one without a ring on her finger. Well, part of the reason.

She'd loved everything about her job, from the staff to the pa-trons to the amazing aerial view of Charlotte. It was like throwing a party every day. She'd made the restaurant the most important thing in her life, had made Nick runner-up, and now they were both gone.

"Honey, you've got, like, twenty unopened texts on here. And a bunch of missed calls."

Maddy shook away the cobwebs. "What time is it anyway? And why aren't you at work?"

"It's after three, honey. I just got off. Have you been in bed all day?"

"Maybe."

She was going to have to put out her résumé again—undoctored this time. She could do this. Maybe she'd wind up at an even better restaurant. But they didn't come much better than Pirouette. Was she willing to move away from Charlotte? She didn't even want to think about that.

Holly held up the phone. "Who's this from a 910 area code?"

"Telemarketer probably."

"They've called five times. Look."

"I don't recognize the number."

"They left a bunch of voicemails."

Maddy took the phone, put it on speaker, and tapped the arrow beside the oldest one, which had been sent yesterday at 3:12—just about the time everything had gone down at Pirouette.

"Um, hi, my name is Connor Sullivan. I'm a friend of your grandmother's over in Seahaven. I was hoping you could give me a call as soon as possible if you would."

Maddy frowned at the cryptic message. Her grandma lived alone at the beach. The same cottage where her family had once spent many an idyllic summer.

"I hope everything's okay," Holly said.

"Me too."

She played the second message, sent a couple hours after the first. "This is Connor Sullivan again. Um, I really need to reach someone in the family, so please call as soon as you get this."

Maddy's heart sank at his urgent tone. What if something bad had happened to Gram? "This doesn't sound good."

"Call him."

Before she did, Maddy played his most recent message, sent early this morning. Her heart squeezed in dread.

The story continues in *Summer by the Tides* by Denise Hunter.

The Summer Harbor Novels

"With her usual deft touch, snappy dialogue, and knack for romantic tension, inspirational romance veteran Hunter will continue to delight romance fans with this first Summer Harbor release."

—*Publishers Weekly* on *Falling Like Snowflakes*

AVAILABLE IN PRINT, E-BOOK, AND AUDIO

THOMAS NELSON
Since 1798

THE CHAPEL SPRINGS ROMANCE NOVELS

"... skillfully combines elements of romance, family stories, and kitchen disasters. Fans of Colleen Coble and Robin Lee Hatcher will enjoy this winter-themed novel."

—*LIBRARY JOURNAL* ON
THE WISHING SEASON

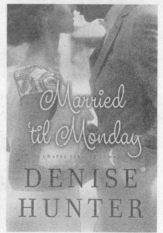

AVAILABLE IN PRINT, E-BOOK, AND AUDIO

THOMAS NELSON
Since 1798

About the Author

Photo by Neal Bruns

*D*enise Hunter is the internationally published bestselling author of more than thirty books, three of which have been adapted into original Hallmark Channel movies. She has won the Holt Medallion Award, the Reader's Choice Award, the Carol Award, and the Foreword Book of the Year Award and is a RITA finalist. When Denise isn't orchestrating love lives on the written page, she enjoys traveling with her family, drinking good coffee, and playing drums. Denise makes her home in Indiana, where she and her husband are currently enjoying an empty nest.

l

DeniseHunterBooks.com
Instagram: @deniseahunter
Facebook: @authordenisehunter
Twitter: @DeniseAHunter